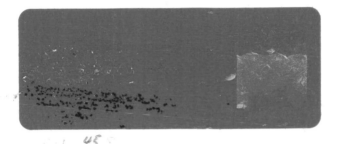

45
9/0 9

Death of a
Garden Pest

Also by Ann Ripley
Mulch

Ann Ripley

Death of a Garden Pest

St. Martin's Press
New York

This is a work of fiction. All the characters and events portrayed in this novel are either fictitious or are used fictitiously.

A THOMAS DUNNE BOOK.
An imprint of St. Martin's Press.

DEATH OF A GARDEN PEST. Copyright © 1996 by Ann Ripley. All rights reserved. Printed in the United States of America. No part of this book may be used or reproduced in any manner whatsoever without written permission except in the case of brief quotations embodied in critical articles or reviews. For information, address St. Martin's Press, 175 Fifth Avenue, New York, N.Y. 10010.

Library of Congress Cataloging-in-Publication Data

Ripley, Ann.
    Death of a garden pest : a Louise Eldridge mystery / by Ann Ripley.—1st ed.
        p.   c.m.
    "A Thomas Dunne book."
    ISBN 0–312–14311–7
        1. Women television personalities—Washington (D.C.)—Fiction.   2. Women gardeners—Washington (D.C.)—Fiction.
    I.   Title.
    813'.54—dc20   95–53296
                                                            CIP

10 9 8 7 6 5 4 3 2

Acknowledgments

Thanks to the kind people who assisted me during the writing of this novel. Trux Simmons, KRMA-TV; Mrs. Elizabeth Campbell, WETA-TV; Paul Iams; Keith Jackson; Susan Tews; Jamie Keiffer; and Stephanie Stashak helped me understand the world of TV and voice-overs. Garden writer Barbara Hyde and garden experts Jessie Lew Mahoney and Irene Sinclair reviewed the horticultural essays. Fairfax County police, magistrates, and public defenders told me about criminal law in that county. Other expertise came from John Mohr, cement plant production manager; Jeralene Green and Craig Kubik of the Environmental Protection Agency; Jim Mahoney; Bob Sinclair; and my husband, Tony. I am indebted to Margaret Coel and Karen Gilleland for their thoughtful critiques. Jane Jordan Browne, my agent, and her assistant, Danielle Egan-Miller, deserve special credit for their many helpful ideas.

To Eloise Bradley Fink

Death of a Garden Pest

1

Louise didn't notice when the books slid down beside her on the chaise longue. Lulled by the warm shade of the loggia, she had lapsed into a pleasant half-sleep.

It was a garden daydream, populated with Vita Sackville-West's weeping silver-gray pear tree swarming with white climbing roses; D. H. Lawrence's "Adonis-blood" anemone of pure condensed red with a "velvetiness without velvet"; and Henry Mitchell's yellow and red spring daffodil, as outrageous and gaudy as a harlot.

A bird screeched in a nearby bougainvillea. She awoke feeling disoriented and had to look around before she even remembered where she was. She sat facing the Caribbean, wearing a bathing suit that revealed the ugly history of a violent struggle.

She touched a scab on her arm and another on her leg, and the bad memory oozed back. Peter Hoffman with his hands around her neck. The hot stove burning her legs. Her jabbing attack with pineapple-like leaves on his eyes until blood spurted out. Picking up the poker stand and bashing him on the head until he couldn't rise again.

"No," she moaned. She closed her eyes and put a trembling hand to her forehead. There was sweat there despite the languid breeze.

Where was her family when she needed them?

The cushion on the chaise moved imperceptibly, as someone sat beside her. Startled, she opened her eyes. Her husband Bill pulled her into the circle of his arms and, gratefully, she rested there.

"Still having flashbacks." It was a statement, not a question.

She nodded. He was in bathing shorts, looking her over at close range, angry at the damage inflicted on her body, angry at the torment that caused her to dissolve in tremors like this. He had none of her guilt—he didn't care that she injured a man for life. He only cared that his wife was alive.

Louise pushed her long brown hair back from her face and sat up straighter. She knew how much Bill wanted her to be well. Softly, she said, "Maybe a swim in the pool would help."

"I was thinking more of the ocean," he murmured. He gave her a final gentle hug, then relinquished his hold on her and stood up. "The girls want to go. Why don't you try it today?"

During these past six days in St. Martin, she had felt the loneliness of the sick child who must languish in bed and watch others play. Bill, Janie, and Martha frolicked in the waves, while she stayed on shore, stretched out sleeping on a towel or brooding in a beach chair, her body not ready yet to venture into the sea.

She pitied her husband. He held high hopes for this little vacation at a friend's villa, hopes that his wife would come back to reality.

With absolute composure, she had testified at the preliminary hearing that sent arms dealer Peter Hoffman on his way toward trial for murder. With the grace of a movie star, she had given a post-hearing interview to reporters, following which she went home and collapsed. Then, a few days later, her family packed her up and got her on the airplane.

Now she was here in paradise, depressed and frightened, one step away from a psychiatrist's couch. She had never felt so low in her life.

She looked at Bill, lean and handsome, standing now with his arms akimbo, his blue eyes challenging her. How illogical of him, she thought, to hope that she would put aside her nightmares and take up her bed and walk. And at the same time, how lovable. She had always cherished him for his optimism.

It was the little spark she needed. She rose from the chaise, feeling immediately the sore and burned places, but refused to cry out in pain. She slipped her feet into thongs, then looked up at him and said, "I'll go in the ocean with you."

"That's my girl," said Bill.

At a call from their father, Janie and Martha drifted out of the house and the family walked down the sand trail that led to the beach a hundred yards away, passing silent, sun-drenched groves of six-foot-tall scrub trees. Each step on the scorching sand gave Louise a little more strength.

She noticed that her husband's casual growth of beard and newly acquired tan did not disguise the unhappy lines on his thin face. Occasionally their hips touched as they walked, and it roused a wave of remorse. She had been hospitalized briefly in the burn trauma unit, and after that was still so wounded and exhausted from the attack that she had seemed to forget husbands were to sleep with as well as talk to.

"Bill, you're not happy, and it's not just because of what happened to me."

"Let's talk about that tonight," he said. Then he deliberately bumped her hip and winked at her. "And maybe you'll feel like trying a little togetherness."

She moved even closer to him. "I think I will," she said softly. "My burns are about healed. My ribs are better. What more does a girl need?" She squeezed his waist affectionately.

"After that," she persisted, "we need to talk about what's wrong at work." Greater than Bill's hatred of Hoffman was his discontent with his job. He had lived a double life these past two decades, employed by the State Department while operating as a deep-cover CIA agent.

They walked for a while in silence before he answered. "I feel like Walker Percy's hero in *Love in the Ruins*—you know, the fallen-away Catholic near the end of the world. Except I'm a disenchanted spy near the close of the spy age."

"The whole world of spying changed when they arrested that Carlos," she said. "An overweight alcoholic killer who once held the whole world in thrall. Too tired to play the game any more, and not much left in the way of clients."

"Oh, there are still clients—that's the agency's continuing job, of course, intercepting the transfer of nuclear material to irresponsible countries." He looked at her cautiously. "That's why they want me in Vienna: The IAEA is there."

"You can't mean it," said Louise incredulously. "Move to Vienna? We just *moved* to northern Virginia eight months ago."

"Not until next year. But I'm thinking, no more moving: Get out, take early retirement, do something new. I didn't mention it to you, but a couple of private-sector people have made overtures." He patted the pocket of his beach coat where his cellular phone resided. "In fact, one of them's going to be calling me."

The girls were catching up. He looked at Louise. "I didn't mean to bring it up now. Let's continue this later. But it's good to be able to talk about the future with you again." He bent over and kissed her on the lips.

Martha, as tall now as her mother, but with even longer brown hair, came up and put two hands on Bill's shoulders. "Okay, no making out! Come on, let's get in the water!" She ran by them, a nineteen-year-old sylph. Janie, sixteen, trailed after.

"Ready?" Bill asked her, carefully arranging their beach coats and towels on the sand.

Louise's heart started thumping fast. What did she have to fear from the surf? She forced a smile. "Ready!" The four of them held hands and ran in together, like children. It took but an instant to start each of her burns and cuts flaming with pain. "Oooh!" she yelled.

"Wonderful, isn't it?" cried Bill, mistaking pain for pleasure. He splashed onto his back and watched her, happy that she was back with him.

She stroked smoothly, trying not to grimace as she got used to the briny sea touching her wounds. Soon, she was enjoying herself, sensing a unity now with the warm water swirling around her like an organic force. They lined up beyond the breaking waves, caught a green mountain of water, and rode in, but Louise waited a second too long to extricate herself from the water, and was tumbled upside-down against the low bank near the shore. She came up gasping for air, with gritty particles of sand clinging to her body inside her bathing suit. Her burns felt as if they had been scraped with a knife. Trembling, she struggled up the bank and slunk to her beach towel like a wounded animal. Longingly, she looked at the scrub trees, wishing she could hide in their shade.

After a few moments prone, she recovered a little. She raised herself cautiously on her elbows and looked around. Martha was sitting near her, staring at her, a strange expression on her face. "That guy really did a number on you, Ma. Your neck, your arms, your legs. I can't imagine anyone being that bestial. *Why?*"

Louise realized Martha, away at college during the fall, had no real idea of what she had endured. "He tried to kill me because I'm the only one who can tie him to that murder. The man's a psychopath. And a womanizer, of course. When they offered him the big Defense job, they warned him to quit his running around. His girlfriend wouldn't go quietly, so he murdered her."

"What a fool!"

"The body parts we found had been stashed in bags of leaves he set out on the curb."

"Which you recycled, as usual. And . . . he had actually hidden her head and hands . . ."

"Yes—in a secret compartment inside his house." She stared into the blue sea. "Monstrous," she whispered.

They fell silent for a moment. Then, Martha said simply, "No wonder you've had nightmares."

Louise reached out a hand, and the young woman scuttled across the sand a few inches so she could take it. "We love you, Martha. We missed you these past five months." College had taken her away, and the phone had not done her justice: The social butterfly freshman she thought they had deposited at Northwestern in the Chicago suburbs had changed.

Martha said, diffidently, "If we ever have any time alone, I need to talk to you." Louise's neck muscles tensed. Could her daughter be pregnant?

"Let's make the time. How about now?"

Her daughter drew up and sat with her long brown legs crossed in front of her. "Now, it's *not* what you probably think: It has nothing to do with sex: I have that all taken care of."

"Oh." It was all Louise could do to refrain from asking for details. "Of course you have. I realize . . . that you are perfectly capable of handling that."

"This is much more important than sex," said Martha. She picked up a pink shell and traced her own name in the sand. "Here I am, nineteen, and you and Dad think of me in the same old way." She shook her head. "And yet I'm not that person any more: I'm changing."

"Funny, I was thinking the same thing."

At that moment, Janie sprinted onto the beach and slung herself between the two women. Sand sprayed into Martha's face. "*Oops!* Now, everybody, please don't yell at me," said Janie, brushing sand off Martha's leg. "It was just an accident." She turned to her mother. "I need to ask you something quickly, before you conk out again and before Dad comes." She looked pointedly at Martha.

"Oh," said Martha, sarcastically, "could that be a hint? Okay, I'll go back and swim." She stood up, made a try at pulling down her high-cut bathing suit, and stared at Louise. "You know, Mother, at the rate we're going, we will never, I repeat, *never*, be able to talk. And you will never, I repeat *never*, know the real Martha Eldridge." With that, she turned and strode back into the water and disappeared in a dive through the rising crest of a wave.

Louise sighed. "Jane, you drove Martha away. She was talking."

"Oh, that's all right. She'll forgive me. She *likes* me." She picked up Martha's pink shell and examined it, not looking at her mother. "I'd like to talk about guys."

"Oh." Louise knew this concerned Chris, the eighteen-year-old who lived across the cul-de-sac from them. Chris and Janie had helped her stop Peter Hoffman. It had given the two teenagers something important in common, maybe too much. Louise's heart began to speed up again, and a wave of fatigue settled over her. She slumped back on the sand, shrugging a towel into a makeshift pillow under her head. "Now. Go ahead. Tell me what's what."

Before Janie could start, a few drops of sea water that fell on Louise's leg announced someone else had come ashore. Bill slid down beside her. "Any calls?"

"No."

She felt like an animal that had just crawled out of its hole and reached the light, only to get pounced upon by predators.

She closed her eyes in an effort to shut her family out.

"Uh-oh, Ma," declared Janie, "you're—losing it again. I'll catch you later."

Louise opened her eyes just a slit. Bill looked distracted. He said, "Maybe I'll call our home number to see if they called there."

"Pretty fancy phone arrangement you set up for this trip. This call is really important to you, isn't it?"

"It's about as important as anything ever gets."

He scrounged the cellular phone out of his beach jacket and tapped in their number in far-off northern Virginia, then lay back with her to listen for messages. She began to drift off.

He was silent.

Curiosity finally overcame sleep. She slowly turned her head and looked at her husband. There was a strange expression on his face.

Abruptly, he sat up and extended the phone toward her. "No message for me, but one for you."

She struggled to a sitting position, took the phone and pressed the repeat button.

"Hi," the friendly voice said, "I'm looking for Louise Eldridge. Louise, this is Marty Corbin. I'm a producer at WTBA-TV, Channel Five. That's WTBA-TV, Public Television. Heard you in an interview about a week ago, and I've been thinking about you ever since. You talked about gardening: Y'know, burying garbage in the garden, and picking up everything that isn't moving to put in your mulch pile. Forgive that last remark: It wasn't very tactful, after what happened to that poor lady. But what I'm getting at is, we need someone for our show on gardening—a more or less *organic* gardening show. WTBA's is the producing station, but it's carried by seventy other PBS stations in the country. I'd like you to try out for cohost, or *hostess*, if you prefer that title. First, we'll need an audition, and if that goes well, we'd sign you up on a trial basis. Then, if it works out, we'll make it permanent—one show a week. The audition should be no problem; I can see already you photograph well—yeah—you're a natural." The voice was warm and low and assuring. "So call me." He gave his number and urged her to reply soon.

She dropped the phone on the beach towel and gazed out into the Atlantic, her family forgotten for a moment. In the east there, she could see a star rising: "Louise Eldridge, Organic Gardener." She laughed at herself.

But if this call was for real, she might be headed for a genuine career. The thought was frightening. For twenty years, she had been a foreign service wife, a mother, and an amateur at everything else: gardening, volunteering, writing. Could she emerge instantly as a full-blown career woman?

2

When the receptionist at Channel Five told her Marty Corbin had been delayed, Louise was grateful; it gave her a chance to collect her thoughts. The misgivings she had had about this interview had been shoved well back in her mind.

They had arrived home from vacation the day before, so she hadn't even had time to review anything in her standard books on gardening. This morning, however, she had brought a black leather folder with a pad of paper for notes. She had already written down a few hasty ideas: "the easygoing way to make compost," "unveiling the spring garden," "a recipe for soil."

The busy receptionist, a woman with her sandy hair in a French twist, glanced over at her. "So. I'm Berta. And you're Louise, the gardening expert?"

"Sort of." She chuckled, and it had a phony sound to her own ears. "Mr. Corbin is auditioning me for a show on organic gardening."

The receptionist smiled. The woman had a know-all, see-all aura about her. "Well, that certainly fits."

Of course. She knew all about Louise and the mulch murder.

"I'm sorry," the woman amended, her eyes sobering. Louise could see a woman with malicious instincts that she tried to hold in check. "I shouldn't have been so flip. I bet you hear all sorts of smart cracks like that. So, have you ever worked in television before?"

Louise shook her head. "Only plays, and that was years ago, in college."

"It's not that hard to learn. Just make friends with your shooter."

"Shooter?"

"Photographer."

"Oh." Louise laughed. "I get it." She went back to her own thoughts.

Although her family was delighted by her TV prospects, it hadn't stopped them from pouring out their troubles. If she snagged this job, she wondered if she would be able to handle everything, career, two nubile daughters with lots of issues, and a husband who despised his job.

Unfortunately, no call came for Bill on the beach that day. And Martha clammed up, once interrupted by Janie, so Louise never did find out what she wanted to talk about.

It was different with their sixteen-year-old. Janie and Louise had talked, and talked again. She wished she knew the single right thing to say to her child to steer her away from the sexual shoals. Then she had an inspiration. "Janie," she said, "when I think of sex, I think of outcomes, babies, for instance. Did I ever tell you what fun it was to bring you into the bed with us when you were a baby? You'd be all smiles, warm and irresistible and smelling of pee."

She had looked at her mother with alarm. "How disgusting. Why didn't you change my diapers first?"

"Sometimes you just seize the moment and you don't worry about cleaning up first. You know those after-dinner talks we have. We don't worry about cleaning up the dishes right then." She looked at the vulnerable child-woman sitting in the sand in front of her. "Or, since you want to talk about sex, let me tell you about lying there after making love." The girl was hanging on her words. "Talking, not rushing to wash ourselves, but just lying there, enjoying an incredible peace. That's part of life. That's part of sex."

"It sounds kind of *messy*," said Janie.

"Well, you've had sex education: You know there are lots of fluids."

"When they taught us in sex ed, Ma," she said dryly, "they didn't exactly spell it out in ounces."

The receptionist interrupted her thoughts. "Pardon me, Mrs. Eldridge. Marty's ready."

Louise's heartbeat speeded up. The worry shoved to the back of her consciousness came straight to the surface: She had done so much boasting to Marty Corbin. Hadn't she practically lied? Now she had to prove herself. When she had returned the producer's phone call, she had assured him that she was a gardening expert. "Oh, yes," she had said during that phone call on the beach, "I've done just about everything there is to do in gardening," although that was far from true. She was the consummate amateur here, as well as in everything else she had ever done in life.

"Great," he had said. "Then all you have to do is show us your stuff on camera."

She stood up and clutched her purse. Her hands were clammy. Now was the moment. She would have to conjure up every bit of garden knowledge she had ever learned, from her darling bent-backed skinny old grandmother, from books, from grubbing in the soil among the worms and bugs so many happy, experimental hours, and prove that she was the genuine article.

Unsteady even on her low heels, she walked to the office the receptionist indicated. The door swept open and a large, bearlike man grabbed her by both arms. He had a majestic head of wavy brown hair and liquid brown eyes, an aquiline nose, and other patrician features somewhat obscured by his being slightly overweight. He wore a white dress shirt with sleeves rolled up, and he smelled good. Was it just his body smell or a scent?

"Louise, my garden expert," he murmured, and his breath, she noticed, was also sweet. "You look *dynamite!*" The man couldn't seem to take his eyes off her. In a millionth of a second, she thought: Womanizer, and then, but I can handle it.

With his big arm around her back, he slowly moved her into the room, like a mover sliding a piece of furniture on wheels.

Another person was already present. The aura of intimacy projected by Marty Corbin evaporated as she met the green-eyed stare of the handsome young man standing near the desk. He had risen with tigerly grace from one of two chairs placed equidistant from Corbin's desk.

It was a knowing stare from this tall, slim, brown-haired young man. His expression, for her eyes only, said, You're not a player.

She took a deep breath. It was clear that he viewed her as someone who had hit a lucky strike. Well, too bad, buddy, she thought, as she sat in the other chair. Rank beginner or not, she was a player now, after a lifetime of amateur roles. And she knew she could do it! Hadn't she risen to the occasion when her husband had asked her to be a courier of secret documents? Or when he asked her to entertain the enemy in their own home at dinner parties for the express purpose of gaining information? This was only more of the same. She exhaled the breath, crossed her legs at the ankle, and relaxed.

His name was John Batchelder, and, according to a quick run-through by Marty of his credentials, he seemed to have years of television experience despite his seeming youth. Louise quickly realized John was not in his mid-twenties, as she first thought, but probably ten years older. Sitting near him, she saw the delicate fatigue lines around his eyes.

It was the eyes, she noticed, that were the defining point of this beautiful man: They were fringed with thick black lashes. They made him resemble a Caravaggio painting of somebody—a minstrel?—that she had seen in Italy. As so often with beauty, it was the mixture of elements—southern European with northern European in John's case—that made it hard to tear one's eyes away.

John flashed her a perfect smile. "And *I* am to be your Mister Greenjeans, the cohost of *Gardening with Nature*."

"Oh, I didn't know." Flustered for the moment, she turned to Corbin, and then recovered herself and resumed the sophisticated yet friendly exterior she was determined to project. "Of course, I don't know anything yet about this show."

The producer waved a big hand. "Of course you don't. I just wanted you to meet John before he had to dash off. *Yeah*." Corbin said "yeah" with such pleasure that it was as if he had found the answer to a long-standing problem. "We'll have the two of you in the first couple shows, anyway. You, Louise, can be knowledgeable, explain things, reeling off Latin names of plants. John will be the equivalent of the ingenue, the learner." He grinned, and gestured John's way with his big hand. "He'll be the dummkopf, the guy who hasn't heard of a . . ."

". . . *bromeliad?*" said John.

"Bromeliad—Louise's weapon of choice." Marty chuckled, then looked at her guiltily. "Sorry, Louise, I couldn't resist that."

She said nothing, and the producer continued: "The show will have authority, and at the same time it will seem accessible. We've had a kind of 'elegant garden' host on WTBA-TV for a few years now. A garden dreamer, reminiscent of the Romantic Age. I'm sure you've seen Madeleine Doering—she's done a *great* job within the confines of the concept for the show."

"Yes, yes," drawled John, " 'Lady Madeleine,' we call her. Not an idea of her own, so Marty's always feeding them to her."

Marty frowned at his desk inkblotter. "Listen, she had presence, we all know that, and that's worth something. But times are changing and we're looking for a different approach." Then he turned pointedly to the young man. "Sorry you have to leave now, John. But the three of us will powwow soon with Rachel the writer." Louise smiled inwardly at "pow-wow." Marty's personality was as different from an Indian's as any man's she had ever seen.

As John left the office, understanding began to sink in. Marty Corbin was not entrusting this show to a newcomer. He had the outspoken but experienced John Batchelder right there to take over in case Louise bombed out.

The producer settled himself back in his chair and turned his attention fully on Louise. "Now, let me tell you first what I have in mind; then you can give me your reactions." He sat back and put his elbows on the arms of the chair and opened his hands, as if willing to accept gifts from above. His eyes were locked on Louise. "You, Louise, would take over as hostess the middle of March. He spread his arms wide open. "It's true that Madeleine's always been like a Lady-Jane-in-the-Garden, dreamy and"—he shrugged his massive shoulders—"*effusive.*" His voice piped out in a pseudo-sophisticated soprano: " 'Let's see where we can place the lilies and the roses, my dears, to best remind us of the Tuileries.' "

He leaned forward and narrowed his eyes. "You're younger, hipper, more representative of the environmentally aware gardener. You'll have a little more missionary fervor—not completely organic, but tilting in that direction. And you'll not be afraid."

"Afraid?" she repeated.

Marty beat a big fist on the desk. "You're not afraid to tackle the issues, any more than you're afraid to drop a Latin plant name now and again." He sat forward. "Why? Because of the thousands, no millions of new gardeners in this country, you know where they come from?"

"Well, no, I guess I don't."

"From the baby boomers!" he cried, the brown eyes exultant. Marty got more action out of just sitting than anyone she had ever seen, his body fairly bouncing with enthusiasm, his Roman nose in the air, his arms waving, his head wagging to emphasize his points. "And we know what *baby boomers* are like: better educated, more thoughtful, more concerned about the planet. Spending big bucks on their gardens."

He shuffled his big hands through his curly dark hair, which Louise noted presaged a new speech. "The boomers," he declared. "They started out as flower children, metamorphosed into the 'me' generation, suffered the treachery at the hands of their employers in the eighties, and now they're returning to something they can count on. The land. The earth. The soil." He made a zigzag motion with his hand. "That little garden in the backyard represents it all to them."

"And younger people . . ." she ventured. But he wasn't finished.

"*Busy.* These boomers are busy, Louise." His bushy eyebrows elevated alarmingly. "They want to do it in a hurry. Remember, the average American never has enough time. So we want you to make it complicated but simple."

She stared at him for an instant, and then at the wall behind him, where numerous broadcast honor awards proved this man wasn't as nutty as he sounded. She broke into a smile. "Forgive me, but that sounds contradictory, though I'm sure you didn't mean it to be."

He looked at her, puzzled, then grinned. "Yeah. It was contradictory. I see you've got my number already; I'm always overtalking, throwing in too much garbage, confusing issues. But *you* know what I mean; I can tell. Smart people always know what I'm tryin' to get at."

"And there's a writer? You don't want me to help with scripts, then?"

"We can't do without a scriptwriter; that's Rachel Gordon. Little thing, not a hundred pounds sopping wet, but smart as hell. But we need help from you, from your vast experience. How long did you say you'd gardened? Since you were a child?"

She recalled her exaggerated claims and blushed. "Taught at my grandmother's knee."

He waved both arms victoriously. "*Super!* That's charming—*you're* charming. We'll make it 'most of your life,' for the publicity department," and he scribbled a few notes on a pad. "Okay, so we need a few things right away: some publicity stills, a press release, some story ideas for our first shows. We'll do most of the shooting on location. A little in our studio. For the first show we'll fly south, to Southern Country Gardens, or one of those other places in the Carolinas. We need blossoms." His brown eyes were filled with good-natured sincerity, like a cow's. "Blossoms are essential in gardening shows, believe me."

"You said there are people who underwrite this show. I guess that means there are not a lot of money worries."

Marty threw up his hands. "*Never* say that, Louise, if you work in public television! There are *always* money worries. Money has never been in big supply in public broadcasting, and the temper of the times"—he frowned at her—"well, you know. *This* show is funded for *this* season, but you always have to look to the future. The development department's talkin' to a couple of potential future underwriters. One's a guy named Bruce Behrens." He frowned again. "But that may not be a go. The other is Atlas Mowers. Atlas would be a great affiliation. Yeah. *Always* be on the lookout for possible underwriters. Now, as for your pay." He described her tryout period, which if successful would put her on fulltime staff. In her mind came a vision of something she hadn't had for years: a real paycheck. Then he talked about script ideas.

"We gotta keep those scripts coming"—he hit his open hand on the desk repeatedly—"bam bam bam bam bam! And they gotta match, *you know*, nature's cycle: the time the dogwoods bloom, the time the tulips pop open . . ."

". . . the time the slugs show up to eat your garden—I get your drift."

He grinned, pleased with her. "Yeah, you're gonna do just fine. I see lots more stations picking up this show once you become hostess. And now I want you to audition—just a little talk between the two of us in front of the cameras."

17

They got up to leave the office when there was a hurried knock and the door flew open. "Marty, darling," said the woman at the threshold. Her face lit up when she looked at the producer. Then she turned to Louise. "And who have we here?" she asked coldly. As Marty introduced her, Louise got a closeup look of a woman, a little older than herself, a Nefertiti-like sculptured quality to her face, a peerless makeup job. This was the woman she was replacing, whom Marty had not described physically. And no wonder. Madeleine Doering was a few inches shorter than Louise, but with the same hazel eyes, and, embarrassingly enough, the same big mane of shoulder-length brown hair. It made Louise determined to go right to her hairdresser and get a trim. She was a smaller, older look-alike of Louise, and from her expression it was clear she did not fancy having the younger version around.

Louise glanced quickly at Marty Corbin, looming beside her. Some men liked blondes. Some, like Marty, liked brunettes.

The woman halted right at the doorway, stopping their progress, and pulled an English cigarette out of the pocket of her emerald green suit. Marty, as if accustomed to this, produced a lighter out of his pants pocket and lit it for her. At this close range, the intimacy between the two, the electric eye contact, could not be disguised; it was reflected in everything they said to one another—a private world that intruders would enter at their own risk, thought Louise.

Madeleine ran her tongue over her wide, brilliantly colored top lip. "An environmental gardening show. That sounds pretty boring on the face of it, Louise. Lots of luck." She reached up and placed a proprietary hand on Marty's white-shirted chest. "But I'm sure this brilliant man here will pull you up, and make your program an audience pleaser— at least for people who like to muck around in manure."

Then she reached over and tugged delicately at Louise's black folder. Louise was so surprised at the gesture that she nearly dropped it. "What're these?" she drawled. "Garden notes from all over?" Her voice held a slight sneer.

"As a matter of fact, they are," replied Louise, readjusting the folder.

"We are late, Madeleine," said Marty as he put a hand on Louise's waist and firmly steered her out of the office. "Louise is auditioning. Gotta go."

"Don't let me hold you." She gave Louise another looking over. "Do your best, Louise," she said. "Newcomers with no experience often have a difficult time."

Marty turned Louise in the opposite direction. "Yeah," he said, sounding discouraged, "you didn't need that, now or any time."

Maybe she had been wrong about that intimacy; maybe it was his general office procedure with all women. Now, with his arm around her shoulders, he said, "Madeleine has been treated very fairly by Channel Five. She's becoming cohost of our show for the senior crowd, *The Best Years*. And that's considered a bigger prize than the gardening show; it has an enormous audience. Let's get back to your show. There's going to be one heckuva lot of work to do, because we have a commitment for twenty-eight programs!"

"Wow!" exclaimed Louise. "Twenty-eight?"

He caught her enthusiasm, his eyes filled with excitement. "Louise," he whispered, clamping his big hands on her elbows and blanketing her with his wide-eyed gaze, "I really think we're on to something with this series. I want you to *sleep it, eat it,* and *breathe it.* Put the show right there on top of your priority list, before your dog, your kids, your husband. Can you do that?"

Begin at the Beginning:
The Good Earth

Happily for us home gardeners, we can tell if we have good soil simply by looking at it. It should resemble chocolate cake—rich, dark, and light-textured.

Since this chocolate cake ideal is not easily reached, let's use some other visual tests as well. When you squeeze a handful of your garden soil, it should hold together, not turn into a depressing clod or fall apart like sand in a child's pail. If worms or roly-polies crawl out of this handful of earth, consider yourself blessed: Worms are nature's little rototillers, and the armadillo-like roly-polies may *look* tough, but they are among the good guys that eat bad bugs near plant roots. One more simple soil test: Wet the soil slightly and squeeze it; if it becomes a shiny-looking ball, you have a heavy clay problem, and it needs fixing.

After these little tests, gardeners often go down different paths. Seat-of-the-pants–type gardeners dig, plant, and let the results tell whether their soil is any good. Others, probably with more scientist in their souls, pack a pint of soil into a bag and send it to the cooperative extension agent to get a soil test. It can be worth that small price, because soil can lack subtle ingredients. Remember that plants, just like people, have complex nutritional needs.

So where does our soil come from? It is a mixture of minerals from weathered rock and organic matter from plant remains. The soil under our feet today started forming before Columbus came to America, and continues to change right before our eyes. The minerals come in forms we're familiar with: tiny platelets of clay, larger bits called silt, and, the biggest particles of all, sand. The ideal soil has a balance of these three, and when we get this balance, we've hit pay dirt! You've heard of it—it's called "loam."

But soil needs two other crucial ingredients from us, the gardeners. One is the continual addition of organic matter. This stuff contains millions of unseen microorganisms, tiny bits of life that are rather like the digestive juices in our stomach—they busily break down food so it is made available to plants. Add at least an inch of organic matter a year over the top of the garden, more if your soil is top-heavy with either clay or sand. The other thing soil needs is air space—lots of it—to allow oxygen, water, and fertilizer to reach the plant roots. That means dig your soil, not too often but well.

So, whether you're gardening on a balcony or in a backyard, be kind to the soil. No farmer would let a year go by without replenishing the fertility of his soil, and neither should you. Your plants are gobbling up the nutrients like a hungry man at a dinner table. And don't just use fertilizers: Remember, organic matter—manure or compost—is what provides all that microscopic life. You can get manure from the circus (they call it "zoo poo"), the horse stables, or the farmer. Biosolids are given away free at your city waste water treatment plant.

A few other quick tips. You can sweeten acidic soil by adding lime. But there's no easy way to acidify an alkaline soil. Sulfur will help, but don't overdo it. The best way is to add a generous amount of organic matter each year. Is organic matter beginning to sound like manna from heaven? Your garden will think so.

Here's an easier way to approach the gardener's least favorite task—digging. Dig the depth of your spade blade only, incorporating your fertilizers and organic materials as you do. (Some swear by the torture known as double-digging, but it is overkill.) Rototillers also can be used, but you'll still need to finish the job with a hoe, rake, and the back of the shovel to achieve a fine tilth. No getting away from it: The word *tilth* comes from the Middle English "to labor"—and good soil demands just that.

As you dig, raise the garden beds above the level of the ground. Any raised bed is more vibrant than a ground-level one. Besides being more attractive, the raised bed drains better and warms faster in spring. Your goal, remember, is that chocolate-cake look: fluffy, rich soil that allows the entry of air, water, and nutrients. Seeds and plants you put there will never have it so good.

3

She and Bill had been having a peaceful Saturday morning, until she started reading the local-news section of the *Washington Post*. "Oh no," said Louise, looking in disgust over the rim of the paper. "How would you like to die *that* way?"

"What way?" said Bill.

"In a rock crusher. Listen to this." First she took a sip of her coffee. " 'The general manager of a local Maryland cement company, who was interviewed Thursday night on Channel Eight on the controversial subject of burning toxic wastes at cement plants, was killed late Friday night when he fell into machinery designed to crush limestone rock.' "

She looked meaningfully at Bill. "Sounds like no accident to me."

"That's because you treat everything suspiciously."

"Why not? Well, reading on . . . 'it is true there was only a twenty-inch-high rim around this large open hopper. It's called a "primary" crusher.' . . ." She kept on reading. "Oh, yuck!"

"What? They could only recognize him from bits of his shoes and his hardhat? Maybe bits of the papers in his wallet?"

Louise looked hard at her husband. "You read this story."

Bill, his head into the sports section, said smugly, "Nope. But it's only logical."

"Hmh." She read further, then said, "This man had just given an interview to Channel Eight about emissions into the air when they burn toxic wastes. Wish we'd seen it. Gee, isn't it comforting to know they burn toxic wastes in the metro Washington area?" Then she began reading another story.

"Watch out, Louise."

She looked over her page again. "Why?"

"You're broadening your horizons even before you get your first program off the ground."

"How d'ya know that?"

"I can smell it. You want to plunge straight from gardening into heavy environmental issues."

Just then the phone rang. "Where is it?" he asked, looking around for the cellular.

"Bedroom," she said.

She read the story of a carjacking in western Fairfax County from start to finish, then frowned, and pinched her lips with the fingers of one hand. Fairfax—that was *their* county. Maybe the suburbs weren't as safe as she thought. Yet their immediate neighborhood, Sylvan Valley, seemed like a little pocket of calm in the midst of a sea of violence.

Enough of crime, she thought, closed the newspaper, and drank the last sip of coffee. She needed to do some research on making compost, subject of show number two. The first meeting with the producer and the scriptwriter was alarmingly close.

January had given her a chance for her wounds to heal completely, and to get back into shape with the aid of aerobics classes, and now it was February. She stretched a long leg up in the air and pointed the toe. The movement sent a surge of strength up her thigh and through her whole body. She smiled. Back to her old self, only better, because now she had a job and soon would be bringing home a paycheck.

Their financial plight was almost amusing: After twenty years in government, Bill was making almost eighty-five thousand a year. But once they subtracted enormous mortgage payments and college tuition for Martha, his take-home pay was near the poverty line. Her paycheck, though modest, would make all the difference. Now, for the first time in her marriage, she would be pulling her own financial weight.

Bill had been on the phone for a long time with someone. He returned to the living room and stood with hands on hips. "You're not going to like this, Louise."

"What?"

"Hoffman's out on bail. That was Detective Geraghty."

In as casual a voice as she could muster, she said, "I'm not surprised. What did Hoffman do, pay the world to say what a good guy he was? Maybe that wife of his testified."

"No," said Bill. "Business associates, mostly, talking about how responsible the sonofabitch is. How he provides jobs for five hundred in his small arms factory in Alexandria. How he's a paragon."

"Will it be safe for us?"

"Geraghty has charge of that angle. He says Hoffman can't come anywhere near you. And they will monitor his comings and goings."

She was silent for a moment. "I'm glad I'm not just staying home anymore. I think that would make me nervous."

"Louise, the guy won't be hanging around his home anyway. Although the fact that he lives only a half mile from here is not comforting. But Geraghty says that at the bond hearing Hoffman stressed how he wanted to get back to running his business and resuming a normal life. Apparently he's even got contractors at his house, just like an ordinary suburban fellow."

"Huh," Louise scoffed. "Ordinary suburban fellow, my foot. How can a man accused of first-degree murder be called ordinary?"

"Well, listen to this. Hoffman's lawyer is leaking the story that they'll try and pin the murder on *Mrs.* Hoffman."

For a moment her mind tried to twist the story of Peter Hoffman around to fit the scenario that the wife did it. "I can't believe it," she said. "That's totally crazy!"

"The scenario goes like this: She was jealous of that mistress. *She* killed her and used Peter's saw to cut up the body. Can you believe *that*?"

"No, I can't. And neither will anyone else—will they?"

"I don't know. Continuing this scenario: *She* could have put the body in the leaf bags and stuck them out at the curb, just before you came along and picked them up. She could have concealed the head and hands in the secret compartment in their house."

"God," she said softly, "incredible."

"She knew the layout of that house just as well as he did."

"Where's she now?"

"Gone. I guess she's finally discovered what a treacherous guy Peter Hoffman is."

Louise could easily call Peter Hoffman up in her mind: big, graceful, straight blond hair, pale eyes behind aviator glasses, a wily mind that twisted words and thoughts to his own purposes. And yet attractive, in a primitive way that perplexed her and that she had never wished to analyze. Her gaze retreated to the comfort of her gardening book. "I don't want to know any more. I'm going to forget that man ever existed until the trial comes up and I have to testify."

"And that's the other news. The trial's been delayed. They claim they need more time to develop this theory of theirs. It's set for July."

"Good. That gives me even more time, five months, during which I don't have to think about him at all."

She stared out of their floor-to-ceiling windows, into a deep forest of tall sweetgum trees, only black skeletons now. In a world filled with crime and stories of crime, it was hard not to wonder what was out there prowling in the dark.

Shakily, she got to her feet and went to the windows and drew the curtains on the cold winter woods.

The President of the United States was a little drunk. Jack Fairchild needed courage in a bottle right now. He looked at his watch, then pushed his dyed-blond hair into place, and picked up the phone. Fairchild felt a little funny calling Tom Paschen after midnight. He hadn't spoken to his chief of staff for a month. Officially, the man was on vacation. While

Fairchild waited for the call to go through, he poured a bourbon from the drinks tray on the table that sat between couches in the White House family quarters. He drank it neat, then poured another. When Paschen was finally on the line, the President didn't waste words. "I called to ask you to come back, Tom. I need you. Especially now that Hoffman's out on bail, I can't trust the situation."

"Hoffman? Why worry about him? He's not going to bother you. If you think he'll run out on nearly a million in bail, you've got another thing coming. Anyway, why should I come back? You threw me out, Jack." His voice was cool and bitter.

Fairchild could imagine his chief of staff standing there in his Middleburg home, cocky, loving the humiliation of making the President of the United States grovel to get him back. Paschen was a smart, ruthless Washington insider. Yet he was honest enough to be considered a treasure by people who needed smart, ruthless people around them. Like Jack Fairchild.

"Tom, Tom, you notice I kept my mouth shut. I didn't fire you. I didn't even publicly blame you, for not vetting Hoffman properly."

Paschen laughed heartily into the phone, until it jangled the President's ears. "Jack, I'm the Cassandra who warned you all along the guy was a loser. And now you're stuck with the situation."

"I know," said the President morosely. "The damn press have had a field day. Who's that woman, Eldridge, who bonked him on the head? Now she's in the news again. Has some TV program. Unfortunate. It just keeps the topic alive, when it should be dropped. Too bad *we* couldn't have discovered that Hoffman killed his mistress and stuck her in the leaf bags before that woman did."

"You mean, then we could just have covered up the murder? Hey, that would have been great, Jack."

"Oh, for heaven's sake, no. Not a coverup. I mean *we* could have uncovered it, and wound up looking good. Right now, the publicity is bad. And not only that, I've lost the services of Hoffman to the Defense Department."

"I really feel for you," said Tom, his words larded with sarcasm.

This pissed the President off. "Tom, are you screwing around with me? Well, no matter. I need you, I want you. Christ, I'm not playing the blame-game. I'll never accuse you again of driving the guy to kill his mistress." The President felt as if he were pleading with Paschen like he would a lover. "I'm here, you know I'm drunk, I'm eating humble pie. Asking you back. It isn't just handling this scandal. It's everything. Telling me what's important and what's not—I *miss* that. And then the campaign. I don't even want to *think* about planning a campaign without you."

Paschen was silent for a minute. "What's in it for me?"

"What do you want?" It was obvious to the President it wouldn't be anything with a trail attached, like money.

"Let me think about it," said Paschen. "I'll let you know soon. Probably before your ship of state totally founders. One other thing, Mr. President: Use that woman, Louise Eldridge; just don't carp about her."

"Use her?"

"Get in on the action. She's smart. She's got a show. She's an environmentalist; they're not all bad. Maybe you could be a guest on her show."

"Bullshit. You're kiddin'."

"No." Paschen laughed. "Cowshit: That's more what her program deals with. Yeah, I'm kidding. But just remember: Everything that happens can be used to your advantage, if you only know how to do it." The President heard the sound of challenge in Paschen's voice, and knew he'd won. The man was coming back.

4

It should have been the height of romance: Janie and Chris had abandoned the basketball game in the cul-de-sac and gone for a walk in the woods. Taunts from their friends followed them as they left. But Chris had retrieved a long stick to bat snow off branches, strike dead wood off trees, and tease Janie by tapping the top of her head. She was exasperated. "Do you ever wonder about yourself? You just *never* can be still. Don't you have any—"

"Any what?" he asked, threatening to spear a curious ground squirrel with the stick.

"Inner serenity?"

Chris, handsome, windblown, and red-cheek, guffawed. "That's the stupidest thing I've ever heard. Even my mother doesn't say things like that."

"Maybe she thinks them, though," said Janie, grinning. "I bet as a baby you never lay still, and always had to be entertained."

"Oh, boy, I don't know. I'll have to check on that."

Soon they had arrived at the deepest part of the wooded park, deserted at five o'clock on a schoolday. "Let's go over there," said Chris, pointing with his stick. There was a small rocky area underneath the bank of the looming hills that bounded the park. They went and sat down on a big flat rock.

"So here we are."

Chris put the stick carefully aside and slid over and put his arms around her. Then he pushed her mass of blond hair aside and gave her a short kiss. "Like that? That's what's on *my* mind."

She felt stirrings in her body. "I—I liked it a lot." They kissed again.

Chris's eyes were alight with interest. "We could do it like they do in the movies, like two fishes kissing." He puckered his lips loosely and she puckered hers, and they parodied what they had seen in romantic scenes. Suddenly, his tongue was in her mouth, and hers in his, and the pretense was gone. The kiss lasted a long time, as they squirmed as close to each other as they could get in their big parkas.

He looked at her, as objectively as he would have looked at his specialty, a math problem. "I think I love you, Janie."

She shook her head slowly. "I'll probably never love anyone just the way I love you right now."

"Then, you know what the next step is." His voice sounded hoarse. "Sleeping together."

There. He'd said it. They'd barely kissed before today, just a few embraces back when they'd saved her mother from Peter Hoffman, and then Janie had gone away on vacation.

"Chris," she said quietly, "having sex is pretty serious. Is that what you want to do?"

"Oh, yeah, that's what I want to do."

She cringed a little, remembering those discussions with her mother about smelly little babies. "How? Your mom's home all the time, writing poetry."

"What's wrong with your place?" he countered. "Your mother is doing a gardening show: That ought to keep her out of the house."

"There's the neighbors."

Chris sat back, picked up his stick, and tapped it on the stone. "Look, Janie. You know the neighbors can't see anything that happens at your house; it's too hidden. Maybe you just don't want to do this."

The weight of Chris's disappointment came down upon her.

She jumped up from the rock. "Hey, *I'm* modern. If we're going to do it, we have to get some stuff." She looked at him warily. "You know."

"They have them in the drugstore in the shopping center. The rack is right near the front of the store now." They trailed off down the path, Chris tapping ahead with his stick, as if looking for hidden traps in the forest floor.

All in all, it had been more fun to play detective with Chris than to play sex kitten, but he had lost all interest in detecting. She guessed it was all part of growing up.

Louise immediately liked Rachel Gordon, the writer. A thin young woman in a tailored gray suit wearing large, round, horn-rimmed glasses, she got right down to business in the first planning meeting. They blocked out sequences for the first program and talked about future topics.

When she got home, it was almost six, but Bill wasn't home yet. Janie was in the bathtub, singing a slow song with which Louise was unfamiliar. She was happy to see dinner was in the oven. As she walked down the hall to her bedroom, she paused at the door of Janie's pretty blue bedroom. It looked out of kilter. Her almost compulsively neat daughter had thrown her school clothes on her bed. Poking from underneath the clothes was the corner of a paper bag. Her curiosity piqued, she looked inside. It held only one item: a small package with "Trojan" emblazoned on the side.

Louise exited quickly and went to the kitchen and set her books on the counter. Here was one of those definitive moments. To speak or not to speak. To have been discovered nosing around, or to pretend not to have seen. To worry, to anguish, over this child-woman with new breasts, new curves in her hips, new depths of feeling in her shining young eyes.

She caressed the book bindings and felt a sharp sense of unease. Instead of these tomes on gardening lore, what she needed at her fingertips was a book on sex and the teenager.

5

The neighbors across the cul-de-sac from the Eldridges were having a party, a party that hostess Mary Mougey hinted might end up being profitable for Louise. Two wealthy potential PBS sponsors were among the guests. Louise was learning more each day about how gravely in need of funding WTBA-TV really was, so she was anxious to meet these moneyed people.

The Mougeys' living room was elegant, its comfortable couches and chairs accented with highly polished antique pieces from Europe. Mary Mougey was filling Louise in on the history of the house. They had added a large bedroom suite and doubled the size of the living room. Extending a graceful hand to encompass the crowd, she explained, "My job involves a lot of entertaining. I raise money to combat world hunger and it takes more than impassioned pledge letters. A little discussion over dinner sometimes is much more effective."

Louise noticed how well this pale, blond woman in a dull claret velvet hostess dress blended with her old-world antiques. In attractiveness she was matched only by Nora Radebaugh, the acknowledged neighborhood beauty who at the moment was engaging Louise's husband Bill in close-headed conversation. With Mary, it was the pale eyes, watching always for the feelings of others, and reflecting her genuine concern for starving people around the world, as if she, personally, could feel the pain of these millions of victims of wars and drought.

Louise looked around at the rest of the people, all in party dress. The majority were neighbors from Sylvan Valley, people she had known for less than a year but who were now friends. They had paid her condolence calls after the Hoffman incident, as if she had suffered a death in the family. Mary's husband, Richard, in the State Department, like Bill. The chubby, balding Sam Rosen, a congressional aide, who was the Eldridge's next-door neighbor. The buxom Nora Radebaugh, who was a poet, and her businessman husband, Ron. People from the wider neighborhood—Sarah Swanson, a large, handsome woman in flowing caftan who was a potter and one of Louise's favorite people, and her husband, Mort.

The hostess smiled and smoothed the velvet bodice of her dress with a graceful hand. "A few newcomers you must meet." With a delicately curved finger she pointed at a middle-aged man in a well-cut suit. "The good-looking but awkward gentleman nearest us in the group by the windows is head of the Behrens conglomerate—Bruce Behrens. He mothers its chemical company and is one of our heavy contributors. The young woman next to him is his latest wife." She smiled at Louise. "But something tells me she's bored with him. What do you think?"

"The body language is pretty obvious," said Louise. Although the man devotedly clasped one of his wife's hands, the young woman leaned as far away from him as she could, like a horse pulling against a tether.

"Whatever his personal problems," Mary said practically, "the man *gives*—and *gives*. Probably to assuage his guilt about one of his biggest-selling pesticides. The EPA is doing tests and may withdraw it from the market. Now that you have your own gardening program, you particularly want to talk to him."

"Come to think of it, Marty Corbin mentioned something about him. Although I don't think he'd like my program."

Mary's expression was wise. "Don't be so sure. Why do big

oil companies, who by their very nature cause catastrophes, underwrite nature programs? It's part of their argument to the public that they're good corporate citizens, even if they do mess up once in a while." Mary smiled. "Anyway, didn't you tell me you weren't going totally organic?"

Louise said, "Yes, and that's a disappointment."

"His name is Bruce; his wife is Tina. Try him. He is generous, terribly generous." She looked at her tiny evening watch. "Now I need to check dinner."

Louise sniffed. It was a mixture of smells that reflected the height of fine living—of an utterly clean, elegant house; of women's expensive perfume; and of a well-cooked dinner in the kitchen. "Ah, the smells of India," she said. "It must be curry."

"Curry, indeed. Now go meet Bruce, my dear."

She went over to the lively group of which Bruce Behrens was the centerpiece. The crowd opened and welcomed her in, almost as if she were a celebrity. As she was introduced, he took her hand in both of his and said, "Mary told me about you; I'm excited about your program." Behrens was handsome, she decided, despite having lost most of his hair. He said, "Your show is just the kind of project Behrens might be interested in, depending on how it's presented."

Louise cocked her head and smiled. "And that's pretty much up to the producer."

He suggested Louise sit with them during dinner, and without waiting for a yes he scooted Louise along with one hand, his wife with another. "Come, Tina," he said, as if urging a pet to cooperate.

His hand on her elbow faintly annoyed her. For a fleeting moment, she considered excusing herself, saying she had to sit with her husband; then she remembered Mary's words about the man's generosity, and meekly sat down. Sam Rosen joined them and spun some witty tales about Congress, improving her temper as well as the temper of Behrens's pouty wife.

In Louise's peripheral vision she spied Nora, her breast touching Bill's arm as they stood together in the buffet line. Her husband seemed to be Nora's favorite person.

Behrens captured Louise for a solo narrative of how he became a self-made millionaire. It only took a few minutes for her eyes to glaze over, as his monologue dragged on. His success despite no college education. His lawn-care company. His farm pesticides company. His cement plants. All offshoots of his chemical manufacturing concern. Cement plants?

Her hopes sank. How could this man ever put money behind her environmental gardening show, when his company was forever trampling on the environment?

She never realized that being a player could make one so tense. Oh well, she would try the oil company president next. Oil seemed so much less controversial.

It was their usual after-church Sunday brunch of bagels, lox, cream cheese, sliced tomato and onion, eaten at the old pine dining room table littered with Sunday papers.

The phone rang, and Louise went to the kitchen to answer it. It was Martha, who liked to call from school at this time. She came right to the point: "Ma, I'm going to change my major."

"Why, darling?" She wandered back to the dining room table with the portable phone and sat down. Bill looked at her inquisitively and she mouthed, "Martha."

"Because Urban Studies is the *only* action on this campus. I was veering toward Women's Studies, but the people there are too sexist. But there are great people in the Urban Studies department and they have summer internships. You know, in Bed-Stuy—Bedford-Stuyvesant to you—and in Detroit, with Father Harrington."

"Bedford-Stuyvesant? Detroit?" Just the kind of places, thought Louise ruefully, she would want her very attractive, innocent nineteen-year-old to spend the summer

34

months, among the dope addicts, criminals, and dropouts. She bit her tongue and said nothing further.

"I wanted to tell you at Christmas, but who can talk about the underclass while you're sunning yourself on the beach of a fancy resort?"

"Well, honey," said Louise, rushing to hers and Bill's defense, "I can't help it if someone lent us their posh place in the islands."

A sigh from Chicago. "See, Ma, that about says it for inequities in our society. We go to the islands for Christmas, and the poor just fester in their overcrowded apartments, or maybe on the street. Think of all the street people! They only live *eight miles* away from you! Do you ever drive through Washington's non-marble neighborhoods? Try southeast Washington. Try northeast. People are destitute. No jobs. Drugs are the only way they can make money."

"That must be why they're killing each other at such high rates," said Louise reflectively.

A silence from Chicago. "See? I can tell from your tone you're just like the rest of the whites in the Washington area: I could hear it in their voices when I was home for Christmas. They're scared to death of minorities; they think they're all criminals. I'm going to help do something about all this."

"Martha, please don't damn me by tone of voice. Actually, I think it's a wonderful goal. If this is what you want to do, your father and I will support you."

"You know who influenced me on this? It wasn't you or Dad. I really don't see anything in what you do as something I would want to do. It's our neighbor, Mary Mougey."

"Oh," said Louise hollowly. Nothing like realizing where you stand with your own child. Then Louise simply told the truth: "I can't agree with you more, Martha. Mary is a role model for me as well."

Bill talked to his daughter briefly, said good-bye and offered the phone to Janie, who declined with a curt shake of the head. She kept her head buried in the Sunday funnies while Louise filled Bill in on details. "I really admire her, Bill."

"I only wish Martha didn't go into things headfirst," said Bill. "Yet it's better she changes her major now than later. I only hope she means it, switching out of literature and into saving the world."

Louise stared out into the woods through their big floor-to-ceiling windows and said, "You know, I thought this might happen. She's a wonderful person who really cares about people."

"Yes," said Bill, "but couldn't she express it in a less hands-on way? Why does a person have to start out a new major by immediately going into the field with an urban internship?"

"Because she's brave. She's braver than you and I were, even though we were just as idealistic at that age." She smiled at her husband. "I think we can be very proud of her."

Janie slammed the paper down and glared at her parents. Parents and child stared at each other in silence for a moment. Then, in a trembling voice the girl said, "It's so weird how you talk about my big sister. Your voices are so funny. You're so respectful. It's just like you were talking about somebody who'd died."

"Well, honey," said Louise, "I guess we are respectful. Martha is pretty terrific and she's in the process of change."

"How come you never talk about me that way?" demanded Janie. "Aren't *I* brave? Don't I count for *anything* in this house?" Tears overflowed her eyes and she rushed from the table to her bedroom and slammed the door.

Bill picked up his coffee cup and sipped thoughtfully. After a while he said, "What would you think of a little spring ski trip to Vermont next weekend, you and me and Janie?"

Louise was silent a moment. "I think it's a great idea. It's just that I can't afford to go." She shook her head regretfully.

"I'm so involved in these shows. Could . . . just you and Janie go?"

He looked at her, disappointed. "It'll be okay this time. But let's not make it a habit, okay?"

6

Channel Five had done all the travel arrangements for the trip to North Carolina, where spring truly arrived in March. Now, on location in Southern Gardens, the weather was perfect, and things had come into bloom as if responding to a cue.

Everything was perfect, except Louise: She was a wreck.

"Louise," said Marty, "we've walked everyone through the paces. We're almost ready." He looked at her closely. "But I'm worried about you. What's wrong?"

"I'm nervous. Can't you understand that I might be nervous on my very first shoot? And besides, I-I have to go to the rest room again."

"So go!" he said, impatiently. "We've walked everyone through the script and we're ready to roll."

She trotted up the path to the garden headquarters, noticing John Batchelder ambling toward her. "Going the wrong way, aren't you?" he said.

"Be back in a second," she said, panting. Then she thought how foolish it was to run; after all, they couldn't start without her, and what good would it do to arrive breathless? She walked the rest of the way up the hill, realizing with every step that she had to get a grip on herself. So on the trip back down, she tried an experiment. She deliberately slowed her gait, half-closed her eyes, and drew up a recollection of her grandmother's June garden, bursting with roses, oriental poppies, delphinium, and iris.

The entire crew was waiting. "I'm ready," Louise announced in a calm voice.

"All right," said Marty, encouragingly. He came up close to her. "There's the girl. I can tell by your expression you're going to do just great."

Under Marty's expert guidance, they taped all morning. They took a lunch break, and then continued until the producer was satisfied. It was when they were shooting among the trees that Louise noticed John was expanding his lines. This made it difficult for her to fit hers in during the remaining time. She was almost amused by the fact that every time he shoehorned in an extra phrase, it was straight out of a garden book. It forced her to scramble and improvise. After the third time, it was all she could do not to shout, "Quit stealing my lines!"

John stopped embroidering his lines while they taped a segment in the native gardens, but Louise grew anxious again as the final sequence approached. "Okay," said Marty, "ready, everybody?" Then, he came out with the cold words: "By the way, John, let's quit making Louise's job more difficult; let's stick to the script." John put up his hands, as if being threatened with a blow from an enemy.

"I am chastised, Marty." He recovered immediately, however, and Louise knew it was just more posturing. "I'm ready to stay with whatever Rachel has written for me."

Louise launched into her description of what makes good soil. Then she and John got into it, digging, throwing in soil additives, rototilling it into place. The scene ended with Louise and John leaning together on the rototiller, touching shoulders, exuding phony good fellowship. She turned and looked into those Mediterranean eyes and found herself blushing: Good grief! Even she was not immune to the physical charms of this otherwise worthless person. John smiled, as if reading her mind, and she felt like giving him a good kick where it hurt the most.

Marty came over to them. "Congratulations, particularly to you, Louise."

Then the producer put his big arm around her and took her aside. He found it hard to disguise his obvious pleasure.

"Now don't rest on your laurels just because you're good. This is only the first program and we shoot again next Thursday. We have a planning meeting on Monday, and you get to sit in when we do the online editing Tuesday. *Capisce?*"

"*Capisce,*" she repeated automatically.

He gave her a long serious look. "Louise," he said quietly, "you were great, just like I knew you'd be."

She looked up at him and smiled. "If I was great, it is largely due to you." This kindly, temperamental, talented man was enabling her to find a professional identity for the first time in her life.

But euphoria was eclipsed by exhaustion. Her back muscles were tight and her throat felt sore. At least there had been no problems with the shoot, or their night flight out of here would have been changed; as it was, she should be home before midnight. It would be good to get out of the thrall of her television life and back to just plain Bill.

7

After dropping Bill and Janie off at National Airport for their skiing weekend in Vermont, Louise drove on to the station. She was looking forward to this weekend alone, and felt confident a few days' skiing would improve her daughter Janie's psyche, and her husband's too, for that matter.

But for two days, she would put aside thoughts of her family. It was John Batchelder whom she needed to think about. Her cohost had become a problem. It was surprising, for John talked frequently about how he had been in television since graduating from college, and even lived with a woman who was a TV news anchor.

But yesterday, during the show on compost, John had acted strangely once again on the shoot in Rock Creek Park Farms. Rather than adding lines for himself as he did in North Carolina, he seemed to be erring on the side of reticence. Marty finally had exploded.

"Don't be a wimp!" the producer had yelled. "Speak your lines with some conviction, John. Don't you love compost? I want you to care about compost, and how it's made. Dammit, John, let's put some life into it."

She wondered what kind of nasty little game her ex-host was playing. She heard John had expected to take over the gardening show host spot from Madeleine, instead of having an unknown like herself step in as lead host. Would it be a fight to finish every week? She had to talk it over with Marty today.

Louise hurriedly parked, and went in. As she approached

Marty's office, two strange things happened at once. She saw a flash of color that turned out to be Madeleine. The woman cast a long, malodorous glance at Louise before dodging into an office. Louise stopped in her tracks, like a deer trying to dissolve from the sight of a predator. How the woman hated her!

Even more curious was the janitor. Henry Aiken stood there in the hall watching every move Madeleine made. He was a tall, husky man with a troubled face and a disorderly mop of dark hair. He was purportedly scrubbing the hall carpet, but his every movement inclined Madeleine's way, in the time-honored tradition of infatuated males. Louise knew lust when she saw it, and she would not want that man looking at her the way he had at Madeleine.

When she entered Marty's office, Rachel had the script spread out on a round worktable. "Hi, Louise," she said. "I think we're fat on this script."

"I'll be glad to help pare it down. Where's Marty?"

Rachel, oblivious to all but her editing, said, "With Madeleine. He'll be right back."

The show's subject was nativism. They had scoured through the whole script before Marty returned, looking furious. She had never seen the amiable producer in such a foul mood; his temperamental bursts were always short and easily passed over, like small storm clouds, but this was more like a tornado ready to descend upon them. It seemed as if he was suffering from an affair that was overripe and sticky, with a woman already unhappy about her position in the WTBA-TV universe. No time, perhaps, to talk about her paltry problems with John Batchelder.

Then the phone rang, and it was for Louise. "Want to take it in here?" asked Marty.

She nodded. "Hello?"

"Ma, it's me," said Janie, her voice sounding hollow. "I'm in the hospital."

"Oh, God. What happened?"

"Just chill out and I'll explain. We got here, no problem.

Got settled. Got dressed. Went up the advanced hill. Whammo! Dad fell down and broke his leg in three pieces— well, not three pieces. It's just that there are two small breaks."

"Ooh," Louise said, grimacing. "Can I talk to him?"

"He's dozing for a few minutes in the bed, and then they'll kick him out of it. Can you pick us up tonight? He said he wants to come home as soon as possible."

"Of course."

"And Ma, be warned, he's not in a very good mood."

Louise got details on their arrival and hung up the phone. "Sorry. Bill and Janie were skiing, and Bill's broken his leg rather badly, I'm afraid." She looked at her watch again. "I . . ."

"You're distracted," said Marty, staring at her without sympathy.

"Yes, actually I am. I guess I need to go home and get organized for his coming home."

Marty's eyes darted over to the desk clock. "What a day, and now it's gotten worse." We haven't treated this script fairly, but you can leave, of course. But let's not make a habit of it, okay?"

Getting Off to a Good Start:
Gardening the Organic Way

Something strange is happening to Americans. Once, they went down to the garden supply store and without hesitation reached for products with "DANGER" and "WARNING" prominently written on the label, the equivalent of a skull-and-crossbones.

Their objective was to kill: Kill bugs, kill fungi, kill everything that was injuring their garden plants or trees.

Today, a virtual revolution has occurred. Now, gardeners pause at the counter and ask a lot of questions, looking for a safer way to get rid of garden pests and to fertilize their plants. They buy boxes of lady beetles and praying mantises to take home and feast on "bad" bugs in their garden. They hang homemade pest catchers on their trees and count the numbers they catch. They spray bugs with a solution made of liquid detergent and water. They put pans of beer out to catch slugs. They're going organic.

Even if they don't call themselves environmentalists, they have read and heard enough so they can no longer adhere to their old garden habits. Overflowing refuse dumps, contaminated home wells, and disappearance of native flowers under the bulldozer—these are the kind of stories we have long read about. But it's finally hitting home, and home gardeners are doing something about it.

But a language barrier exists: We hear the words, "xeriscape," "making compost," "chemical-free gardening," "integrated pest management," and "nativist" gardening, and our eyes glaze over.

After all, it's one thing to be environmental, but why can't these environmental folks talk straight? Yet it isn't hard to learn what these phrases mean. Here is a primer on the latest phrases that will help you understand what it's all about.

- **Chemical-free gardening** means just what it says—using only natural products. This is an even stricter concept than **organic gardening,** which permits the use of some minerals in the gardening process.
- **Integrated pest management (IPM):** This sounds dry, but it's fun. It's a fancy phrase for common-sense pest control. Pes-

ticides, like chemical fertilizers, ruin our soils over time, since they kill everything, even the beneficial life within it. IPM also has four simple rules: 1. Use good garden practices such as mulching to discourage pests; 2. choose disease-resistant plants; 3. plant things that attract beneficial predatory insects to do battle with pests; and 4. monitor the number of pests. Then, only if necessary, use an organically based pesticide. Realize caterpillars and box elder bugs won't kill you, and that predatory bugs are your best garden friends.

• **Xeriscape (or low-water) gardening.** It has four simple rules: 1. Grow plants that suit the local environment; 2. reduce the size of turf lawns, which are proven water "hogs"; 3. group plants with the same water needs and then water them wisely (try irrigation hoses and emitters); 4. improve the soil's water-holding ability by adding organic matter and mulches. If Americans followed these practices, they could reduce home water use 50 percent, creating a total *25 percent* reduction in national water use.

• **Compost:** It's the great stuff that results when organic matter decays. Make it in your backyard or haul it in from your city's biosolids center. Municipalities produce tons of the stuff; gardeners are the logical people to take it off their hands. Don't add to the city compost pile—it is 20 percent of the bulk in crowded landfills—keep organic wastes in your own yard. Composting is simple, and your garden will love it. It not only gives your soil nutrients and body but also can be used as a protective mulch.

• **Nativist gardening.** This is the earnest effort of American gardeners to save and encourage native species. Some plant and nurture a few, while others plant whole fields of flower species that might well disappear if not encouraged. They see wilderness shrinking all over the globe, with the loss of many plant and animal species. Their answer is to turn their own yards into ecological sanctuaries.

Did you understand all that? Then, you're on your way to becoming an organic gardener!

8

The response of others to her first gardening program could have turned her head, had she not been so busy nursing Bill. Her closest human companion was held in a codeine dream, fighting the pain in his leg, and could hardly focus on the show, much less comment on it. But neighbors and friends called all weekend with their congratulations, and when she returned to work on Monday, Marty and the rest of the Channel Five staff were ecstatic.

The producer gave her a bear hug that nearly toppled her. But he immediately released her: "Sorry—I gotta quit doin' that. These days they call a friendly hug 'harassment.' But *Louise, geez!*" His big brown eyes shone with excitement. "We've really tapped into something here—you are a fantastic success!" He scooped up a sheaf of papers from his desk. "Look at these overnights! We've got something to sell to the whole PBS system."

She looked at him and couldn't help smiling. Again she forgave him his excesses. The man knew how to create shows the public liked: His industry-wide reputation was proof of that. Good thing, because his effusive character occasionally raised eyebrows in the quiet, intellectual atmosphere of WTBA-TV.

Everybody at the station seemed to have watched the program, even Jack Lederle, the renowned anchor of the station's hour-long evening news show, who worked with his staff in splendid semi-isolation in his own separate studio. He passed her in the hall, smiled, and said archly, "Good job." Funny, what a friendly small town Channel Five was turning out to be. Rachel was pleased because Louise's success meant hers.

Feeling as if she had a little more clout to do so, she now brought up the subject of John Batchelder with her producer. "It's the one thing that concerns me about the show, Marty. I admit, something good comes out of it. It doesn't matter whether he shortens his lines or lengthens them—it forces me to improvise. So at least I'm learning to think on my feet."

Marty agreed John was a problem. "Don't know what's goin' on with the guy, but he's gotta fish or cut bait." His tone was grim. "He's not going to ruin this show—it's a damned good show!"

Madeleine Doering struck the only sour note, and Louise should have predicted it. She barged into their story conference and congratulated them all. "I hear you have a little hit on your hands." Louise could see from her eyes and the sag of her mouth that she was near tears.

"Marty," she said, in a voice just short of a whimper, "I just hope since I have gone from gardening to—geezers!—that you still will have a little time left over for me."

Then she looked down at Louise, and Louise could see the fine lines under all that makeup, and was reminded of the cracked glaze of antique china.

"See if you'd like it, Louise," she complained. You know what's next on the Best Years program? The five identifying signs of Alzheimer's disease! So just don't think I'm happy." She turned and flounced out of the room.

Marty looked stunned and resentful. This woman was dragging him down, day by day.

After a moment, the producer seemed to recover himself. He shrugged his big shoulders. Those warm, brown eyes were cold now. He growled, "So she's not happy. Let's get back to work. It isn't as if we don't have another show to do."

9

Carrying an art case she borrowed from Janie, Louise trudged up the hill toward the Swanson's house. Rather pompous, it stood like a large glass box on one of the higher hills in Sylvan Valley. It had won so many design awards that Sarah Swanson was embarrassed, wishing the slick architectural magazines would find other houses to write about. The place contrasted sharply with the Eldridges' low-slung one-story, with its freestanding addition, that they dubbed the "hut," and was attached to the main house with a grapevine-covered pergola. Of the two houses, Louise preferred her own.

She remembered the first time she came here for a board meeting of Sylvan Valley Swim and Tennis Club last fall, before all the tumult of the mulch murder. She discovered, in swim club life spans, Sylvan Valley's was an aging relic, the cedar shake roof on its quaint, two-story clubhouse rotting from too many Virginia rains; its pool and tennis courts displaying wrinkles and cracks. All this presaged some serious spending on repairs or replacements.

She pressed the bell, releasing joyous chimes within. Sarah, who had become her friend, was a potter and conducted her thriving business out of a studio on the ground level of the house. Strictly mail-order, of course, so as to comply with Sylvan Valley's touchy zoning laws that, although ultraliberal in all other respects, sternly ruled out commerce, and that of course included selling out of one's home.

Sarah was the regular hostess for Swim Club meetings. She

opened the door, a large woman with gray-blond hair wearing a majestic wine-colored caftan of Guatemalan cotton.

"Louise, my dear," she cried enthusiastically, "we were just starting." She led Louise up the flagstone stairs to the airy living room looking out on thick woods. The other board members had just voted on a motion to repair the modest clubhouse before opening. They interrupted their business to tell Louise how they enjoyed her show. Then came her turn to make a report as new grounds chairman. She opened the art case and showed them sketches of her planting schemes, reeling off the names of all the plants. "I need help with the digging, all the more since my husband's off his feet with a broken leg—a little skiing accident." While she accepted their condolences on behalf of Bill, she made a quick count on her landscaping sketch. "I'm talking here about three dozen generous holes."

"Generous holes?" mocked Mort, Sarah's husband, a debonair-looking man with a receding hairline, who was an attorney with Washington's most prestigious law firm, Wilson and Sterritt. A memory nagged at her: Wasn't Peter Hoffman one of Mort's clients?

The lawyer continued to tease her: "Is that in contrast to nongenerous holes, holes that give nothing?" He sat back in a handsome leather chair, grinning. Louise was used to this. Men often felt compelled to twit her when she talked about gardening. Yet she could feel some new sensibility in her rising.

"Yes, Mort, generous if you want things to grow. At least twice the diameter of the plant. You may never have put those hands to a shovel, but this may be the time to start." She smiled, to soften her words.

Tart words, but no tarter than his. Louise didn't know what was up with her: She wasn't taking anything from anybody these days without answering back. In fact, she had just snapped back at her husband before she left for this meeting. Sitting on the couch with his cast propped up and his mouth in a pout, he suggested once again that she was overextended with her TV job and Swim Club responsibilities. "There's no turning back, now," she had told him. "I'm afraid I'm a career wife now, and career wives by that very definition are overextended."

She looked at Mort. Her teasing words, like most teasing words, were true. He had the hands of an eighteenth-century dandy, his beautifully manicured nails covered in a dull, protective polish.

"Now, Louise," said Mort, sitting up, "you wouldn't have recognized me when I was young and lived in the country."

"And that was some time ago, right?"

"Touché," said the lawyer, smiling. "Okay. I'll be the first to volunteer. What say we get a bunch of diggers out next weekend. I'll come; I'll show you how I used to do it back on the farm."

When the meeting was breaking up, Sarah asked her to stay for a moment. "I'd like you to do me a favor, Louise." The potter smiled, putting her strong hand on Louise's arm.

"I will if I can."

It was as if Sarah were asking her a very personal service. She lowered her voice. "I would like you to come over to my studio some day and pose for me."

"Pose. For what?" Then she chuckled. "A planter, maybe?" Sarah was known for her production of vases and planters, which she sold to places like Bloomingdale's and Smith and Hawkens.

"Exactly!" cried Sarah, taking Louise's hands in hers. Having Sarah's hands touch her was always a visceral experience, since every surface was like sandpaper. "You are such an *embodiment* of a gardener, tall, willowy, graceful."

Louise grimaced. "Oh, please . . ."

Mort had come up to join them. "But she's right. You are a perfect subject for Sarah." He patted Louise on the back. "We know you're a busy TV personality now, but sit still for it, Louise." Then he drifted importantly away.

"And I'll end up as a planter?" She couldn't suppress a smile. With her two agile hands, Sarah fashioned a complicated figure in the middle of the air. "Here you are, your figure. Leaning against the planter. Maybe with your hand spread to the side, touching it. We'll call it 'The Gardener,' how about that? Denim jacket, tan Japanese gardening pants. How does that sound?"

"Well, it sounds okay to me." Louise grinned widely. "It's better than a planter made out of my empty head, for instance."

Sarah laughed, then paused, thoughtfully. "Now, Louise, that's not a bad concept, either. So. When can you sit?"

"Soon, Sarah," said Louise. "My life's moving too fast. But I'll make the time."

10

No one had warned her except John. Her cohost lounged around in the audio studio and watched while Louise conducted an interview with the Green Club environmentalist. Marty decreed Louise would handle it solo. "More impact. We don't want any chitchat on this one. We're dead serious."

She came out of it feeling euphoric, as if the environmentalist and she were teamed up against the enemies of the planet. Pesticides were the woman's particular target. This interview, plus footage they shot of natural gardens in North Carolina, would become the first of several programs on "nativist" gardening, and was to identify the program strongly with the nature conservation movement.

"Look," said John matter-of-factly, "I don't want to make you unhappy, but you're going to get in deep doodoo when that baby airs." The two of them were watching the environmentalist soundlessly walk out of the studio on her run-down Birkenstocks. She was a woman of about fifty who had worn gray natural-weave clothes in spite of hints from the show's floor director that brighter colors would photograph better. At first, she had even objected to having pancake on her face, but finally gave in on that issue. A woman not used to giving in. Her hair was pulled back in a bun that was twice as severe as the one Louise's dear old grandmother, another conservationist, used to wear.

Though she may have been dull-looking, the woman's words were explosive. She condemned pesticides, citing court cases where one of the most commonly used ones was being investigated by the EPA. Louise recognized the chemical as one produced by Behrens Enterprises. The green woman had wound up by suggesting colorful alternatives to kill bugs and fertilize gardens.

"Collecting your own urine for the garden?" said John, laughing. "Come on. You've got to edit that bit."

"John, what do you think garden fertilizers are made up of? They often contain urea, animal urine, or animal manure. Anyway, she mentioned the collection of human urine as an extreme in recycling. Don't scorn it. What do you think the pygmies have done in Africa for centuries?" She smiled slyly. "You could try it on the flower boxes at your apartment."

John fidgeted. "Yuck, Louise, stop putting me on. And those stories about pesticides she told, like the family that croaked when they came back in their house after it was sprayed for moths? How do you think that's going to go over?"

"People need to know these things. All our data came from the EPA and the National Coalition Against the Misuse of Pesticides. There's proof of the harm some of these chemicals do to people, to say nothing of animals. Do you think we operate in a vacuum?"

John shifted from foot to foot, but stood his ground. His exotic, dark-lashed green eyes locked on hers. "The weird thing, Louise, is all these pronouncements you're throwing around, down there in North Carolina and again today. Put the two segments together and it will reek of kook, just what this station doesn't need if it wants to hang onto federal funds: 'Planting in drifts.' 'Pruning trees so they grow crooked.' 'Avoiding rectangles and straight lines.' C'mon, some people are going to think that's radical—the same people who swung this country back to the conservatives. Some folks like straight trees and neat little gardens. What's wrong with a row of, say, zinnias, like my mom always plants in front of her house back in Urbana, Illinois?"

She sighed, trying to be patient. "Do you think I'm saying square gardens are conservative, and natural gardens are radical? John, this has nothing to do with politics. I'm not laying out marching orders for you, or your mom, or anybody. This is just one way of gardening that actually is less work than formal, rectangular gardens."

She could tell from his eyes he wasn't buying it and probably never would. Mom had done her work well with this boy. He did not seem sly and sneaky now, just down-to-earth, but naive. Totally out of synch with the show. How long would it take for Marty to figure that out?

Just as predicted, trouble came. John apparently had a keen sense of how the public would react to things. It took only two days from the airing of the nativist show for the rowdy pickets to show up.

She met them coming in the following Monday: two derelict men, looking totally out of place in front of WTBA-TV's dignified marble entrance. Their signs read: WHAT'S WRONG WITH LAWNS, ANYWAY?; ENOUGH OF ENVIRONMENTAL FREAKS. WE HAVE A RIGHT TO SPRAY! They marched around in a little racetrack formation, loudly chanting, "Green lawns don't kill, green lawns don't kill!" When she stopped and asked them where they came from, one practically spit the answer into her face: "Ever hear of the Society for Traditional Gardens?" Her face turned crimson, and she hurried into the studio.

As she walked through the lobby, she saw Marty and Madeleine conferring outside his office. He quickly broke away and came toward Louise; she could see a malicious smile on Madeleine's face.

"Okay, I'll bite," Louise said, as they went into his office. "Why are those men out there?"

Marty spread his hands wide. "You know the program's been getting great mail and phone response; I can't figure it out either. That nativist show wasn't *that* far out." He went to his desk and grabbed a handful of message slips. "You know Bruce Behrens? He was polite, mind you, but apparently very unhappy with the tilt of the program." The producer peered at her over his dark, bushy eyebrows. "He's hot to become associated with your program, you know, but probably it will never happen. He's just calling up as an— interested donor. You know, to tell you what he thinks."

Louise noticed Marty didn't say "our program," like he usually did. At the hint of controversy, surely he wouldn't distance himself from responsibility for the show.

She frowned. "Can I see those messages?"

He handed them to her. "There're plenty of 'em. The response is still mostly positive. Quite a few jokers wanted to make hay out of that urine thing, but hey! Jokes are not necessarily negative."

"Then the pickets stand alone. They said they were from some 'traditional' garden organization."

"Could be. Oh, I almost forgot. In that pile you have one from the guy I talked about. The Atlas Mulching Mower Company guy." Marty leaned forward. "Louise," he whispered, "this is right up our alley. Treat this man right, and he'll come through for us. But now let me take you next door."

He led her out of his office into the small one adjacent. "Your own office," he said, smiling. "And I got you a little bouquet to start you out." The room was white and antiseptic, with only phone and computer on the gray desk, so her eye was drawn immediately to Marty's casual bouquet of massed blue iris.

"Marty, how can I thank you . . ."

He put a hand on her arm. "Don't. I'm thanking you."

When he left, she looked around, pleased. An office of her own. Experimentally, she attempted to put her feet on the gray desk, but the skirt she had worn today was too tight. Another day, then.

She got down to the messages next. She separated out the ones from the mulching mower company and Bruce Behrens. The first message sounded promising, but she frowned when she read the second. More trouble. She could feel it in her bones.

She walked briskly up the sidewalk toward her house, whistling a tuneless little version of "Downtown," which she'd always liked for its funky rhythm. She had so much to tell Bill. When she reached the front door, she noticed the white of a cigarette butt protruding from the leaves and kicked it with her boot. Muted pink lipstick on the end. Stooping over, she picked it up. English: Nora's brand, and probably left over from a visit a month or so ago. She would throw it in the kitchen trash, since she didn't tolerate butts in the yard.

She went in, gave her husband a quick peck on the cheek, threw off her coat, gave the air a couple of quick sniffs, and started spilling her good news. First, she described her new office. Then she told him about the Atlas Mulching Mower Company call, and how they wanted her to audition for the job of spokesperson, in company ads. "I'd appear on their national television ads all through the country." She rubbed her hands and grinned. "Big bucks, Bill, if I should get picked. It pays something like twenty thousand dollars!"

Her husband, lying on the couch with his leg cradled in pillows, hadn't been listening closely. Now his forehead wrinkled in a frown. "What company did you say?"

She felt a little deflated. "Atlas Mulching Mowers. You know, you mow, you leave the clippings on the lawn . . ."

"Oh, yeah, I get you," he said dismissively. "I bet that Madeleine woman you talk about will try out for that job. That'll give the two of you something else to dislike each other for."

Subdued, she went in and fixed dinner, realizing her husband's mood would get no better until he got off that couch. She brought in their dinners on trays. "Good," he said. "Maybe we can have a quiet evening by the TV. There's a good show on tonight."

Louise looked at her watch, and drew a breath in between her teeth like a little whistle. "Gosh, I forgot! I'll have to eat and run: Sarah wants me to sit for my statue."

Even as despondent as he seemed, Bill smiled wanly at that. "You seriously are posing so you can become a planter, right?" Then his mouth fell again. "I must say, Louise, I can't keep up with you; no one can."

She squeezed his hand; she had felt so high when she came home. Now, she realized her husband was on one end of the happiness scale and she on the other. But that was not so strange. While she had been experiencing one career triumph after another, Bill was dead in the water as far as his job went. Not only was he incapacitated on a couch for the indefinite future, but the promising phone call about a new job had never materialized.

11

"So it seems those who don't love her and her show, *hate* her and her show. And so they picket, they write nasty letters, and they threaten to sue." Bill said this lightly, and Nora laughed, a silvery sound. That was his summary statement on Louise and her career.

Their neighbor had been with him for a while, sharing a lunch of soup and hot buns she had made and brought over. She had talked in veiled terms about her current unhappiness; Bill already knew from Louise that it had something to do with menopause. He looked at Nora and could hardly believe she was old enough.

And they talked about him; he seemed her favorite subject. Nora, more than any woman he had ever known, with the possible exception of Louise, really listened. He laid out flat his total frustration with his job, carefully circling around its secret component. She picked up all his clues, seeming to know things before he even spoke.

Another disconcerting thing was her delicate spring-like perfume that just barely reached him as she sat opposite in an upholstered chair.

Then she got up, moving quietly and smoothly across the room. For an instant, he thought she was coming his way. He noticed what she was wearing: old gray pants with wide legs, black tunic top, no makeup except pale pink lipstick, nothing to distract from her gleaming black hair. She was going out on the patio to smoke. "Sorry," she tossed over her broad, bony shoulder.

"Just keep the sliding door open and stand in it," he suggested. She did that, lighting up, tucking smoking supplies in a deep pocket, puffing deeply as her gray eyes narrowed in pleasure. Looking curvy and flushed with pink. This was her third visit. He could tell by the tumult in his system that something was going to happen. Nora had a wild look that did not presage well for either marriage.

They talked back and forth across the space between the couch and the door, and it was like an electric charge. As Bill looked at her there, with every right to look since they were talking, he saw a woman who wanted him. Unfortunately, that had not been the case with his own wife for some time now. He guessed it was the leg cast, or his perpetual bad mood.

Nora tamped out her cigarette, flipped the butt in the woods, and slid the big door closed.

"Lock?" she asked, with one brow raised.

"Please," he said, sitting up straight so he didn't appear concave.

She came over to the couch and perched next to him. Then she reached over and picked up a picture of Louise that was sitting on the end table. "The wife with the flowing hair. Lovely." She replaced it and turned to him, shutting out the table, the picture, the room, everything but the two of them. He could feel the warmth of her body. The look in her eyes was unmistakable.

For some reason, both of his arms tensed, as if he were going into a defensive mode against an enemy. "Now, hey, Nora." The arms went out, whether to fend her off or to embrace her, he wasn't sure.

Then the phone rang. "Excuse me." Nora straightened up. Bill reached for the phone on the table. "Hello."

"Dad, this is Martha. Where's Ma?"

Bill had always thought it rather odd for the girls to call their mother, forty-two, long-legged and beautiful, 'Ma.' "Your mother is not home, Martha. Everything okay at school?"

"Well, actually, it sucks. Look, Dad, can you have Ma call me as soon as she comes home? I'll be here studying for my dumb exams."

"But how's Urban Studies, that transfer you talked about?" He noted Nora was looking at him, attentive to every word.

"It's the only bright spot in a gray, gray world."

"Okay," said Bill. "I'll have her call you."

When he hung up the phone, Nora chuckled. "Our children are always with us." She looked at him, a penetrating look from no more than inches away. He felt hot. "Bill." She leaned in again and parted her lips slightly, and when the phone rang again, they remained parted and a low laugh floated out from her throat.

He grabbed the phone. "Hello."

"*Bill*, you sound so tense," said Louise. "What's that noise? Laughing? Are you watching TV? Is everything okay?"

"I'm fine," he said tersely. "Why are you calling?"

"I just wanted to tell you how our meeting came out with the chemicals manufacturer. Bill," said Louise plaintively, "he's trying to bend Marty Corbin. Trying to influence our program. I've never seen anything so bald in my life!"

"Louise . . ."

"Then, next crisis of the day is John. I'm the only one who can possibly save his ass."

"Louise!"

"Sorry," said his wife. "They're so profane around here— I pick it up like a sponge. But back to John. The only one who can reconstitute him is me, and I don't even like him much. But if something isn't done, Marty's kicking him off the show. Darling, would you mind if I brought him home for dinner? Maybe together the two of us could recycle him. He's thirty-nine and he sure needs it."

"Do I mind?" Bill sighed. "Of course I don't mind, dear. Bring him home. It all fits with your desire to save stray puppies." When he said this, Nora got up from the couch and went over to where her coat was slung over a chair.

"Thanks!" said Louise. His wife sounded like an enthusiastic kid. "It'll do the guy good. Even meeting Janie will be good. A real, live, human teenager who is nice, and my terrific husband, who is grumpy but great."

"Louise . . ."

"Good-bye, darling. See you at five or so."

He hung up the phone and looked at Nora. He smiled gently and didn't move an inch. "Might as well give it up, Nora. It'll never happen."

She laughed. "Guess not. You're an interesting man, Bill. We can be friends, can't we?"

Her eyes pleaded: Don't tell, don't condemn.

Then, before he could answer, she turned and walked out the front door.

Louise said good-bye to a grateful John Batchelder and closed the front door. She marched back to the couch where Bill reclined and stood in front of him, hands on hips.

"I enjoyed that," said Bill. "John's not such a bad sort. I'm glad you brought him here. Funny guy—he operates at two levels. There's the midwestern schoolboy and would-be actor, from a strictly middle-class family. Now he's playing in the big leagues, he thinks, and he seems torn between the superficial and the real. I think Janie brought the best out of him when she asked him all those questions about what he really wants to do for other people. All he has to do is quit horsing around and giving you guys a hard time. Start acting like a human being."

If he weren't so busy chattering about her less-than-competent cohost, he would have noticed how upset she was. At the rate he was running on, he would never notice! She sat down next to him. "Bill," she said ominously, "let's get right down to it."

"What? Get down to what?" he asked, in innocent surprise.

"Nora's been here. Been here today. Been here other days, too, I bet. Isn't that true? Why didn't you just tell me?"

Bill hit his head with the palm of a hand. "God, Louise,

don't do this to me! I should have known to tell you that our neighbor, a very kind woman, as you know, paid some calls on me. Brought me a few lunches."

"Calls? Like formal calls, huh? Lunches? I thought you were eating liverwurst sandwiches. I wondered why those kitchen utensils were put back wrong. Why didn't I catch on to this?" Her voice was ascending, and so was her anger. She slapped a hand on her knee. "Why do I have to find out by picking up her cigarette butts in my gardens, and smelling her smoke in my house, in which I do not permit smoking. Even a picture of me is out of place on your table."

Bill leaned forward. His eyes widened. "I can't believe you. You are applying all your excellent little detecting skills to proving that your faithful husband has been unfaithful."

She got up in disgust and strode back and forth in front of the couch, her arms swinging, her mind churning with thoughts. "You know what that woman is, Bill? She's *adventitious.*"

"Come on," groaned Bill, shaking his head hopelessly, "what the hell does *that* mean?"

She pointed a finger at him as if he should know. "Adventitious—you know, like the roots." Her eyes flashed dangerously. "Those upright roots that spring so ingeniously and so unwelcomely out of the base of trees and out of branches and intrude themselves on the scene." Her voice rose. "And need to be pruned out! That's Nora all right—she needs to be pruned right out of our lives!"

"Bull!" he yelled, and leaned forward and grabbed his leg with both hands so he could guide it down to the carpeting and escape from the couch. Through sheer force of habit, she handed him his crutches, which were leaning on the end cushion.

"That's it, Louise. I have lain here on a bed of real pain for three weeks now. No work, few calls, nobody's interested in talking to me. Boredom, little family support . . ."

"Lack of coitus: I suppose you'll charge that next. Well, whose fault is that?"

He struggled to his feet, grabbing the crutches, freeing a hand to wave wildly. "You're so full of yourself you pay no attention to me! Huh! I'm getting out of here, doctor or no doctor."

She came nearer to him, afraid he would fall. "Bill, please be careful. I . . . I didn't mean to make you so angry."

"Louise, *you* are angry, and *I* am angry." He stood, waving slightly, recovering himself until his expression settled into a polite, impersonal mask. "If you wouldn't mind terribly, I would prefer it if you would sleep in the guest room tonight. I would myself, but the sleeping getup for this cast works better in our bed."

She barely stifled a sob. In their twenty years of marriage she couldn't remember a moment like this. Tears came to her eyes and coursed down her cheeks. She didn't wipe them away. She shook her head. "Sorry, Bill, but no. The guest bed's all filled with piles of garden books. Anyway, I don't care if you're angry; I can't sleep without you, and that's that."

They went to bed without speaking, and Bill, as usual, turned away from his wife. As usual, she faced him, and put a tentative hand on the soft curve of his waist, and immediately began the downward path toward sleep.

Getting a Little Wild:
Nativist Gardening

It is easy to be humbled by nature. It only takes a ride on a western river, a hike in the Appalachians, a visit to California's dunes, bluffs, chaparral and grassland, or a walk near a mighty river in the Midwest. Nature is the ultimate garden designer. More and more of today's gardeners are stepping off the well-worn path of formal gardening and using nature as a model. In the process they are creating a revolution in the appearance of our cities and countrysides.

Fifteen years ago or so, adventuresome gardeners began digging up their emerald-like lawns and replacing them with indigenous plants. Neighbors raised their eyebrows. In a few places they even called the police, protesting the outrage. It looked strange then, but not any more. Many yards in cities across America have become nativist gardens. Even apartment gardeners, who traditionally plant neat rows of pots, have caught the spirit, and garden balconies are overflowing with flowery vines and native species. Those with larger acreage have planted whole colonies of native plants. They are helping propagate and continue species that are threatened with extinction as more and more open land is turned over to development.

Before nativist gardeners choose plants, they check carefully to determine the type of soil with which they're dealing. It is much easier to grow plants that suit the soil than to attempt to change the soil to suit a plant. Nativists mulch bare earth heavily both to discourage weeds and help water retention. They arrange plant life in drifts, sometimes very large, colorful drifts, the way we find them in the virgin woodlands, meadows, and prairies. Straight lines are avoided: Nature dislikes straight lines and so do native gardeners. Trees and bushes are pruned from the top and the sides with subtle irregularity, to conceal any hint of human intervention. Gardens flow and complement the lay of the land, with subtle transitions between the wild and more traditional parts of the yard.

Rocks, streams, dunes, stone outcroppings, and hills are the skeleton of the natural garden. But suppose the site has no natural wonders? This does not stop the intrepid nativist gardener, who simply introduces them by digging depressions, making hills, and importing soil, natural stones, and clusters of rocks. A hillock, or series of hillocks, a small pond, or a recycling waterfall can be added to a yard and made to seem as if it were always there. Water will attract more wild birds and animals to the native enclave. If there are low spots in the land, it's an opportunity to plant things that need higher moisture. This is doing it the xeriscape way—by grouping plants with similar watering needs.

While large tracts blooming with native species are a beautiful sight, the process involves hard work and persistence, not over months but years. Grass and weeds must be removed before planting; this alone is a major task. Then comes faithful watering of the native seedlings, and careful weeding. Early fall mowing will help thwart weeds, but there is no substitute for a lot of hand weeding to get rid of these intruders in the wild garden.

If you aren't a gardening dynamo, rest assured that smaller-scale efforts also are effective. Plant drifts of native plants in an irregular border to separate "wild" from formal gardens. Plant them near fences to achieve the look of a hedgerow. Or tuck pockets of these plants at the base of a tree or a turn in the path, as a delightful surprise.

Big or small, the rewards are great for the gardener. There is nothing quite like a field of brilliant wildflowers, a hillock covered with waving grasses and daisies, a low swale abounding in joe-pye weed and native iris, or a bubbling waterfall tucked in the homemade wilderness, luring the birds and animals.

Nativist gardens reflect the philosophy of people who want to work with our entire ecosystem, both insects and plants, and restore what was there before "civilization" came along to disturb it.

12

Things were getting wild. It wasn't the hate mail—people attacking Louise for being an environmentalist and a nut. It wasn't the pickets: They wouldn't go away and were a continual embarrassment that caused even Jack Lederle, their prestigious news star, to raise his eyebrows at Louise. It wasn't the enormous gulf that had opened at home between her and Bill. What was bothering her most was Bruce Behrens. He was threatening the integrity of her entire show.

"There's trouble for us, Louise," Marty Corbin had warned yesterday. "Behrens has almost persuaded the general manager that we need a program telling the 'other side' "—he tweaked two fingers in the air to indicate quotation marks—"that we're not living up to the high standards of Public Broadcasting. They called our lawyer in on the meeting."

"Letting prospective underwriters call the tune certainly isn't living up to the high standards of PBS. Why does the man have all this clout?" asked Louise.

He looked at her warily. "Louise, I don't think I have to elaborate on the temper of the times and our station's perilous future—and the philosophy of fairness, of presenting both sides, that is written into PBS's conscience. Behrens isn't exactly making demands, but he is asking for a definition of the show and where it's going."

Today, they sat together at lunch at Fisherman's Wharf—she, Marty, and Bruce—for what Bruce called an "explanatory" meeting. They sat in a corner where they could look out through big glass windows at the Anacostia River Yacht

Basin. Boatmen were walking back and forth on the sunny gangways, getting their crafts ready for the season.

The chemicals manufacturer, sitting there looking tanned and handsome and maybe even a little thinner, told them in detail about his powerboat berthed at Alexandria. It just figured he would choose power over sail, thought Louise. She could picture him trading out of his expensive suit into expensive boating togs.

Then he ran his next spiel, a description of his estate on the Potomac River, complete with stable. To her, the place sounded pricey, colonial, and boring. But she was surprised to know the man lived only four miles south of her.

What he carefully *didn't* talk about were his chemical production plants, and how one of his pesticides might be recalled by the EPA. Or how his cement plants, like others, were involved in the questionable business of burning toxic wastes. She wondered whose talkative cement plant manager it was who bit the dust in that rock crusher. Could it have been Bruce's?

As he talked, Behrens nonchalantly gobbled up hard rolls and sipped his wine, confident about what was going to happen at this Washington luncheon. He launched into his main speech when the lunches arrived. In between hurriedly chewed bits of beef tournedos, he laid it out. "Your general manager and I agree. You people have put yourself in a very radical mode."

Louise looked at Marty. The producer was busy with his beef Stroganoff and obviously wasn't going to make any rejoinder to Behrens until the man finished. But she was.

Even though Marty had asked her to listen today and not talk too much, she had to say something. "You know, Bruce, 'environmental' does not, ipso facto, mean 'radical.' "

Marty gave her a warning look.

"Sometimes it does. Depends on how it's handled. That's what I told your general manager." He waved his fork at Marty, as if he were the other power source at this luncheon. "You guys—and I'm including you in that, Louise—have gotten off to a leftish start. Unbalanced. Marty told me the show would be IPM, not party-line organic. But do you know when the trouble started? It was when you had that green woman for a guest. First of all, I must say she was drab. A show like yours needs color, if you want my opinion, not drab. She's one of the most far-out environmental spokespeople in the country—you know that, of course?"

Marty came alive. But Louise didn't like what she heard. "Bruce, I talked this morning to the G.M. I think we can analyze this whole problem with a legal definition: Then you will know if you want to underwrite this show or not. Organic doesn't mean chemical-free. This is a nature gardening show, within limits. You can see that title gives us lots of latitude." He gave Louise a stern look. "Louise and I reached that understanding before the show even started." Then he turned back to Bruce. "I like the 'Integrated Pest Management' position of most county extension offices throughout the country. They recommend trying organic methods first, and only when necessary using a chemical product."

Louise drew in her breath and put down her fork. Her broiled fish had lost its luster. "Marty," she said, trying to draw him back, "wait."

Marty gently gestured with a hand, as if to tell a child to be still. "It's apparent, from the pickets and some of the mail . . ."

She looked earnestly at her producer. "Marty, you know as well as I do: The more organic our slant is, the more good mail we get. We've had *basketfuls* of good mail," she pointed out. "Two volunteers had to be assigned to help me handle it."

"I said *some* of the mail, Louise." He turned deliberately to the chemicals manufacturer. "I'm sure Louise can accept a balanced, IPM approach."

For a moment, she felt as if she were suffocating. By next week, she could foresee them recommending chemicals to eliminate every moving creature in the garden! She picked up her goblet and took a large gulp of water.

Like a man who had already won the argument, Behrens reached over and tapped her wrist. It was peculiarly invasive, and she withdrew her hand to her lap. "Let me mention a few more bromides of yours, Louise, that kind of get me—even though they aren't crucial. Like planting crooked, instead of in straight lines. Like pruning irregularly instead of shearing bushes. Where are you going to go with all that?"

Louise was speechless. "There's no chemical input in that, Bruce," she said testily. "That's just artfulness, if you could but recognize it."

Behrens finished with the clincher: "Funny thing, folks, Behrens Enterprises was thinking of underwriting your gardening show. But I can't see that happening right away, with the kind of program tilt you've had so far."

That did it. Here Marty had essentially kissed the guy's ass, and he still was wavering on the decision to become a sponsor. What more would the station do next to assuage this man? She could feel the blood throbbing in her head. She was furious and opened her mouth to speak. Then she shut it again; after all, that's what Marty had asked her to do, just listen. She had already said too much.

13

Janie had that guilty weight on her shoulders that comes from being late. A faint picture of a worried mother came to mind. She and Chris had dawdled their way down Route One and ended up in Super Hamburger, where she was now attempting to finish a large burger. She took small bites, while Chris gobbled his quickly. He crumpled up the hamburger wrapper, looked at her square in the eye, and got down to what they really had wanted to talk about since they left school.

"Look," he said, "I didn't mean to be avoiding you. I just thought I'd leave it up to you." His eyes were serious under his blond hair, which hung over his brow, in need of a haircut.

She took a fry and popped it in her mouth. "Well, I've been thinking about it. We both have supplies." Chris had bought two packages that day, each holding six condoms, handing one off to Janie, and keeping the other. Twelve condoms! That would mean twelve times, when she couldn't imagine doing it *one* time.

Suddenly she knew what her decision was. "I just can't do it."

"Oh. Why not?"

"For one thing, my dad's still home on the couch. And your mom's home all the time. I'm *not* doing it just anywhere." She looked straight over into his disappointed eyes. "But that's not all of it. I think it would be fun to be in bed with you, especially if we were in our pajamas." She looked down at the table. "But I don't think I'm ready for sex." She mouthed it quietly.

Her glance slid past Chris's face and up at the bright ceiling. She was remembering her mother's descriptions. "Because there are so many fluids and everything."

"Fluids," said Chris in a normal voice.

"Shhh," she warned, looking around at the other booths to see who might be listening. Nobody seemed interested. They probably thought she and Chris were talking about a car.

"Nothing wrong with a few fluids," he said quietly. "So, what you're saying is, you're not ready for all this."

She smiled weakly, feeling very faint. "I'm sorry. Maybe . . ."

"Well, you need to grow up a little, that's all," he said philosophically. "And it may take some time. C'mon, let's shove along."

Outside, looking at the traffic of Route One, Chris looked down at his books. "Darn! I need to go back to school. Forgot my physics book. Can you make it home by yourself all right?"

"Of course," she said. "It's only a mile."

He gave her a little kiss on the cheek. "Be careful. It's getting dark."

She crossed the highway at the light and started down the stretch of dimly lit road that eventually would lead her into Sylvan Valley. She felt lighthearted and light-footed, her thoughts all on Chris. So the dark figure behind her could have been tracking her for some time before she noticed. In a glance backwards, she caught the light gleaming off the person, a button, perhaps, on the person's coat. She started walking faster.

With horror she heard the footsteps behind her turn into a run.

Stretching out on either side were half-empty fields, with just a few modest houses with no lights on, the people living in them probably working overtime to earn enough to

71

live. But in one of them, an old white place, was a friend of Chris's. With a rush of energy she sprinted across the uneven fields toward it.

Reaching a dirt road, she swerved sharply, and, keeping as low to the ground as possible, raced down the block to where she could see the lights of the white house. It was surrounded with scraggly big pine trees. She ran toward the light, but knew the large, dark figure would catch up with her before she reached it. She let out a helpless moan, then turned on the overburner she used when running the fifty-yard dash at school.

She glanced over the shoulder. The figure was so close behind her she could see the ski mask.

On it were painted two big, scary eyes! She started screaming in sheer terror and couldn't stop.

And then her salvation arrived in the person of a scruffy white dog. It wheeled around the bushes and started barking like a machine gun. She eluded the darting, snarling little creature, which then went after her pursuer. At that moment, the front porch light flicked on. It was the most wonderful light she had ever seen. A young man opened the rickety door and she ran up the walk, took the steps two at a time, and stumbled forward into a tiny living room.

"Please, please, quickly close the door! There's someone out there after me. And he's running toward the back. You'd better lock the back door!" He hurried through the back of the house, and as she grappled with the bolt on the front door, she could hear him throwing a lock.

She cowered against a wall, trembling. When the young man returned to the living room, he looked at her quizzically. "You're Janie, aren't you, from school?"

"Yes," she whispered, shoving her hair back off her face. Her eyes darted around the room, staring at the curtainless windows with black beyond. "And someone chased me just now. He's out there. Can I call home?"

The young man thought about that for a moment. "I'd say, let's call the police."

Louise came home from work in a low mood.

"Not a good day?" asked Bill.

"It sucked," she growled, and plopped onto the couch next to him.

"Louise, that language . . ."

"Got it from your daughter, Martha. Sorry. State Department wives don't talk that way, do they." Her voice was edged with cynicism.

"Well . . . so tell me what's wrong."

"Everything. Marty and I had lunch with Behrens. It's totally against station rules for underwriters to get involved with the program, but he's making inroads, I can tell. And he hasn't even given any money yet. And then that extra sign. I hate those pickets!"

Bill sat up straighter. "What did the sign say?"

"They added one today. It said, 'Adolf Hitler Endorsed Natural Gardening.' "

"Well, did he?"

"Apparently, yes. Marty and I had the research department check it. Hitler did promote a big natural gardening movement through the thirties. But so what? He was also supposed to be a vegetarian; does that make every vegetarian guilty of Nazism by association?"

Bill swung his cast down onto the floor. In a droll voice he said, "I, of course, believe you are free of any Fascist taint. Now, we have a dinner date, haven't we?"

"Yes." She looked at him warily from her slumped position on the couch. This dinner was a reconciliation attempt. He stretched out a hand and took hers. He almost looked like the old Bill. "Louise, we'll both feel better after we talk and clear up these misunderstandings."

She squeezed his hand and they looked at each other for a long moment. "I need you," she said. She said it simply, without smiling.

"And I need you." She thought he might kiss her, but instead, supported by crutches, he made his way to the bedroom. She slouched back on the couch and stared moodily into the woods. She knew it would take time to get back to their old comfort level. Then her mind wandered back to work. It was frustrating, the way controversy had intruded on what was becoming her comforting little world of work.

When Bill's cellular phone rang, it was within easy reach.

Detective Morton of the Fairfax County police was a man of few words. She and Bill had met him at the time of the mulch murder and had not been fond of his blunt approach, preferring the more reasonable Detective Geraghty. Morton said, "Your daughter is at the police station and you'd better come pick her up."

With some prodding, he told Louise of how the police were called to trouble at a house near Route One.

"Is Janie all right?" asked Louise, standing now, pacing with the phone.

"She's all right; she's just scared. It's not good to allow a teenaged girl to walk home in the dark, ma'am, right near Route One. You can only expect trouble if you do."

Louise looked at her watch. It was a little after six. She was so wrapped up in her own problems she hadn't even noticed Janie wasn't home. "I realize she shouldn't have done that. But, a stalker? Could it be someone we know?"

Detective Morton was silent a moment. "Oh. I get it. You maybe want to hang this on Mr. Hoffman?" Louise could picture Morton, sitting at his desk, his large upper body giving him a giant quality, his mask-like face revealing nothing. "It wasn't Hoffman; a police car just cruised around and checked on him not fifteen minutes ago. What you better do is tell your daughter that it's a dangerous world out there."

"All right," she said, chastised. "I hear what you're saying."

The detective coughed self-consciously at the other end of the phone. "Consider another possibility, Mrs. Eldridge. I see on the TV new that you're raising a ruckus with that program of yours. Could it be somebody connected with *that* who's harassing your daughter? One of them sorry-looking fellows picketing the TV station calling you a Nazi?"

Could her job, her career, have created this danger for her daughter? It took a tactless person like Detective Morton to drive it right home, like a sharp blow to the solar plexus.

14

Louise kept her nose delicately lifted in an attempt to escape the encroaching smell of mildew in the hot waiting room. Her guess was that they kept it either super-heated or super-cooled in here so the little spores that lingered in the wall cracks and carpeting didn't come out and grow and turn the place green. Her eyes went to the only thing of note in the room: a huge movie poster, from a Clint Eastwood spaghetti Western. Clint was sighting a huge rifle right out at the world. Tacked onto the poster was a handwritten sign that warned, "Shhh, casting next door!"

The warning worked: People were mostly silent, straining to listen to the directions being given by the director in the adjoining casting room: "More projection, please. More emotion! And you'd better swallow: We don't care for the — — obber effect." Louise couldn't quite hear. Did he say slobber effect?

She looked circumspectly at the others sitting with her in this low-budget casting office. She didn't know every name, but she recognized them as the elite of the Washington television corps. Of course: Why wouldn't the local stars audition for a plum job like this? Big envelopes with publicity photos were clasped in their laps as respectfully as if they were the Holy Grail.

They all knew each other. Like old friends, they bantered quietly back and forth whenever there was a lapse in conversation next door. She was the outsider again, just as she had been a couple of months ago when she started at WTBA-

TV. Slumping in her seat a little, she realized her chances of getting this job were nil.

Things were now escalating behind the thin walls. The director was getting irritated, and it became easier to hear every word. It was a raw, rude voice. "Move in on the product. Surround it. Circle it, do something, get some emotion into what you're doing. You're not relating to this mower. I want you to relate to this mower!"

She could feel sweat forming in her armpits under her suit jacket. What would she do when she got in there with that mower? Temperamental people screaming at her was something she wasn't used to. She looked at the others; they were unaffected by the rough words from behind the partition. She took some deep breaths, trying to find a comfort level in this alien environment.

"Hi," said a mellow voice. It was the well-made-up young woman sitting beside her. She stared at Louise curiously. "You look familiar." She pointed a long red-lacquer-tipped finger right at Louise. "Now I've got you pegged: You're the Channel Five gardening lady. Gee! Now, *that's* an in. How did you get here?"

Louise said she was invited to audition. "And how about you?"

"This is how I make my living: voice-overs, TV spots."

"Is it a good living?"

The woman was no more than thirty, if that. Her whole person, the pretty face, the shapely figure in beige silk suit, the long, well-turned legs, was overshadowed by her leonine blond hair. Her eyes were an unnatural shade of violet, redolent of pansies. "Well, I'm paying the rent on my condo," she said. "And I occasionally have enough to vacation in St. Kitts. But it is mercilessly competitive. Especially for women. Believe me, it's a man's world here. Wait until you get into that casting studio. And in the industry there is maybe one job for a woman to every six jobs for a man. We girls really get desperate."

The young woman put a hand inside the protective cage

of hair to touch her honey-and-peaches-complexioned face. She smiled brightly at Louise. "Just look around you." She cast a polite glance at the others in the waiting room. Through Edgar Bergen lips, she tallied them off by name. "Most of them are local superstars. That ballsy guy over there: Recognize him? Channel Thirteen. Not only does he pull down two hundred thou for his newscast, he also is the voice-over for, oh, at least half a dozen companies, everything from bras to bedsheets. They love his voice. He'd love this job."

She looked at Louise again, as if checking to see how she was holding up under this information. "Now, competition is such that, if you should walk in there and get picked, six people will be willing to murder you for stepping in as an amateur and taking away the prize."

As if to verify that, the man from Channel Thirteen stared at her with eyes as cold as stones. "This is a great job," continued the blonde, "because the company isn't the kind, like McDonald's or one of those, that's going to change their ad campaign that fast."

"And I hear you get paid every time the ad runs."

"Every time." The young woman shook her head, and the blond hair shimmered. "God," she muttered, "I need this gig. Though need has nothing to do with it, believe me."

With a tactful side glance, she checked out Louise's sporty blue suit with its oversized jacket. "Let me tell you, outside of the fact you're a little old for this kind of job, you look great today. Just the right touch: You are a good-looking woman."

"Well, gee, thanks." said Louise.

"As long as the mower company doesn't agree with those pickets who are calling you a Nazi, you'd be a great spokesperson." She grinned. "Darn it. But good luck to us both."

At that moment, another person came in the anteroom. Madeleine Doering.

She looked as beautiful as Louise had ever seen her, wearing a tailored dress in a becoming muted green, her long brown hair fashioned in a pageboy, her eyes bright and rested. Her face was made up with its usual skill, today in burnished brown and bronze tones, as if to echo nature. Quite in tune with mulching mowers, observed Louise.

"Oh, oh," came out of Louise, before she could stop herself.

The blonde looked at her, and then at Madeleine. "You work with Madeleine, don't you? Oh yes, and she used to have your show. Well. Must be a snakepit over there at WTBA."

Madeleine stood in the doorway, but when she saw Louise, she stepped back as if recoiling from a blow. Others in the room greeted her casually but she barely responded. She walked over and stood in front of Louise. Her perfume, heavy and expensive, was like a separate presence. Quietly, menacingly, she said, "What on earth are you doing here?"

"Madeleine. Hello. I was asked to audition, just like you were."

The woman pressed on. "You don't even have an agent, do you? You're a total amateur. I'm at a loss as to why you were included here. Was it Marty's influence?"

Louise stared up at Madeleine. She was getting tired of being her favorite punching bag. In a low voice that only the blonde next to her could hear, she said, "You will have to get used to the idea that I live and operate in the same world as you do. I am not here to destroy you, and I wish you would stop acting as if I am." She held Madeleine's hate-filled look, refusing, for once, to back down and be a wimp.

Mercifully, at that moment the casting secretary hurried into the room. She checked out the crowd and then came directly over to Louise. "Excuse me, Louise Eldridge? Can you please come with me?"

Louise glanced at the blond woman to whom she had been talking and shrugged her shoulders in guilty bafflement as to why she was being called before others.

The blonde's eyes narrowed speculatively. "Gee," she said, "I had a sneaky feeling you had an in." She gave Louise a half-hearted wave.

When Louise got up out of her chair she was face to face with Madeleine, who stood immovable. She said nervously, "Take my chair, why don't you," and fled the room with the secretary.

As they hurried down the hall, the secretary thrust a one-page script at her and gave her a quick fill-in. "This company's auditioning in a number of cities. The client, well, you'll find this out right away in there: He's unfocused. He wants a certain feeling out of someone who will be selling his product, but he's not a hundred percent sure just what feeling he wants. So it might take them a while to get back to you is what I'm warning you."

The studio was as modest as the waiting room, with the same sickening Washington basement smell. It was about half again as large, with one camera, and several people sitting behind a folding banquet table. Glaring lights were aimed at an object, which Louise expected to be the company's major product, the mulching mower. Instead, sitting in the pool of light was a dented metal folding chair with a hand-printed sign on it reading "Atlas."

"All right, Ms. Eldridge," said the director, "are you ready?"

Louise had not even had time to look at the words on the sheet of paper clutched in her hand. "Right now? Could you just give me a few minutes?"

"Minutes?" he repeated, in a high, incredulous voice. "Ms. Eldridge, we have a schedule to maintain. I'll give you a minute. Then let's roll."

The secretary guided Louise into the circle of light and took her purse. She stood there, frantically focusing on two double-spaced paragraphs of words in bold capital letters.

She couldn't quite believe what she read. It alluded to the mulching mower as a savior of the world, just like the mythical Atlas. She looked dubiously at the dark faces beyond the circle of light. "I guess I'm ready."

"Now, Ms. Eldridge," said the director, "you're going to pretend that chair is a mower. We want you to react with this mower, and tell us how wonderful it is. Ready? Let's tape." She had done some research on mulching mowers, as much as she could lay her hands on. She realized the writer of this copy had done none.

"Can I improvise?" asked Louise, quickly. "You don't mind a little, do you?"

A querulous woman's voice asked, "Can't she just read the script?"

The director sighed heavily. Her words probably signaled to him that she was an amateur, not a professional like that macho Channel Thirteen newscaster or the other smooth-talking, fast-read candidates in the outer office. "Just do what you can, dear," he said resignedly, as if he were talking to a mentally deficient person to whom he was obliged to show charity.

She slowly approached the chair, trying to call up the pictures in the books she had read about these contraptions. Mentally, she transformed the chair into a bright green machine with fancy controls on top, for which a gardener would be willing to pay $1,200 or more.

"We remember the old story about the mythical Atlas," she began. She could feel the adrenaline kicking in. Here was the payoff of two months of slaving before a television camera with an unreliable cohost who forced her to improvise at every turn. She began to enjoy herself. After all, a woman who could make compost into a provocative topic should have no trouble selling a mulching mower! "Atlas held the world upon his shoulders," she continued. "And as gardeners know, today we all hold on our shoulders part of the responsibility for maintaining our planet. Here's a way we can do it that is easy and effective."

She made eye contact with the camera, then gracefully caressed the top of the chair, as if smoothing her hands across a set of controls. She described how the mower worked by spitting grass right back into the turf. Then, using the pivotal leg-and-hip motion that Marty had taught her, she whirled around and gracefully swooped down at the front of the rickety chair, which had *become* a mower as far as she was concerned, and told how to convert it into a mulcher. She circled the mower, still talking, and ended where she started, a hand resting gently on the dented chair, a serene smile on her face aimed right at the camera.

There was a moment of silence. Then a victorious whistle floated up from the banquet table, followed by enthusiastic clapping. Louise was acutely aware that Madeleine Doering and all those other competitive people could hear this through the paper-thin walls.

"Hey," said the director, in a robust voice. "Who'd have thought it? We've got what we need on the first take." The writer continued to grumble about a sabotaged script. The third man at the table got up and walked over to Louise. He had a friendly face and thinning white hair, his face bronzed as if from sitting on a tractor all day. But his suit was an Armani.

"Ms. *El*dridge." The voice reeked of the Midwest, as warm as a summer day in Iowa. "I've seen your show, and I think it's great. Let me introduce myself. I'm the president of Atlas. They say I have more sittin' in to do at auditions in a couple of other cities—but believe you me, ma'am, I'm pretty sure I've found my spokesperson already."

15

Louise had come home from work and changed into her jogging clothes for this walk in the woods with her daughter. It was a perfect, early spring afternoon, with a faint breeze blowing, and new leaves on trees seeming to unfurl even as they walked through them.

A few months ago, it might have seemed contrived to have to make a date with her own child to talk things over, but with the way Louise's life had changed, it felt perfectly normal. It gave Janie the chance to grumble about her mother's absences.

She had little to answer the girl. What could she say, that she would give up a career that she had just started four months ago? She kept to herself the euphoria she felt after the successful tryout today at the casting studio; it would only worry Janie more to think Louise might get a second job.

They sauntered over to the Swim Club and she showed Janie the several dozen holes dug by her volunteers for new trees. As she rattled off the tree names, Janie stopped her. "You're working again, Ma: Your next show must be on trees, right?"

Sheepishly she acknowledged this. The last thing she had wanted to do was to talk about her job; she was hoping Janie would confide something about her feelings for Chris. The amount of time she spent with Chris alarmed her, some of it on the basketball court with Chris' sister, Melanie, and the neighbor kids, but more of it alone. For all she knew, sex between them was a fait accompli. Her shoulders dropped a little at the thought. Janie's whole recent life, with sex included or not, was an unknown. What kind of a mother was she getting to be?

They continued down the path, with the hill jutting up beside them on one side, the stream running along the other side. "I haven't heard you talk that much about Chris lately," Louise said casually. "Are you still friends?"

Janie skipped away in front of her down the narrow trail. Louise could barely hear her words. "Yep, Ma. We're good friends. That's it." Her daughter's heart-to-heart discussions of a few months ago had been reduced to sentences with a maximum of three words.

16

Ever so carefully, she had followed the script for her program on pesticides.

Magnanimously, she had allowed the visiting pesticide management specialist to put in a plug for use of "friendly" pesticides when all else failed.

Ever so gently, she had handled the ancient bottles of banned pesticides she filched from a neighbor's garage, and brought to contrast with organic controls now on the market.

She had treated her newly purchased plastic containers of pest-eating ladybugs and praying mantises like two little infants.

Then her nervous fingers somehow flipped the ladybug container over and flying bugs swarmed all over her, her co-host, her guest, the table, and the studio, throwing the staff into a nervous frenzy, except for the cool cameraman, who at the director's orders just kept shooting. Marty himself and those with him in the control room lapsed into paroxysms of uncontrollable laughter.

Magically, it turned out all right. The little orange-and-black creatures began their diaspora near the end of the show. Although she was sure she had blown it, she made the whole thing into a joke. While a couple of ladybugs climbed up her lapels, she deadpanned into the camera, "At least I can be sure of one thing—there will be no pests on me!"

She could see Marty was euphoric: This was the kind of live stuff he loved. Even John Batchelder rose to the occasion and helped improvise the way through the crisis. John was happy because he had been given an integral third voice in the interview. Louise noticed that he no longer tried to grab lines that were not his.

The visiting horticulturist, a tall, gray-haired man, was smitten with Louise, especially after she upended the lady-bugs. "You just wanted a little more action, didn't you?" he teased, in an indulgent voice.

But she earned the undisguised wrath of the surly janitor. After the show, Louise helped him chase the little bugs for almost an hour, with no assurance they had caught them all. While she apologized profusely, his silence rebuked her clumsiness.

Later, she saw Marty again, hovering in the first-floor hall-way among a swarm of volunteers, who had come to the station to help with one of its biennial fund drives. Marty looked at the volunteers and chuckled. "They'll get a surprise tonight. Just when they're answering a call with someone pledging a hundred dollars or so, a bug will fly in and land on their neck."

She apologized again, but the producer said, "Stop apol-ogizing: When I tell you it worked, I mean it was great! It's those little spontaneous bursts that make your progam what it is. And that bit on how to dispose of poisons safely—hell, I got stuff in my garage I've had for years. And now I'm gonna get rid of it right away."

"Well, thanks for the kind words." And there he did it again: supported and praised her, reinforcing her loyalty. And just when she should be terminally disgusted with him for wavering under a proposed sponsor's pressure.

"How about a drink?" The liquid brown eyes were close and inviting.

"Well—sure, but it would have to be a quick one because . . . I should get home."

"Great," said Marty. "Let me get my things. Come to the side door; we'll avoid the pickets."

Louise frowned. "Let's talk about those pickets, Marty. A

reporter called me this afternoon for an interview and told me at least one of those men was what he called a 'picket for pay.' They're phonies! Plus some other things, like Bruce Behrens. I saw him around today; I wish you'd tell me what's going on with him."

It was as if a curtain descended on Marty's face. She decided to stay off that subject for now. "But it's those pickets— I wish we could at least find out who hired them."

The producer frowned and rubbed a hand across his five-o'clock shadow. "That's interesting. I'll talk about it to the front office. Be back in a minute with my coat."

He insisted that he drive, and they went to the nearby Joe's Raw Bar, one of Northern Virginia's older neighborhood watering holes, where the smell of malt and fish had crept into the worn wooden floor and would stay there as long as the place remained standing. They hunkered down in comfy captain's chairs, their attention undistracted by the decor, whose high points, Louise had noticed, were a neon Schlitz sign and a modest stuffed fish hung over the bar. When she ordered a Poland Water, Marty protested. "Hey, we're celebrating another good program, your fifth, and getting better all the time."

"Sorry, I don't drink, Marty." Of all the times she wouldn't bend this rule, now was it. Marty had been a little too affectionate from the start. She hoped maybe she could make it clear to him this afternoon she was not one to stray from her marriage vows.

After some shoptalk, Marty said, in his low, mellow voice, "So I can tell, Louise. You've made up with Bill: You were on the outs there, for about a week."

"And you could tell we made up." She looked at him without smiling.

He grinned, unabashed at her discomfort. "Hey, look, Louise, I work with you four days a week. Yeah, I can notice changes in women. Things got sort of bad when he broke his leg there. Then they got worse, over something, something that made you really angry. Then, as of two days ago, it's the

87

old, happy Louise, whistling little tunes under her breath, the fire back in her eye. So I figure you made up with Bill."

Louise couldn't help smiling. "You're very observant. Everything you said is more or less true." She leaned forward, the better to give him the message. In her best imitation of a temptress, she said, "It was that *da-a-mned* cast—got in the way. But now it's off, and you just don't know how good it is to be back in my sweetie's arms."

Then she sat back and crossed her arms, trying to smother a smile.

"Okay, I get it." He sighed and sat back with his draft beer, and his expressive face lost its good humor. "You don't know how good you've got it, when you're really in love with the person you married. And nothing's as bad as getting all fouled up in a relationship outside of marriage that goes nowhere and ends up in fights." Then he threw down a couple of bills from his wallet and they left the raw bar.

Awed at his mood change, she didn't have much to say to him on the way back to the station. Both of them had things to pick up. Inside, Marty glanced scornfully at the volunteers swarming about the lobby. "Would that these eager beavers could save our financial asses."

She looked at him. This was no longer the amiable Marty, but the Marty disillusioned with his clinging mistress, his marriage, and the future of the PBS station where he worked—a man who took every rebuffed pass he made at a woman as some kind of personal failure.

Louise had to make a stop at a women's rest room. Because of the crowd of volunteers, she chose the less public one at the end of the hall. She pushed open the door. The perfume odor reached out and assailed her before she noticed Madeleine Doering standing near the sinks, applying eye makeup.

"Hi," Louise said neutrally. "Going home?"

Madeleine sniffed, "Improbable that you'd care, Louise,

but no, I'm staying. As an experienced, on-camera talent, I volunteer my time for fund-raisers."

"Oh, that's good of you." Louise somehow hadn't realized the Channel Five staff worked free on these fund drives. She went into the lavatory, and when she returned to wash her hands, found Madeleine still there, working on the other eye, her head close to the mirror to see better.

The woman stood up straight, mascara brush poised in midair. It was as if she had been waiting for Louise. "You're not a professional, you know." She bit off each word. *"Don't think you are."*

Louise tapped the lever on the soap container; an unsatisfactory little dribble came out. She turned on the hot water and rubbed her hands. "I'm under no illusion that I am a professional. But I am trying to learn." Out of the corner of her eye she saw someone with light-colored hair come in and quickly hurry by to the lavatory stalls.

Madeleine turned her blazing eyes on Louise. "I suppose you think you did pretty well in that audition. You play dirty when you try to move in on the commercials. You're going to get yours from somebody." Her voice was growing louder and shriller. "You haven't paid your dues, Louise! I bet *I* get that mower contract. But if I don't by some chance, you won't hear the end of it."

Cautiously, Louise sought out the words of a peacemaker. "You're probably right about deserving things, Madeleine. I haven't paid my dues in terms of working in the business for a long time, but I have worked awfully hard since I started this job."

"You have a mealy-mouthed answer for everything, don't you? You are such a good suburban person, with your suburban family. While I am divorced, putting a kid through college, struggling my way through life."

Louise knew Madeleine lived in an attractive condo in northwest Washington and her daughter attended Smith College. Her clothes certainly outclassed Louise's.

Suddenly, all the weird things that were happening to her flashed through Louise's mind. The released ladybugs. The pickets. The little black cloud of Peter Hoffman's presence. The threat of Bruce Behrens ruining her show. The worry over her daughters. And nearly losing her husband to a sub-urban siren.

She had it just as bad as Madeleine, maybe worse! Her patience evaporated.

"Oh, just cut it out, Madeleine," she snapped. "My life is *not* easy. As usual, you have it wrong." Immediately regret-ting the outburst, she reached by Madeleine for a towel, anx-ious to get out of the crowded little room.

At that moment, Madeleine cried out, "Oh! See what you made me do, get mascara in my eye!" Blinded for an instant, she whirled around and her long fingernails swept across Louise's cheeks, painfully scratching her.

"My God, that hurt!" cried Louise. In the background, she heard a toilet flush and someone hurry out, understandably not wanting to get involved. And then she discovered she was caught, entwined somehow with this woman. Madeleine's hair had tangled in a button on Louise's suit jacket.

"Madeleine," commanded Louise in a calm, firm voice, *"hold still."* Madeleine stopped moving. "Thanks." She pulled a couple of clean paper towels out of the holder and put them into Madeleine's hand. "Here, you can use these for your eye. Let me untangle your hair. It's caught."

"And my eye is stinging like hell."

"Sorry. If you just wouldn't get so angry at things. Now I have to yank a little to get this hair loose. But it'll only hurt for a moment." With a jerk and a whimper from Madeleine, she was free of the woman, leaving the removal of hair strands from her button until later. "Now, can you bathe your eye all right?"

"Yes, I guess," moaned Madeleine.

"I'm going now," said Louise, "unless you need me to stay and help." She sighed. "I wish you could be more reasonable about things, Madeleine." She hurried out of the rest room, noting as she left a figure retreating hurriedly toward the back stairs.

As she went to her office, volunteers were being collected to go on-air. Some looked vaguely familiar. Since they were all from the Nature Club, she may have met them in her research into environmental issues.

She unlocked her office, turned on the light, and went to her desk to gather up the books and materials she needed to take back home. She put on her coat, hefted up her heavy briefcase, and leaned against one of the white walls for an instant's rest. Then, she turned off the lights and relocked the door.

She wanted to just sneak quietly out of this nerve-wracking place. Still lurking around here were her temperamental producer, her jealous predecessor, and probably her feisty co-host as well, to say nothing of the luckless janitor who had been turned into a game warden.

Then she heard the screams. They echoed like an unearthly dirge from their starting point down at the end of the hall. She rushed to the sound and saw a woman in her sixties, her face crumpled and drained of blood, stumbling out of the women's rest room. Then, as Louise watched, she collapsed in a heap in the hall.

Almost all action stopped. Only the little hum of words from the announcer for the on-air program could be heard. The small conversations between visiting volunteers, even the din of computers and printers and tape machines were silenced, as if to give the screamer undivided attention.

"Jesus Christ, what's going on?" muttered Marty, as if Louise should know the answer. He had appeared from somewhere, with others quickly joining him. She threw down her heavy briefcase and ran to the woman and crouched down. "Are you hurt?" she asked.

The woman huddled up against the wall like an animal repelling attack. Her screams had diminished to whimpering sobs. Louise watched in fascination as the woman extracted

91

a trembling hand from near her body and pointed it toward the rest room door. "In there," she cried. "She's shaking herself to death!"

Someone flung the lavatory door open and they crowded in. First they heard the noises: guttural gasps and scuffling noises on the floor. Louise peered around Marty and saw her.

Madeleine Doering lay on the floor near the place Louise had left her no more than ten minutes before.

"My God!" said the producer, and turned away. Louise put her hand up to her mouth, forcing herself not to be sick.

Madeleine's body was shaking so hard that it was bumping around the floor like a mechanical windup toy out of control. Her face was frozen and contorted in agony, her features appearing to be flying away from each other.

"She's having a seizure!" cried Louise, pushing Marty aside. "We have to do something!" She ripped off her coat and laid it on top of the woman.

With pupils so contracted that her eyes seemed pure green, Madeleine now managed to look at Louise, as if grasping for help from a friend. The mouth, drooling saliva, opened grotesquely as she tried to fashion some words. "I . . . I . . . he . . ." Then another convulsion swept over her, and her jaw locked for good.

Louise knelt near her, holding the coat over her and trying gently to keep it in one place as the body continued to jump reflexively. She knew seizure victims should at least be kept warm. "It's okay, dear," she said in a shaking voice. "We're trying to help you. Hold on—someone is calling the doctor." But as her face came closer to the woman's on the floor, she smelled it, above the strong perfume odor, and she had a hard time keeping her stomach from seizing up. A sick, pesticidal smell emanated from Madeleine's mouth—or was it from her pores, her whole body?

Louise suddenly put it all together. "Pesticide! Tell someone it's pesticide! I hope someone's called the medics—they could save her with atropine!" She leaned down, detecting the now unmistakable chemical smell, acrid in her nostrils. In an automatic self-defensive motion, she leaned back on her haunches and put a frantic hand over her face, desperate for a breath of fresh air, desperate to get away from the stench of this dying woman.

Dying? No, dead. She stared at the woman's face, still at last after that agony of shaking her life away on the cold terrazzo floor.

Poisoned, Louise was pretty sure, just like a bug.

There's More Than One Way to Get Rid of a Pest

Gardeners need a different attitude toward garden pests. Pests are not permanent: They arrive in the garden, they propagate, and even if you do nothing to kill them, they ebb away and disappear. So instead of freaking out and reaching for a can of pesticide, reach for your magnifying glass. Go out to the garden and check out the size of the problem. What you find magnified there might even give you a different slant on pests: They can be quite beautiful, and at the very least entertaining, as they eat your plants and each other.

But it's easy to understand why we panic when big, horned worms suddenly appear on our healthy tomato plants and we see sky through the holes in the leaves, or when aphids swarm over our rosebuds. Insects make us itchy; it's no wonder we look for a chemical weapon to destroy them. But the truth is that if we demolish all those pests, we disturb nature's balance and create worse problems. Or, to put it another way, the "good" bugs will fly off to your neighbor's yard if we don't leave some of the "bad" bugs in place for their food supply. Spray for caterpillars, and we will demolish the natural enemies of spider mites, and that will be our next pest epidemic.

We home gardeners are heavy-handed: We use more pesticides and insecticides than farmers. In the process, we damage nature's balancing act and contaminate the country's well water. Fortunately, a practice called "integrated pest management" (IPM) has been adopted by most cities and counties and many farmers, in an attempt to reduce the amount of pesticides in the environment. IPM calls for using that magnifying glass and traps for monitoring pest problems before just settling for the poison spray. Farmers who have adopted these techniques find they have cut their use of pesticides in half. Backyard gardeners can do it, too. Follow these guidelines:

- Select only plants and trees resistant to disease.
- Soil creates more disease problems than any other factor. Develop and maintain a healthy one.
- Have clean garden habits. Fight the spread of germs by keeping tools clean, pruning and trimming correctly, and removing wastes, especially diseased leaves or plants.

- Measure the size of the problem by using pheromone or other traps. This is one of the fun parts of gardening, because you are matching wits with pesky little insects whose survival record is much longer than that of humans.
- Encourage beneficial insect predators such as green lacewings, syrphid flies and lady beetles. You can buy lady beetles in bulk, and they're cute, but don't count on them not to fly away. The best way to encourage these so-called good insects is by using a variety of plants; this provides them with a constant source of alternative hosts on which to feed. Also, divert pests. For instance, plant rose mallow near your precious raspberry bushes, and they'll leave the raspberries for you to eat.
- Get rid of insects the old-fashioned way, by removing them by hand. Children will love the challenge of picking off rose beetles or tomato worms: Pay them a bounty for each bug. Set out traps, such as a pie plate of beer, to catch slugs. A simple spray with a hose will remove many insects, and a spray with household detergent and water will demolish stubborn ones.
- If the above measures don't work and the problem is serious, use oil sprays or other organic pesticides. *Bacillus thuringiensis,* pyrethrum, and neem tree products are among the most popular. The best news is that more safe pesticides come on the market each year. Chemical cures may soon become obsolete.

After you start looking differently at pests, you might want to encourage one entertaining fellow, the parsleyworm. Attract it by providing its favorite foods: parsley, dill, fennel and carrots. It is a handsome thing, with white, yellow and black stripes. When disturbed, it has a cunning defense weapon: It pulls up a Y-shaped horn from behind its head that emanates a rancid butter smell and discourages its enemy's approach. This worm turns into the beautiful swallowtail butterfly. Children will love it and thank you for attracting it to your garden.

17

"I don't understand what more I have to tell you," she told the detective. She put a hand on her breast. "I don't know anything else, other than I was just in there trying to help Madeleine. But I'll be happy to tell you anything I do know."

Was she being repetitive? She and the tall black officer stood in the hall, not far from Louise's office. Around them, other policemen were rounding up the staff and the Nature Club volunteers and moving them like an unwilling herd of dogies toward the lobby.

The detective, distracted by the activity, took her by the arm. "Ma'am, let's just take our conversation in here." He guided her to Marty Corbin's office.

Casting a last longing glance at the crowd outside, she entered the familiar environment and sat down in one of Marty's visitor chairs. The detective closed the door and went behind the desk and sat down.

"Mrs. Eldridge, I've picked up some information here that ties you right to the scene."

"The scene of *what?*" she asked.

"The scene of the murder, Mrs. Eldridge. All the evidence indicates the victim was murdered. The coroner is here, and we should know pretty soon. Now, back to your part in this."

"I have no part in this," insisted Louise. "I just . . ."

"Oh, yes," he said knowledgeably. "You just had a knock-down, drag-out fight with the deceased, right?"

"Well, not a fight, exactly."

"Ma'am, more than one person heard her yelling at you."

Louise's heart sank. Madeleine's screaming at her. Getting Louise's goat so she eventually spoke back, probably in too loud a voice to be polite. Then Madeleine blinding herself temporarily with the mascara, flailing around and scratching Louise's face, and getting her hair tangled. Louise helping Madeleine to regain her composure.

But no one had seen that last part, where Louise helped Madeleine.

The detective had stood up and slowly walked around the desk and peered down at her face. "What are those scratches, then, on your cheeks?" Then he pointed to her chest and his eyes lit up. "And, what have we here? Is that hair, hanging off your buttonhole there?"

Drat it! She'd forgotten to untangle Madeleine's hair.

"I can explain it," she said, touching the hair, trying to untwine it. "We did have an argument in the bathroom. Then she got . . ."

He put up a warning hand. "Just a minute, Mrs. Eldridge. It is Mrs., isn't it?"

She nodded, wild-eyed.

"Keep your hands off those hairs, if you would, please. They're evidence. And you can save the details for when you are questioned at the station house."

"The station house? Why? Why would I have to go to the station house? I can't really be a *suspect.*" She felt her voice grow more shrill, but she didn't care. "Look, I didn't hurt that lady. She scratched me by accident. Why, she might have died accidentally for all you know."

The man still loomed over her. "Just to be safe, please slip that jacket off right now, Mrs. Eldridge."

"I can't believe this," she muttered angrily. She removed the garment and handed it to him, and felt naked. She realized how like armor a woman's jacket was: safeguarding her from charges of nonprofessionalism, its tailored lines masculinizing her just enough to make her one of the boys in what was still a man's world.

She shivered and folded her arms across her chest. "I suppose you want the rest of my clothes, too, right?"

The detective's friendly brown eyes widened. "We may well want them, you're right."

She leaned back hopelessly. "Oh, no," she moaned, "that's incredible."

At that moment, there was a short knock and then the door opened and in walked a stooped man with a large, dome-shaped head. He cast a disinterested look at Louise, then shuffled over to the detective and murmured something quietly.

Louise could hear a little of the cryptic sentence. "Death by poisoning."

"I heard that," declared Louise. " 'Death by poisoning,' right? Well, detective . . . sorry—I forgot your name."

"Johnson."

"Well, Detective Johnson," she said, starting to get out of her chair, "I already figured death by poisoning, simply from the smell of that room. But poisoning—that lets me off the hook, because I don't have any poison in my possession. I didn't have an opportunity."

He signaled her to sit down again. The bespectacled man peered at Louise over his glasses and shuffled out of the room.

Johnson said, "I beg to differ about opportunity, ma'am. The syringe used to shoot poison into Madeleine Doering was thrown in the wastebasket right next to the body. And you were seen with her only a few minutes before her death in that very same room."

She looked up at the detective standing there holding her incriminating jacket. "I was?"

"And besides that, weren't you fooling around with some poisons this afternoon in some show on pesticides?"

"Huh. If I were going to kill her do you think I'd be dumb enough to bring the poison to the studio and use it on my show?" She slumped back and gazed into space, her eyes alighting on a framed picture of Marty Corbin some time in the past, receiving one of his awards. The picture of a man in his salad days. A thinner, happier-looking Marty.

But who was she to talk? Here she was, sitting in her workplace right next door to her own cozy office, being grilled by a homicide detective about the death of her acknowledged rival. Not only grilled, but maybe even suspected of committing this monstrous crime.

Louise Eldridge, a woman above reproach for the best share of her life, and only just recently brought down by crimes and criminals. She felt a wave of fatigue sweep over her. She had just gotten rid of the nightmare of Peter Hoffman. Now a new nightmare engulfed her.

Detective Johnson leaned against the wall, as if to give her more space to think. Gently, he said, "The reason we want you to come to the station house tonight is because we need to test under your fingernails and take a blood sample from you. And also, I think, take your outer clothes for testing. So, do you have a family who will bring some other clothes to the Fairfax County Jail? It's in the city of Fairfax, you know."

"Oh, my God, this is really happening." She felt as if she were going to burst into tears. She fought to regain control; she wasn't going to give the police the satisfaction of making her cry. "Yes," she muttered. "I have a family that will bring me things." She pressed her lips together hard, to forestall any possibility of giving way to tears. Then she clasped her hands carefully together so they formed a tent. In a quiet voice, she said, "Detective Johnson, do you know who I am? Did anyone tell you? I'm the person who got tangled up with Peter Hoffman. Do you remember him?" She peered over at the detective, who still leaned against the wall.

He nodded. "Sure. Peter Hoffman: He's charged with first-degree murder in the killing of his mistress."

"Yes. Did you know that he came over to my house to try to kill me, too, and that I caught him for the police, the mulch murderer?" She looked at the policeman as if this should have been a great awakening and possibly signal her release from this cloud of suspicion.

Johnson sighed. "Yes, ma'am. I heard who you were. That's why all this comes as such a surprise. It may mean nothing, but we can't ignore evidence."

She stared moodily out the darkened window at the lights of Fairfax County in the distance. Maybe those were the lights of the jail she was seeing out there. "Evidence. Okay, they'll find my flesh under her nails. They'll find it's her hair caught in my jacket. And somebody's already told you about the 'fight,' although it wasn't what it seemed, Detective. So that looks bad."

He pulled himself up straight. "We just have to weigh it in with other things we find at the scene, Mrs. Eldridge. Um, are you ready to go now? Maybe a quick call to your home, so your family can meet you there. Evidence collection on your person won't take more than half an hour. You can come back tomorrow for the interview."

She continued to sit in Marty's visitor chair and slowly shook her head. "This is so incredible. There have to be loads of other staff people out there as possibilities"—she waved her hand in a wide gesture—"plus dozens of strangers, volunteers, running all over the place, with all sorts of opportunities to kill." She leaned forward and glared at him. "And yet you are dragging me to the police station." She sniffed in disgust.

"Now, Mrs. Eldridge . . ."

She wasn't done yet. "And just because evidence is evidence." She plucked at the shoulder of her blouse, as if it too were filled with evidentiary material. She stared at Detective Johnson. "So what happens to this stuff? It gets sent off to a lab, right? And that takes a little time. How long does it take for these things to come back from being analyzed?"

"Anywhere from two to three weeks."

She got up out of the chair. "So that's what I have: two or three weeks."

"That's what you *have?*" he asked, puzzled.

She looked at him, wondering why he couldn't understand. "That's all the time there is for somebody, the police, or me, to find the real murderer of Madeleine Doering."

18

"It was a mixture of organophosphates," said the coroner. "My guess at the moment, methyl parathion and malathion. And injected right into the lady's lungs, where it would work fastest without contaminating the murderer."

"Mixing poisons—that's bad news," said Detective Johnson. He stood alongside the body in the Fairfax County morgue and listened carefully. At the same time he could not draw his eyes away from the sagging mass of flesh that was Madeleine Doering's face.

"As you probably know, it ups the ante," explained the coroner. "We call it 'potentiating' the poison." His round Buddha face with balding head now slowly turned to Johnson. "And that's why this little lady died so quickly—probably within three to five minutes." His lip drooped cynically to the side, as if to cover some other emotion. "That, and the slamming of her head against the sink: You might say it was gross overkill."

"Methyl parathion," mused Detective Johnson. "That's not on the market, is it?"

"It's been banned in the United States for at least twenty years. Even by itself, it can kill a person in much smaller doses than this poor woman received. In fact, about a year ago a toddler in Michigan died after some exterminator sprayed it in the family kitchen to kill roaches."

Detective Johnson said, "But where'd it come from, if it's banned?"

"Easy. Left over in somebody's garage, or fairly easy to

come by illegally. Exterminators like it, because it works so efficiently. So they sometimes cheat and use it. It's still made here in the U.S. and sold overseas—India, Africa—places where there's no EPA."

"Overseas to Third World countries—sounds culpable." Then Johnson continued to gaze at the ravaged body. "So the contusions on the face . . ."

The coroner nodded. "From where she got jammed in the sink."

"I suppose to stun her while the poison took effect."

"That's what I mean by overkill. It wasn't needed: She immediately became paralyzed, then went into convulsions and suffered respiratory failure, while also literally shaking herself to death." His large head jiggled imperceptibly, and Johnson thought it was as if he were steeling himself against this death and all the deaths he witnessed so intimately.

When the coroner finally spoke, there was hidden feeling in his voice. "The pesticides she got shot with were— get this—*full-strength*. Once injected, it took no time at all to lower her acetal cholinesterase levels to nothing. Cholinesterase controls proper nerve function. When levels go down this low, your whole body is out of control. You die in one of the most horrible deaths imaginable."

Detective Johnson slowly shook his head. "Jesus. It's all there on her face. They say she was a handsome woman."

The medical officer gently touched the flaccid face with an index finger. "Now she looks like something out of a Salvador Dali painting, doesn't she? Gross muscular degeneration, just in those few minutes it took to die." He frowned and looked at the detective standing next to him. "Why the hell didn't anyone call for help? A big shot of atropine could have turned this around." Impatiently, he ripped off his rubber gloves. "Although, full-strength poison—I don't know if even atropine would have saved her."

"Atropine?" said the detective. "That's funny. Atropine's what Louise Eldridge was talking about."

"How would she know about that?" he asked suspiciously. "If so, why didn't she get her ass in gear and do something to save this woman? Wasn't she first at the scene?"

The detective felt an illogical urge to explain away Louise Eldridge's conduct. "She's the garden show hostess—you know, the one I was questioning in the office the night of the murder. That's probably why she knows about antidotes to pesticides." He paused, then added reluctantly, "One of our suspects."

The coroner looked at Johnson through narrowed eyes. "She's the one connected to those old poison bottles found in the studio?"

"Yeah. And some skin and hair evidence, too. Mind you, she's not the only one—we're lousy with possible suspects. It's a crime scene with dozens of strangers roaming around—volunteer night at the studio. But we know that evidence will point to her, so finding an old bottle of parathion among her things might only make things look worse."

The coroner was matter-of-fact: "Sounds pretty stupid. Yet killers can be stupid—we both know that—or maybe she's thinking we'd never believe she'd carry the murder weapon around publicly."

"We know poison's more often a woman's weapon."

"We also know a person's looks don't tell you anything, even though Eldridge, the gardening lady, didn't look like a murderer to me." The coroner gave Madeleine Doering's body one more glance, then covered it and slid it away in its compartmentalized cooler space. In a nonchalant voice he said, "You have to take suspects where you find them."

The detective's brow had acquired deeper worry wrinkles. "But why did she bring up atropine at all? And why was she the only one to do something smart at the scene, like keeping the victim warm?"

The coroner shrugged shoulders rounded with years of bending over dead bodies. "Again, she could be tricking you. She obviously brought it up when it was too late. Women killers are just as wily as men killers, if not more so, and some of them may look sweet but they're mean as hell underneath. It would be clever of her to shoot someone up with poison and then come right back and pretend to try to help save her. Was Doering her enemy?"

The detective explained. "There was a lot of animosity between them. But then there's a far reach to believe she is the kind of person who would kill her enemy just like she would kill a bug. Let's face it: The person who did this knew what they were doing. They chose a weapon a helluva lot meaner than a gun even, or a knife."

The coroner extended his hands in an "I told you so" gesture. "Like I said, find somebody with a real mean streak, or a lot to lose. Or both."

19

"Come out in the garden, Bill," Louise called. "Something terrific's in bloom."

He made his way on crutches out to the flagstone patio and around the table and chairs to where she was working. Wearing faded navy shorts, striped T-shirt and work boots with heavy wool socks, Louise looked like a shapely, long-limbed teenager, gardening away as if she didn't have a care in the world. A colander filled with vegetable parings and coffee grounds stood on the ground at her feet.

He frowned. Something was seriously wrong with his wife.

She had dug a deep hole in the garden area that lay between the patio and the woods. Now she took the garbage and dumped it in the hole, and covered it with a little dirt, still leaving a large place where he knew she would be putting a new plant. "There," she said brightly, "more underground compost." Then, with graceful fingers, she touched the flowering bush near her. "Here's what I wanted you to see: a deciduous azalea. It's just come into bloom. It's like a dish of orange sherbet."

"Beautiful."

Now her busy hands were caressing other plants—straightening this one, taking dead flowers off another—never still, housekeeping the flower border as rapidly as she might clean up a kitchen filled with dinner dishes.

"The whole yard is full of surprises, Bill." She looked at him and he knew she wanted him to love this damned garden as much as she did. "Just think," she went on, "the first spring in our own house. There are lots of great things here: azaleas, rhododendron, mountain laurel, wild geranium, meadow rue, columbine. Smell it all." She threw her arms out in a wide gesture, raised her nose and sniffed the air. "Isn't it heavenly?"

"Ummm." He took a deep breath, and it did smell good. He peered at the flowering bushes and emerging perennials. "Looks like there's plenty here already. So what's the new hole for?"

"I thought it would be neat to put a pink azalea next to the orange one. Or would you rather I make it yellow?"

He stood there in silence. Finally, he said, "Louise, are you sure you're just not digging a hole to get rid of the blues?"

"I don't have the blues," she said briskly, and jammed the digging fork into the ground. "We'll pick up an azalea at the garden center after we get home from jail." She began to chuckle, and was still chuckling as she came over and put her arms soundly around his waist and hugged him tight.

He looked in the face close to his and frowned. "You have me worried. You've been up for hours before me. You've had little sleep. Then you act as if nothing's happened. Come on, now, get real. A woman was murdered at your workplace, and you're one of their suspects. What's going on?"

She released him from her embrace, her face sobering. "How about coffee?" she asked. Without waiting for an answer, she darted inside the house and prepared a little tray with coffee and sweet rolls and brought it out. The cellular phone also lay on the tray. She pointed to the phone. "That's in case we get more calls. Now, back to your worries: How can I forget what happened yesterday? I've already heard from three people at work."

"Who called? Marty, I suppose, for one." He had a slight discomfort level with Marty Corbin, even though he had yet to meet the man. Louise painted a picture of a big, rather handsome, free-wheeling guy with a zest for life and for women. She was attracted to him, though Bill hoped no more than she was to any other man or woman with lots of spirit. She was talking fast. "Marty called early. Poor guy. He's pretty upset. After all, Madeleine and he were very close. And she was cohost of the seniors show. He has to find someone new right away. Then the receptionist—huh!" Anger flickered in her eyes. "Berta—she's the one who squealed on me to the police. She called to apologize for telling them about the quarrel in the rest room. So I put her guilt to good use. First, I teased her—threatened to call her 'Benedicta Arnold.' "

Louise chuckled. "Good thing she thought that was funny. She's going to give me the address of the janitor at work for me, the one who liked Madeleine."

His wife paused to fidget herself into a more comfortable position in the garden chair. "And guess what else? Berta said she had another person I might be interested in knowing about, namely, John Batchelder's *girlfriend*." She made a dismissive gesture with her hand. "Oh, it may be nothing, but Berta gets vibes from the way people treat her on the phone. And this woman emanates bad vibes. Berta's heard conversations that would make your hair stand on end . . ."

"Louise, wait: Don't get too carried away here . . ."

". . . and John Batchelder called, too, of course." She smiled wryly. "Let's face it, he's not the smoothest guy. He just wanted to know what they're going to do to me. After all, if I go to prison, he gets my show, right? Think this anchorwoman chick could have put him up to murder?" She put up an admonitory hand. "Just a wild thought, because"—and she laughed nervously—"this woman's name is Wilding."

More concerned than ever, he watched as she poured out two cups of coffee, reflecting that the last thing Louise needed was another shot of caffeine. His wife was headed in some direction that he feared.

She handed one coffee to him, took up the other herself, then propped her booted feet on another garden chair, and chomped into a sweet roll. He took a roll, too, although he would have preferred something more substantial for breakfast.

"Don't mind me, Bill," she said, "I'm totally wired. Up early. Drinking coffee. Thinking." She permitted herself an abbreviated sigh. "I talked to Janie, before she went to school. We all have plenty to do."

"Do?"

"As in 'investigate.' "

Bill took a sip of coffee, feeling a yawning trap opening up under him. "Last night, I was really worried about you because you were so angry and depressed. Now, you are totally hyper. What exactly is going on in your mind?"

"Thanks for last night," she said, reaching over and squeezing his hand. "You were great. There's nothing as good as a husband who will hold you in his arms while you sob yourself to sleep."

She stared into the woods. "It's funny. For a long time, I had that nightmare of Peter Hoffman attacking me. What I couldn't get out of my mind last night was the image of Madeleine, lying there, kind of dissolving in front of my eyes . . ."

She looked at him, her eyes haunted. Then she smiled. "But my mood changes so rapidly, no wonder it puzzles you. This may only be the coffee talking, but I feel full of hope. *I* didn't murder Madeleine, so why should I worry about being a suspect? And yet, there's lots of physical evidence that is troublesome, to say the least."

"Louise," he said, feeling the trap opening under him, "let the police have a chance . . ."

"Honey, you and I both know the police in Fairfax County are just as good as any others, so you'd think they could find the real killer. But we've just seen a recent example of where they failed to find a killer, until Peter Hoffman came right to our door. So for insurance, you, Janie, and I had better do a little investigating on our own." She took a bite of roll and waved the remainder at him. "We can start tonight," she said, her mouth full.

He studied his wife. She roosted temporarily in the chair, and now her bare legs were tucked under her like a nervous bird poised for flight. She had come to the very perilous conclusions he was afraid of, wanting to turn the Eldridge household once again into an amateur, and not very effective, detective agency. He frowned. "Louise, I don't think it's a good idea. Look at the trouble we got in with Hoffman. You darned near got killed. I can't have you in danger again."

"This is nothing like that," argued Louise. "That all centered around the neighborhood and our home. This crime had something to do with Madeleine Doering at work." In one limber motion, she unfolded her legs, leaped up and paced the patio, tracing its perimeter like a prowling animal.

"You know what?" she said, stopping in front of him. "The murder might even be related to Madeleine's life in the voiceovers; that's a viciously competitive bunch of people."

She plopped unceremoniously down into her chair again, picked up her coffee cup, and smiled confidently at her husband. "I'm sure, Bill, that we can find things out. It will take some doing, but at the very least we can see to it that the police don't overlook the basic capacity of people to kill."

He looked at her skeptically. "And you think you can detect this?"

"Yes," she said. "I think I am particularly good at it."

"Well, it's a good thing my leg's getting better: just in time for me to go out and play sleuth."

"You're so good at it, too," said Louise. "You can use that career expertise of yours."

"You can romanticize my spying career just so much. Remember, two-thirds of it is talking and one-third is action . . ."

"All I want is to get Marty and me off the suspect list—because he will be a natural suspect once I'm exonerated."

She reached over and grabbed his forearm. "Bill, no one except you and I and the police will know how high I rank on their list of suspects, not until a couple of weeks from now when that evidence returns from the forensic laboratories. I'll keep right on doing my television programs. I can even accept the job of spokesman, if they offer it. But when that evidence comes in, the police had better have the real murderer identified, or I could go to jail."

"You'd think they would know a woman like you couldn't have committed that crime."

Louise smiled at him. "You mean, a woman who is above reproach? That Detective Johnson explained to me last night, when I dragged out my spotless, denim-dress, suburban housewife reputation: A good rep doesn't matter much when all the physical evidence at a crime scene points right at you."

He reached over and took her hand and held it. It was like feeling a seismic rumble. "You say you're not nervous, Louise. Then why is your hand trembling like a leaf?"

Her big tormented hazel eyes looked into his. "I'm not nervous, Bill: I'm just plain scared silly. All this brave stuff is my cover."

"Shhh!" said Bill quietly, as Janie started to come in the bedroom. "She's still napping." They backed out together and he closed the door.

"Your mother's exhausted," he said, as he limped his way slowly down the hall toward the living room. Janie followed patiently behind.

"Dad, when do you ditch those crutches?"

Bill slumped down on the living room couch. "I know what you're thinking. In a couple days, barring a mishap. I go slow because I'm so afraid I might trip and get resentenced to the damned things for an extra term."

"I guess I didn't realize how much you hated them." She spread her hands matter-of-factly. "Whatever. But Ma's on a tear, you know. You have to get off those crutches. If she has her way, we're going to be running all over the place, checking out people."

Bill looked over at his daughter, who had sprawled in her favorite chair opposite the couch. She had on her blue denim

111

jacket and pants and yellow hightops. Her blond hair was in braids and her cheeks looked to be permanently rosy; she probably had spent most of the time while he and Louise were gone playing basketball in the cul-de-sac.

"And what do you think of a little investigating, Janie?"

The teenager's face lit up in a smile that touched his heart. "I *love* it. Can I ask Chris to help?"

"Well, maybe, if he can keep a secret. We don't exactly want the whole world to know your mother is implicated in another murder."

"Why? She's innocent. She doesn't really have anything to worry about."

"The question of innocence is not quite that simple, dear." As usual, he sounded like he was preaching to his daughter. He stared out into the woods, remembering how upset Louise had been after emerging from a two-hour interrogation with the police. She had turned to him in the car and said, sadly, "It isn't fair for people to be suspected of crimes they didn't commit." Then, at home, exhausted, she had buttonholed Janie and talked to her for awhile, then promptly fallen to sleep.

"Okay, so let's grab the moment," said Janie. "Shall we make a list?"

"Sure, if we can manage it without your mother."

Janie ran lightly across the carpeting to the antique Windsor desk and retrieved a pad of paper and a pen, then returned to her former reclining position. Quickly, she made four columns and put a heading atop each. "Okay. We have name, occupation, relation to Madeleine, and motive. First. Marty Corbin. Producer. Boss, because he was Madeleine's boss, too, I know." She looked quizzically at her father. "Motive?"

"You probably haven't heard this, but your mother believes he was trying to break off an affair with Madeleine. Apparently they were a big romantic item for several years."

"Oh?" said Janie, one dark eyebrow cocked. "What motive do we call that? I'll just say 'love affair gone wrong.' "

"I bet your mother will refuse to consider him a suspect. She's very high on Marty."

"How about that cute John guy who came out to the house?" Janie busily wrote the name down.

"John Batchelder. Competitive sort. But why would he kill Madeleine Doering?"

Janie sat with pen poised. "Why indeed?" They sat in silence for a moment, thinking.

"You want to know why he might have done it?" Louise stood in the doorway, having awakened from her nap. "Madeleine's job is now open. And as a bonus, it turns out I'm implicated in the murder and could be out of my job."

"Louise, I'm glad you're here," he said. "Come sit beside me." She joined him on the couch and he took her hand in his. "So John Batchelder could win either way."

"It's awful to think about, but yes. Next, put 'janitor' on your list."

"What's his name, and why would he be on the list?"

"Henry Aiken. As I told your father, I'm getting his address from Berta, the remorseful receptionist," said Louise. "He's a large, moody young man who doesn't wash enough, and who was obsessed with Madeleine. He worked afternoons and evenings, and he followed Madeleine around like a puppy." She stared into space, trying to remember. "And I think I remember seeing him or someone his size when I left the lady's room after my little argument with the woman. It was some big guy just leaving the back hall."

"Did you tell police all that?" asked Bill.

"Yes."

Janie turned innocent blue eyes on her mother. "If the janitor loved her, why would he kill her?"

"Why, indeed," said Bill, then laughed. "Maybe there are too many 'why indeeds' being expressed around here. Why indeed don't we leave this whole thing to the police?"

Louise, her face softened by sleep, turned slowly to her husband. There was hurt in her eyes. "Bill, you're giving up before we even start."

He felt as if he had slapped her. "Honey, I'm sorry. I'll try. I just don't know what good we'll do. I don't want you to be disappointed."

Louise told Janie, "Put down in your 'motive' column for the janitor, 'unrequited love.' Because I'm sure Madeleine could have let this guy know any time—maybe yesterday, the day she was killed, or maybe the day before—that she despised him. He was the kind of man Madeleine would use as a doormat. I'm sure she thought he was far beneath her."

Janie examined her list. "Back to Marty. Does this Marty guy have a wife?"

"Yes," said Louise.

She pinned her parents with a discerning glance. "She has one of the best motives of all—jealousy."

Louise and Bill exchanged glances. "The girl is good," he muttered to his wife.

"I know," said Janie, smiling as she filled in her columns. "Mrs. Corbin. Occupation, unknown, but we'd better check it out: If she's a nurse, for instance, then she'd be comfortable shooting a big hypodermic into someone, wouldn't she? Connection: only through husband. Motive: jealousy. Now, who else?"

There was silence. Then Louise slowly spoke. "An interesting woman: John Batchelder's girlfriend—Cheryl Wilding. Put her down as someone to look into, not as a suspect, but more of an . . . instigator. I've only seen her from a distance, but somehow I have the sense she was in the crowd with John the night of the murder."

Louise thought for a moment. "Then there's the strangers, those two dozen volunteers. Any of them could have been wearing a disguise, couldn't they?"

"Right," said Janie, noting it on her pad. "Two dozen wild cards."

20

Janie and Chris were on the handkerchief-sized dance floor, transformed by their best clothes into modish young adults who had handily slipped by the man at the door of this jazz club. Bill had limped in on crutches behind them, in the guise of an uncle-like figure.

They had spotted their prey almost immediately. John Batchelder sat with three others, at a table directly in front of the jazz quintet, which was letting loose. Bill reflected that this meant John and his crowd would lose their hearing even faster than the rest of customers.

Louise had known, from John's conversation last week, that he might be making the scene Saturday night at this, his favorite Washington club. Unless, of course, he was overcome with remorse at taking a woman's life.

But John was here, and there was no remorse on his countenance. Bill sipped a draft Moosehead, and kept his eye on Batchelder. No wonder he went into television, thought Bill. What else could you do with those unusual, slightly androgynous good looks? He noticed that Louise's cohost offset this ambiguity in his appearance by wearing Western designer clothes and Western boots—probably from some East Coast designer store.

His mind went back to Louise's last-minute instructions. He smiled at the recollection. "Follow him, Chris or Bill," she had said. "That includes into the rest room if he goes there. It will be too much to expect that you'll get a table near him, but watch him. Rest rooms are great. People talk too much in rest rooms; I'm a living testimonial to that."

After her nap, Louise had been as refreshed and excited as she was that morning in the garden, ready to believe again that her spirit and drive could result in finding Madeleine's killer. But Bill noticed she had only picked at her dinner, and insisted on drinking more coffee. She was eating little and living on adrenaline and caffeine, assaulted again by the trauma of a crime she had nothing to do with.

His hand tightened into a fist; he had to do something to get his wife off the hook.

He was tactfully blocking the sound by putting a finger in one ear, when he noticed a movement of color in the corner his eye. He turned his head and saw a young woman in a skimpy red dress at the next table, shamelessly staring him down. Her head of long hair was a Medusa-like cloud of tangled red curls. It made him glad Janie had combed hers. The woman was a predator, a budding Nora. Her stare began at his hair, which he had in fact washed for the occasion, and moved down his slim body in its sporty jacket and turtleneck, and back to his face. Something there made her faintly interested. Then she noticed his crutches leaning against his chair and she looked away in dismissal. Probably thought he had hardening of the arteries. After all, guys in their forties seemed ancient in this crowd. The preponderance of people were in their twenties. It amused him to realize that John Batchelder, whom Louise assured him was in his late thirties, was also one of the older crowd.

Occasionally, he saw his teenage daughter's blond hair flying as she and the handsome Chris did a funky dance that seemed to be the dance of choice. Just by donning a short, sexy dress Janie had added five or six years to her age, thereby validating both hers and Chris's ages in the eyes of the club bouncer.

Chris, he noticed, could not take his eyes off the girl.

Bill tried to concentrate on John. The man looked morose,

but that, perhaps, was understandable. His date, with her fall of blond hair and demure little dress, looked like an angel but didn't act like one. This must be the TV anchor girlfriend, Bill thought. She was reaming John out, complete with a lot of finger-shaking action. Bill wondered what had made her so angry. Then the two men put their heads together for a moment and lurched up from the table. Bill helplessly watched them thread their way through the crowd to the men's room. He doubted that even if he tried he would get there in time on his crutches.

Then Chris showed his savvy. Noting John's movement, he swung off the dance floor and followed the pair into the men's room. Janie trailed back to the table, looking as beautiful as any woman Bill had ever seen.

He rose a little from his chair.

"Hi, Dad," she said. "You're so gallant. I love being out on a date with you and Chris." She settled down in front of her Coke, put her elbows on the table and looked at him with brilliant eyes surrounded as if with kohl, like an Egyptian princess. He wondered shakily how the kid could resist his daughter.

"Janie," he said sternly, "do you think you need that much makeup on your eyes?"

She looked down in disappointment, then turned her gaze upon him again. "Dad, you're worrying too much. I know just what you're thinking. Ma worries too, but she doesn't come right out with it like you do. Like, 'Janie'—she imitated him by talking like a croaking old frog—'don't you think you'd better wash your eyes?' "

He laughed nervously. But she wasn't done with him. "Dad, you're, like, 'Don't get too attractive or the boys might want to get you in bed.' " She tilted her head and smiled. "Isn't that what you mean?"

"Yeah," he said, nodding.

"Well, it's going to happen sometime, Dad. There are lots of boys and girls growing up and lots of beds. It happens to everybody. It happened to you and Ma, didn't it? Wasn't she really pretty once—I mean, even prettier, maybe, than she is now?"

He reached over and covered one of her slim hands. "Janie, you're great. I like this going out together. And rest assured, your mom was a dish. Still is—don't get me wrong. It's just that we were able to get married soon after we fell in love. But you're too young for that."

"Margaret Mead was *so* right," she said knowingly. "Too bad we don't live in a primitive society, which recognizes when people attain their sexuality and approves of early marriages."

After a moment of agreeable silence between the two of them, she said, "I like your job better now, Dad, because you have more time at home now than when we lived overseas. Although you were a sitting duck, on that couch with your broken leg: You got a lot of visits from Chris's mom."

Bill looked at Janie. "You know that?"

"Oh, I know everything, almost. Chris knows. He's told me *all* about his mom." She grinned at him. "What do you think kids do, go around with blinders on, like horses? They know things—about the neighborhood, about people, about which dogs bite, and which don't. They peek in windows"—she placed a hand on her father's arm—"you guys should remember that, with all the windows in our house . . ."

Bill said, "So, back to Mrs. Radebaugh—although I don't know that in all fairness we should be discussing her . . ."

The girl looked soberly at her father. "Well, Dad, Nora means well—I call her Nora, you know. Some women are just more predatory than your wife, you know. I like Nora no matter what. She's one of my confidantes."

His daughter threw her long hair back in a Nora-like motion, and Bill was startled. What was that term? Modeling? Children were forever modeling their behavior after adults'. It gave him pause to think the woman was one of Janie's models.

"So she's your confidante. Well, Janie, it's good you have

people other than your parents to talk to. And I agree. Nora, at heart, is a wonderful woman."

"Sure," said Janie. "So, back to the important stuff. It's better now than when we lived overseas and you were away all the time, traveling. Don't get me wrong; it's exciting living different places, but it's not like living in the States." She looked meaningfully at him. "Are you going to do that again, Dad?"

"Take you all overseas again? Maybe not. I guess we haven't talked about it that much, but I'm looking around at other jobs. In fact, the man I've waited to hear from is due back in Washington next week."

Chris came back to the table, excited. First, he took a large slurp of the soft drink he had ordered. "Man," he said, and took another long slurp, finishing the brown liquid and leaving only ice. Then he shook his head. "This Washington scene—I can't believe it. The guys were doing coke in there in the stalls. You should hear them giggling. Pretty disgusting."

"Did they talk about anything?"

"Yeah. Let's see, how would you say it?" The young man frowned and shoved his shock of blond hair back off his forehead. "Browbeaten," he said disgustedly. "John's browbeaten."

Then the teenager got down to the story.

"John goes, 'I'm goin' crazy with this woman. She's too ambitious for me, spends all her time telling me how to arrange my career, how to move in now that someone eliminated some of the competition around the station . . .'

"The other guy says, 'Don't let her, man. Does she come across for you?'

"And John goes, 'Sure she comes across, but much later, after she's outlined everything for me to do for the week ahead, to say nothing of the years ahead.' The guy, I tell you, is browbeaten. Henpecked. That girlfriend of his is the boss."

With an authoritative wave of his hand, Chris beckoned to the waiter for a new round of drinks, as if he had done it all his life. He gave Janie a big grin. "Dancing makes me thirsty."

Janie sat back in her chair. "That's very interesting, Chris. I recognize that woman now: Cheryl Wilding, six o'clock news, Channel Eight."

He turned in his chair to get a better look at the woman. She did look familiar, although he was rarely home for the six o'clock news. The two women were being joined now by John and the other man, who seemed lighter-hearted now than when they left the table. No wonder, with a headful of cocaine.

John and his date got up from the table and maneuvered their way through the crowd toward the dance floor. Bill got a close look at the woman's face as they passed near their table, including her distinctive staring eyes.

A cold feeling ran through him. What kind of a murky world had Louise gotten herself involved in, he wondered, with women whose eyes proclaimed an overriding self-love. With a glitzy coworker who did drugs in nightclub rest rooms? And with a producer who was some kind of soft, fuzzy, but sexually insinuating womanizer?

An unwelcome thought came to him. If the murderer had an agenda more complicated than the police knew, how could he be sure his wife wouldn't be the next victim? He felt a catch in his throat.

He shook his head. No, it couldn't be, and it was unwise to indulge in illogical scenarios that just made the family more anxious.

"Dad." Janie shook his arm. "You're shaking your head. Are you just keeping time with the music, or are you thinking dark thoughts you're not sharing with us?"

"I'm afraid they're dark thoughts." He absently twirled his empty beer glass. "It makes me realize we need to keep working. Any little thing we learn could be helpful. We can't rely just on the police."

"I liked Detective Geraghty last time," said Janie, "except he didn't catch the killer—Ma did."

He looked over at his daughter and in a hard-edged voice

said, "That's exactly right. And I will not see your mother suffer again at the hands of some violent person." Then, with difficulty he managed a smile. "Sorry. I didn't mean to sound grim. I really enjoy being with the two of you. Chris, do you want to go out with us again? Mrs. Eldridge wants us to visit the janitor tomorrow night."

"I wouldn't mind it, Mr. Eldridge." He grinned. "I always enjoy being with Janie."

Now Bill was talking only to the young man, on two levels that he was pretty sure Chris would understand. "It's just possible there could be some danger in this, Chris. But it's important, because if the police don't find the answers, my wife could be in real trouble." He gave the teenager a penetrating look to emphasize the danger. "I'm depending on you."

"I take your meaning, Mr. Eldridge," Chris said, in a respectful voice.

The boy could have meant anything by that. Bill hoped Chris understood that in the fervor of the chase, this father didn't want his daughter pressured to grow up before her time.

Gettin' Down 'n' Dirty:
Making Compost

Hip gardeners know the most interesting place in their yard is the compost pile. There, natural recycling is going on right before their eyes: Voracious little bacteria and fungi are chomping away on their compost materials—hay, leaves, grass clippings, kitchen garbage, and plant tops, reducing them and dissolving them and regenerating them into rich, dark brown, crumbly humus.

It's a hot process, and if we stick a thermometer in the active pile, it will go up to 120 to 140 degrees. This heat is killing harmful bacteria and weed seeds. What magic is going on, in that little corner of our yard! All sorts of good things happen again when we put this compost on our gardens. Made through the action of microorganisms, the compost now becomes *food* for soil microorganisms. This action releases minerals and make them available to our plants. Compost also helps our soil's texture or "tilth," lightening clay soil and giving body to sandy soil. It lowers soil temperature and deters weeds. And, most remarkably, compost has now been shown to protect our plants from disease—the rots, wilts, and blights that can ruin flowers and vegetables. Indeed, composting is at the very heart of organic gardening. It is working with nature and recycling all nature's products.

There are as many recipes for making compost as there are for chicken soup. It takes three basic steps: layering materials, keeping the pile moist, and supplying air by turning the pile periodically. You can buy or make containers for composting. The revolving-barrel type produces compost the fastest, but it takes strength to turn the barrel. You can leave your pile on the ground, or tuck it within a low U-shaped wall made of bales of hay stacked two high.

Some gardeners think composting is too complicated to bother with. People who feel this way can drive a pickup to their own city's composting center and get it ready made. But making compost in your own backyard is not only easy, it's fun. And it reduces the amount of waste that leaves our yards by at least half. This is something to think about when our cities are running out of space for landfills.

Here is a recipe for easy composting:

The Lazy Gardener's Open Space Compost Pile

Make the pile about four feet in width and length and depth. That's enough volume to cause it to heat up. Situate it on the open ground, not too far removed from where you'll be using it. Put down eight-inch layers of "brown" carbon-rich products and "green" nitrogen-rich products. "Browns" include chopped leaves and twigs, straw, sawdust, and wood chips. "Greens" include slightly dried grass clippings, kitchen waste, alfalfa hay, manure, and plant residues. If you are short of greens, substitute a sprinkling of bloodmeal or nitrogen fertilizer. This last ingredient is optional: very light layers of dirt or manure. This will hasten the decomposition process but makes the pile a little heavier to handle.

Once formed, mix the pile thoroughly instead of leaving it in layers, to avoid having to turn it so often. Fork it into a compact shape. Be sure it is well watered. Then, do not add to this pile. Instead, start a new second pile. If you have space for only one pile, just remember to shred newly added materials and tuck them into the middle of the pile. Keep your compost heap moist as a sponge, but not soggy. Put a tarpaulin on top to avoid sogginess if you live in a rainy area.

Turn or fork the pile if it becomes compacted or seems too hot—over 140 degrees. Also turn it a few times to move the drier outside materials to the inside of the pile. Do this by scraping them aside, and then moving the moister materials on top of the dried part. If the pile doesn't get hot, it isn't "working"; add a nitrogen (green) product to correct this. If it smells of ammonia, there's too much nitrogen, so add some brown products. Fortunately, there is plenty of margin for error in composting. Temperatures affect the speed of composting. Warm weather speeds it. Cold weather slows it. In warm weather, with proper moisture, your compost should be ready to use within about two months. The finished product will smell sweet and be crumbly to the touch. You will look at it and feel a tremendous sense of joy at having turned nature's leftovers into a tasty treat for your garden.

21

"What a miserable life this guy leads!" said Janie.

"Oh, I don't know about that," said Bill. "He has a place to live," he philosophized, "and a car, which are among the things that make Americans feel as if life is worthwhile." He looked over at an old junker parked opposite them. "I'm assuming that's his car. It may be old, but I bet it gets him to work. And he has his job; it probably even pays benefits."

"Right," piped up Chris Radebaugh. "Without a job you're nothing."

Bill turned and looked at his teenage companions in the back seat of the station wagon, bestowing on them an encouraging smile that they might or might not see in the fading twilight.

He wondered once again about his wife, who intermittently over the years had involved him in after-hour surveillances, even in the days when God knows he had his own surveillances to conduct for the CIA. But Louise, with her penchant for seeking out trouble and finding it, had done it again with this Madeleine Doering murder case, and here he was, on his second consecutive assignment as head of the teenage surveillance group.

Chris was tapping a knee and whistling soundlessly, a jock kid having trouble being confined in an aromatic-smelling car on a warm spring night. Louise's station wagon always smelled faintly of composted biosolids she dragged in big pails from the city treatment plant. Bill had chosen it instead of his new Camry so they could be less conspicuous.

Janie, used to the car's smell, was slumped next to Chris, a pen flashlight trained on the notebook in her lap. Her mouth was turned down in disgust. What bothered her was this run-down condo neighborhood off Route One, with its marginal population that undoubtedly included drug dealers and criminals and, worse in Janie's book, people who were unkind to their pets. They had already spied two little boys chasing a dog and throwing stones at it, and it was all Bill could do to keep his daughter from leaving the car and chasing after them.

Bill said, "Not quite as swingin' as that club scene last night, huh?"

"No," said Janie sourly. "It's like sitting in Ma's compost heap." Chris smiled, and nodded his head in agreement. "And besides," continued Janie, "I left my French undone; this detecting business is cutting into my homework time. It's not worth it, just to come to this truly ugly place."

"I agree it's ugly," said Bill. They looked out on row upon row of connected housing with garish brown mansard roofs above yellow brick walls. The residents had done little to make it more attractive.

"And it's creepy, besides," added Janie. "Not only mean little boys. How do you like those dudes who keep speeding around? It's a wonder they haven't noticed us and given us a hard time."

"Hey, Janie," protested Chris, "I have a friend who lives here—he's as human as we are. The neighborhood just has a little gang activity, is all."

Her father, sitting behind the wheel, held up his watch to catch the yellow light of the sulfur lamp that loomed above them. He grunted. They'd only been parked for fifteen minutes, but it seemed like an hour.

The janitor, Henry Aikens, lived in a first-floor apartment with sheet-covered windows and decayed wooden steps. From what they could see, the door to the place was damaged and barely closed. Bill looked at the entrance with an analytical eye. "This is one of those places where people get fed up with their condo investment because the complex is not kept up properly," said Bill. "So they sublet, and get people like Henry, who also don't do any maintenance."

"I wonder what he's doing in there," said Chris, trying to be polite, but with his knee jiggling impatiently up and down. "We've been here like a half an hour and nothing's happening."

"He's there, we know that," said Bill. He had casually walked by when they first arrived and heard a television blaring. "Would that he would do something interesting. But surveillance isn't like that. It's a long, boring occupation."

"You sound like you know all about it," said the eighteen-year-old.

"Yeah, Dad," said Janie, looking at him shrewdly. He didn't answer. Some day he might tell her about his career, but probably not until he left the government. He was sure Janie already suspected that he was an undercover agent.

Then the apartment door opened. Five gray cats slipped out.

"Cats!" whispered Janie. "Just what we've needed." Before Bill could stop her, she had quietly opened the car door, and closed it just as carefully. Through the partially opened window, he said, "Be careful. Under no circumstance will you go in that apartment." He shook an admonishing finger at her. "Remember, we're right here within shouting distance. In fact"—he opened the driver's door quietly, got out and stood by the car—"I'll be watching you every second."

Chris quietly took himself out of the backseat and stood next to Bill. "Me, too," he said.

She whispered, "Okay, relax, you two. I'm going to be okay. I'll just follow the cats. Maybe I can pretend one of them got caught in a bush, or something."

"Wait a minute, Janie," warned Chris. "People let their cats out to, you know, go to the bathroom. It's going to look funny if you come up right after he's let them out."

She waved impatiently at the two of them, and slipped across the street. "Fuddy-duddies," she whispered to herself.

Eventually, she made her way through the bedraggled thicket to the front of Henry's house. The builders had expected great things of this condo complex: They had planted a small group of evergreens by each entrance. Now, the evergreens were gangly and overgrown, with bald and dying branches, as if having withstood the fierce winds and snows up at timberline. Instead, Janie realized it was the cruel neglect of human beings. These trees were never fertilized or winter watered.

With annoyance, she realized she was experiencing the same knee-jerk reactions as her mother about things like neglect of trees and gardens. She wondered if she weren't being brainwashed into becoming an environmentalist or something. After all, how many mothers made woody perennials the topic of after-dinner conversation? Would she end up in Birkenstocks and drab woven fabrics and recommend people collect their own urine for their gardens, like that crazy guest on her mother's show? At the thought, she quietly muttered, "Yuck."

Then she came upon the cats. They were cavorting among the pfitzers, not seeming to mind their straggly appearance. "Here, baby," she whispered to one of the smaller gray animals, probably offspring of an incestuous relationship between two of the bigger ones. The creature came to her, and soon she was surrounded with purring, pacing cats.

The front door to the place suddenly opened, pouring yellow light out onto her crouching figure. Janie, anticipating this, continued to pat the cats, but her heartbeat increased.

The man coughed. His face was scary, with angry dark eyes, and his shaggy hair was wild around his head. He was very large. "C'mon, now," he snarled, "whatcha doin' out there, anyway, with my cats?" He came down the steps toward her and she could smell marijuana.

Suddenly she was afraid and began to tremble. Had he noticed the three of them, parked in the car near his entrance? If so, she was in trouble.

"Oh, I'm Janie, and I just *loove* cats." She slurred her words a little, in what she hoped was a version of a Southern accent. She had the impression lots of people from southern Virginia came to this kind of place to make their home. She pointed vaguely down the row of condos. "I jus' moved in down there."

Henry came down one step farther and sat on the bottom step. "Like cats, do ya?"

"Yeah, like cats. You sure got enough of 'em. Could I have one?"

Something strange had happened. Janie, who had a deft touch with animals, was losing her clientele. They were all drifting over to Henry. They contended briefly, then one of the two larger cats was victorious and landed the prized position in Henry's lap. The others made Henry into a purring post.

He looked out at her, where she crouched next to him on the perimeter of the light. "Ya look kinda young. How old are ya?" He reached out and laid a big hand on her arm. A big damp hand on her arm, in the warm Virginia night. She felt a chill through her body. For what seemed an eternity the hand lay there, and she knew that if she didn't act, he would tighten that grip and yank her into the disgusting condo.

And yet she needed to make him talk.

"I'm almost sixteen," she said. Then, holding her breath and smiling graciously, she gently attempted to pull her arm from underneath the hand. To her horror, he pressed his weight on her arm, but she continued to pull, until the arm lurched free, and she was almost toppled backward onto the sidewalk.

"Oh," he said slowly, looking at her with those dark, troubled eyes, "so it's like that, huh. I tell ya, you're damn pretty, and maybe a little too friendly, so how's a guy to know? But li'l lady, I can't give away my cats." His voice was scratchy, as if he didn't use it much. She wondered if he had any friends at all. Now his big hands were busy providing the scratching needs of two or three animals. "They're like my

128

friends, ya know?" He leaned forward, and she was afraid he might touch her again, even spring at her, and yet she knew he wouldn't because it might upset the cat he held. "I can tell you're real nice. Ya don't act like most of the people who live around here. But I'll give ya some advice. It's easy to find a cat. Go to the Humane people; folks're always gettin' rid a' cats. 'Fact, it makes me sick, the way people treat 'em." His eyes seemed to bore into her, even in the dim light. "And speaking of humane! Those assholes ain't humane: They gas cats by the carload!"

As if to protect them against even the thought of Humane Society capture, he scooped up the whole bunch now onto his big, bony thighs. "Now, mine are treated special. Special food, bottled water; Washington's water system gives ya cancer, ya know. And right now, they're ready to eat, and I'm ready to watch TV. Ya kin come in if ya want, but your parents mightn't like that, 'n anyway, it's too damned much trouble to get mixed up with minors. Maybe I'll see ya around."

Holding the bouquet of cats in his large arms with gentle ease, he went in the apartment and slammed the door shut.

In case he looked out from behind the greasy draped sheets to see which way she had gone, she ambled down the front walk as if headed for home. Then like lightning she doubled back across the darkness of the opposite lawns and ran straight into the arms of Chris. Not having been in his arms more than twice, it was a nice feeling. Yet she hissed at him: "You scared me! What are you doing here?"

"I came after you. We didn't like you gone so long." They walked back to the car, hand in hand. Her heart was still thumping, and she knew just why. She had been in danger back there for a moment, but she wasn't going to tell her father and Chris. She arrived at the car where her father stood, arms crossed.

"Get in," said her father, sternly. "You were out of sight too long. That's the last time we pull a dumb stunt like this." They climbed in the car and her father started the motor as quietly as possible and slowly moved down the winding road that led out of the condo complex.

"So, what did you find out?" asked Chris.

Janie was busy making notes on her pad. She sighed and shook her head. "He couldn't have done it, no way."

"Oh," said her father. "You're so positive. How come?"

"The cats," she said. "Nobody could treat animals that way and be a killer. Why, he's as gentle as a big bear. He gives those cats special water, special food. I even asked him to give me a cat, and he couldn't part with one. He loves them too much."

"Janie," said her father, looking at her in the rearview mirror, "I'm afraid you might be making a big judgment off one small piece of evidence. I knew a man once. He turned out to be a killer, and he also raised dogs. Treated them better than people. And who was it—John Gacy? Cat lover, mass murderer."

Stung, she retreated into silence.

"Ahem," coughed Chris. "Hey, don't get bent out of shape, Janie. He's right. We need to look into him further, right, Mr. Eldridge?"

"His employment history and criminal record at the very least," said Bill. "I can tap into that information."

Chris put a tentative hand on her father's shoulder. "But she did good, didn't she?" Janie didn't know if she was annoyed or amused by the fact that Chris, her supposed boyfriend, was playing referee between her and her father.

"Just remember what Ma told us," said Janie, folding her arms across her shapely chest and staring out the window at the spooky yellow streetlight. "We're supposed to be looking at things that reflect character, whether we think people have the capacity to kill. In my book, a person who is as gentle as that with his cats doesn't have the capacity to kill."

22

Louise parked her car in the lot and headed into the station. She knew life had to go on, even after someone died. Certainly none of her problems disappeared with Madeleine Doering's death. They were only made more complicated, since two of the people with whom she dealt most closely at work, Marty and John, had the possibility of being a killer.

She walked swiftly, her steps firm. She had two missions: solve some of her day-to-day problems, and find out what she could about the people who could have murdered Madeleine.

The second mission was the more important one. Bill, Janie and Chris had come up with some interesting details from their weekend surveillance, although disappointingly little on Henry Aikens. Bill would run his own check on the man, and on all the people on their suspect list, one of the advantages, she thought wryly, of having a spy for a husband. Janie might believe this cat-loving janitor was innocent, but she and Bill still believed he could have murdered Madeleine.

"Two things," said Bill, when he came home last night from their surveillance. "He's rough cut, and he doesn't have much to lose. You read in the papers all the time about guys like him, guys with little going for them who get so angry when a woman rejects them that they just go and kill her." Vehemently, he said, "The police better give weight to the fact you saw a man outside the lady's room the day Madeleine died, because he fits that janitor's description."

Today she herself would focus on John Batchelder, her handsome cohost. She meant to spend as much time with him as possible in the coming days to see what she could learn about both him and his newscaster girlfriend from Channel Eight.

And Marty. She realized guiltily that she had to take seriously the producer's angry mood change just before Madeleine Doering was found murdered.

Tell the police? Her heart sank. Snooping was dirty business: She didn't know how her husband had made a whole career of it—trained at the Farm, and then sent out into the world to cajole, coopt, bribe, and lie. The only thing that gave him a sense of normalcy in those years abroad was his family—a wife and two little girls who demanded that Bill act like a regular father and husband.

Snooping on people as close as Marty made her feel like a traitor, especially since her producer had been gallant, as usual: He had proposed to the police that both he and Louise were in their respective offices at the time of the killing. She, of course, could only speak for herself, and had no personal knowledge of his whereabouts in those few critical moments.

She only knew she desperately didn't want Marty to be the murderer: Not only did she like him, but he held a large stake in her job future. There were plenty of other people around that night, staff, visitors, volunteers. But like a bad dream, her mind kept going back to the scenario of the producer as the romance-entangled murderer. She had to admit he was a strong suspect in the bunch. And she was beginning to realize how little she really knew Marty Corbin.

She would have to spy on one and all. She squared her shoulders and strode into the building. It was not going to be a comfortable week.

As usual this morning, she walked by the pickets without making eye contact. That explained why she nearly ran into Jack Lederle, who was approaching the door from the opposite way. "Ah, we meet again," the noted news broadcaster said, pausing at the door. He looked grim. "First, pickets. Now murder in the ranks, I see." But his very tone and demeanor said something else, that he and his entourage of news gatherers and producers were appalled at this additional insult to the integrity and dignity of WTBA-TV.

"My God," she said quickly, "we're descending straight into perdition, aren't we?"

He frowned.

Her face turned beet red. She should be apologizing to this great man, shouldn't she? But instead she was making flip remarks that landed like lead balloons. Yet what had she to do with the murder, except for being one of the leading suspects? "It was a tragic death," she said soberly. "I can't believe it happened right here in our midst."

"Well, not in our midst, fortunately," said Lederle, skillfully separating out his news staff. "We were all gone from our studio, of course, well before five." He smiled. "More grim times for you, though, I guess?" He gave her a knowing, patient look, the kind he gave to his interviewees who were well-known, sometimes-admired criminals.

Like Michael Milken and Richard Nixon.

Had Lederle heard she was under suspicion? Probably, by virtue of being the brightest star in the entire PBS firmament, he was dished all the inside information the police were willing to release. They probably had made some amorphous statement to him about "possible suspects being questioned." That was her. She had already stirred up this sedate public television station like a tornado disrupting a quiet Kansas neighborhood, and brought out a permanent set of hired goons who harassed employees each day at the station's elegant marble entrance.

Or was Lederle's remark innocent? Maybe he was simply commiserating about the dreariness of having mayhem committed in their workplace, knowing she had suffered only recently from the effects of another homicide, the mulch murder.

Whatever he meant, she was tired of responding like a sycophantic wimp. She looked him straight in the eye. "Mr.

Lederle—Jack, if I may call you that . . . and by the way, my name is Louise Eldridge. All of us who were there at the time of the murder are being questioned, and some of us may seem to have been involved. However, I'm confident that as the police continue to gather information, innocence will prevail and the guilty person will be found." With that she allowed him to open the door for her, and strode into the offices ahead of him.

As she continued through the lobby and down the hall to her office, she wished she really could believe those haughty words.

23

Marty, Louise, and Rachel sat at the round table in Marty's office, purportedly for a story conference—or "pow-wow," as Marty called it—on the vegetable garden program. While Rachel was her usual comely self in spring suit of light turquoise, she and Marty looked like they hadn't quite pulled it together this morning.

The producer's curly, dark hair, always perfectly styled, seemed overgrown. There were circles under his brown eyes, and his shirt looked previously worn, as if there were a disturbance in the domestic system whereby he emerged with fresh ones each day.

She had no grounds for criticism. She had pulled out of the closet a cocoa linen pants suit with the wrinkles of half a dozen wearings, and she couldn't even remember combing her hair. She only knew it wasn't sitting the way it usually did on her head.

For some reason, John had not shown up, but when he did, he'd probably be suffering the after-effects of the cocaine he'd sniffed Saturday night. Yet Louise knew the painfully beautiful young man never showed ravages of anything, age or drugs. John was rather like Dorian Gray, although of course not that evil—not much different from other single yuppies living in any big city. Maybe if given a few more years, John, like Dorian's secret picture, would begin to display some real corruption.

She looked at Marty, so benign-appearing today, and felt unsettled at the thought that he could be a vicious criminal.

So, too, with John, who was arriving momentarily. She would have the dubious pleasure of spending the entire morning with two likely suspects, while, to add to the tension, police puttered around the place, still combing through things like stray wastebaskets and everything in Madeleine Doering's office.

Marty spent a few minutes filling Rachel in on the scene at the station Friday afternoon and evening. As he did, Louise could feel a depression descending on her. He went over all the ghastly details, but she didn't need them. How well she could conjure up the image of Madeleine's body, jittering across the floor in a macabre dance of death. How well she could conjure up the mixed smells of death, and Madeleine's perfume, and that wretched pesticide that someone had shot into her body . . .

She put her head down in her hands and felt her stomach do a loop-the-loop.

"Louise!" cried Rachel, reaching out and touching her arm. "Are you all right?"

She looked up at them. "All right? No, not really." She took a deep gulp of air. "Are we going to talk about the murder? I know Rachel needs to know everything, but . . ."

Rachel patted her arm. "You've had enough already, I know. So. Are we ready to muck about in the vegetables?"

Marty chuckled and patted Louise's hand. She was dismayed to realize his touch made her flesh crawl.

He told her, "Don't feel too bad. We know what you've gone through. I'm going through the same thing—remember? I saw the same sight you did there on the floor. I'm having the same dicey time with the police. But you'll live through this, and so will I."

"I'm trying, Marty, but it's just that being questioned by police is no fun."

Against her will, a tremble had entered her voice. "Neither is being looked at strangely by your colleagues when you come in to work. I'd like nothing better than to get away from the topic for awhile."

Rachel smiled at her, sympathy written all over her face. Or pity, perhaps? Then she turned to Marty. "One thing, bottom line: This won't affect the *Gardening with Nature* show, will it? I was beginning to like this job a whole lot." Marty grinned. "Not unless Louise, John, or I are charged with the murder. Unfortunately, we're among the possible subjects. The G.M. of course assures me that he believes us all innocent." He reached over and tried to touch Louise's hand again; she pulled it away. "Even you, despite Madeleine scratching you, and catching her hairs in your button, and all that."

"Gee, Marty," she said drily, touching the healing scratches on her cheek, "I'm glad that's become public information, too."

The young woman writer looked over her big glasses at Marty and said, "Let's get one thing clear. I don't think any of you are capable of such a thing." Then she opened a big tan folder filled with notes and said, "Did you people ever hear about Malabar spinach? It's wonderful—deep green leaves, red veins, good for making leafy screens . . ."

"Right on, Rachel!" said Louise. "I love Malabar spinach! What else do you have for the show?"

Marty grumbled, "I suppose there's no way we can use a few innocent chemicals in this vegetable garden?"

Louise and Rachel shook their heads in concert. "Let's stick with organic controls," said Louise.

They were well into the script when the student intern poked his crew-cut head in the door and announced Louise had a phone call.

She looked quizzically at the young man.

"Detective Johnson's on the line," he said quietly, his eyes large with excitement. "We thought you might want to take it in your own office."

Louise could feel her body tense. She looked at the others around the table. "Gee, folks, here I go again."

Marty looked at her strangely, and she realized the truth of it. The more that police questioned her about the crime, the more others would begin to believe she did it.

Quietly, she said, "I'll be back as soon as possible. You're off to a fast start with that script, Rachel. It's going to be a great program."

With burning face, she went into her adjoining office and closed the door. The place was still rather cell-like, with virginal white walls, since she hadn't had time to hang pictures. She was thankful for this serene white; it gave her a sense of tranquillity every time she came in here. And she needed it now. She sat in her chair, pushed it back to the wall, and propped her long legs up on her desk. Dammit, if she were to be a real suspect, she wasn't going to reduce herself to a tense woman with neck muscle spasms.

She picked up the phone and buzzed Berta, the receptionist. "I'm ready to have that call transferred in."

"Right, Louise," said Berta, in a quiet, conciliatory voice. "It's the police, you know."

Wearily, Louise said, "Thanks, Berta."

It seemed incredible at first that Detective Johnson could have anything further to connect her to Madeleine Doering's death, but he did. She listened politely. Then he unwound the skein of facts like a busy woman at a spinning wheel. Her heart felt as if it were falling into her feet.

It was that damned Atlas mower audition. "And so, not only did you have an altercation with Madeleine in the waiting room . . ."

"Altercation! She was ranting at me. Again, it was Madeleine doing the altercating, or whatever you call it, and *me* the butt of her anger!"

"Just a minute, Mrs. Eldridge," said the calm police officer. She could imagine him sitting there, his black, pleasant face undisturbed by her railing. "Then there's the auditions themselves. We've discovered she was a serious contender, along with you, for that voice-over job . . ."

"More than a voice-over," Louise corrected, absently. "It was a job as on-camera spokesperson for the company. That pays lots more than a voice-over."

"It was going to pay very well, right, Mrs. Eldridge?" chimed in the detective. "This all goes to motive. We know you and your husband took on a large mortgage last year, and have a daughter in one of the most expensive private universities in the country."

"What does that have to do with it?" She sat up, plunked her feet on the floor, and hunched over the desk.

Wave after wave of new realities were washing over her.

Her family's innocent habit of living the American, in-debt way became suspicious, once she was a suspect.

A chewing out she had received from the victim became an "argument" once she became a suspect.

People who would not normally believe she could commit murder were beginning to have doubts, once she became a suspect.

"Detective Johnson, I need to come and talk to you."

"Fine. That's just what I wanted you to do. We need to get to the bottom of these things . . . of which I actually forgot one of the most important ones . . ." He paused, as if looking in his notes. "There's a memo they just found, on Ms. Doering's computer, half finished . . ."

"A memo. What does it say?"

"I'd rather discuss this when you get here, Mrs. Eldridge."

"Please—just tell me what it would have to do with me."

"Well . . ." Again, the pause to review notes. "It's to the producer, Marty Corbin. First, she mentions a story for her senior show, what do they call it—*The Best Years*, I guess—about a new Alzheimer's disease treatment. Then, she expresses her 'consternation,' she called it, over her rivalry with you. She wanted to talk to Corbin about your hostile 'attitude' toward her because you want the spokesman contract so badly . . ."

"Hostile attitude? Rivalry? Let me set you straight on that, Detective Johnson. There was no rivalry. I had that thing all sewn up the day of the auditions. The president of the company practically assured me I had the job."

The detective's voice was reproachful. "But surely, Mrs. Eldridge, you heard, because everybody else heard. I guess it's a flimsy-walled studio of some kind. About what a big hit Madeleine Doering made when she got in there. No. Couldn't it have been that you and Madeleine were the finalists, and if anything, Madeleine held the advantage, because she's more of a pro than you?"

Louise pulled in a breath, and it turned into a shudder. She would be no good around here today to help with a script on vegetable gardening. She felt like a dog whipped in battle with its tail between its legs. All she wanted to do was to go to her home and crawl into bed. Maybe even take some kind of pill that would knock her out for a while.

But first, she had to deal with the police. "Detective Johnson, how would it be if I come right now?"

24

She met Mary Mougey as she was driving into the cul-de-sac and Mary was leaving. They paused and rolled their respective driver's windows down, which gave Mary a chance to see Louise's troubled face.

"My dear," said Mary, in her warm, silky voice. She turned off the key in her ignition, got out of the car and came and leaned her arms on Louise's car door. Mary's pale blond hair was in soft waves around her face, and she was wearing stylish powder blue running togs in which Louise was sure Mary would never run a foot. "What *is* the matter? It couldn't be that terrible killing at Channel Five, could it?"

Louise's eyes filled up with tears. She nodded, looking into Mary's concerned gray eyes. "I seem to be at the top of their ladder of suspects."

Mary's mouth fell in amazement. "That's ridiculous. Why, do you want me to call the police and tell them what kind of a person you are?"

Louise touched Mary's arm. "No. There's nothing you can do. It's physical evidence at the crime scene accidentally that points to me. Little fights. She was always confronting me. There was a contract we were competing for, to do a national television ad campaign. A memo she wrote about me . . ." She bowed her head. "After everything else that's happened, Mary, I don't know. It doesn't seem fair. I'm so angry; I'm so tired—and to top it off, the detective I went to talk to had to hurry off to the site of another murder, so I never did hear all the details of what he has on me."

Mary reached in and put a soft hand on her shoulder. "Louise, you mustn't worry. They'll probably find someone close to that woman, a lover, a would-be lover, an ex-husband, who did it. Men are so much more violent than women. That alone should alert them you couldn't have done it. Haven't they found a lover, someone like that?"

Sure, thought Louise, take your pick—Marty, the ex-hubby, or the janitor. "Yes. There's a worn-out lover, an enraptured would-be lover, and an out-of-state ex-husband who they say still pined after her. But there's no evidence pointing to them, just to me."

"Rats! We have to do something about that. Let's see, who else could have done it? Would I know anyone there? Your cohost, of course—cunning young man—how about him? And your general manager—I know him, of course." Louise was aware Mary knew practically everyone in Washington.

Mary snapped her fingers. "I know another: What about Bruce Behrens? Might he have something to do with it? He talks about WTBA—sounds like a groupie—and lucky you, he's practically on board as one of your corporate underwriters." She shook her head. "Now I don't think Bruce could murder someone, but on the other hand, you learn almost too much about people when they're giving you large sums of money."

Louise looked up at Mary. "I don't think he knew Madeleine Doering. The person Behrens might want to get rid of is me."

"Oh, understandably," said Mary lightly. "I read in the *Wall Street Journal* that his lawn spraying business is off. Is that your doing, or does he just think it's your doing?"

Mary thought for a moment, while Louise slumped behind the wheel, content to let someone else worry about the matter. Then her neighbor, ever the romantic, said, "No, not murder over corporate profits: Passion, jealousy, sexual revenge, Louise—it will come down to that. But I have a super idea: I'm headed for the store for a few groceries. Come on over in twenty minutes and have a hot tub with me on the back porch. As it is, you look like you're ready to pass out, and I don't want you to do that. I'd rather feed you a martini, and let you soak at a hundred and four degrees." She laughed throatily. "If you can survive that, you can survive this murder stuff, my dear."

Louise's eyes lit up, but then she remembered Janie. "Oh, maybe I'd better not. The family's shaken up. Actually, they're very involved with this. We're trying a little fact-gathering." She made an offhand gesture. "You know what I mean. I shouldn't leave Janie; I already leave her too much."

"Bring Janie. I've talked to her a little bit recently, although I don't know her as well as your wonderful Martha, so this will be my chance. The three of us will soak together. We'll discuss all these disgruntled lovers and former lovers—everybody we can think of." Mary spread out both elegant hands, palms out, as if warding away evil. "No, we won't accuse anyone, but everyone must be considered, because someone did this, and it certainly wasn't you."

Trees Unsuitable for Her
Enemies to Hide Behind

Every garden can use a few small trees. They do two things—
they make the garden loftier, as if a second story were added;
and they bring down and humanize taller tree specimens that
loom above the yard. Their friendly presence is near eye level,
and is what we see first when we enter the garden.

Since we expect a lot of these trees, we have to choose them
for their shape and bark as well as their flowers and leaves.
After all, they must look like more than pathetic woody skeletons in the off-season. In the tree suggestions following, you
should be aware that some of these delightful specimens do
not grow in arid, harsh conditions. Always check for the zone
of hardiness.

Trees can go in the middle of a flower border, although
sometimes they work better placed in the rear of the garden,
with flowers and ornamental grasses dallying beneath. Pruning keeps trees open and prevents too much shade falling on
plants.

Size is the most important consideration. Even very small
gardens have room for a tree like the weeping Siberian pea-
tree (*Caragana aborescens* "Pendula"). It is droopy-stemmed,
hardy, and disease-free, with pretty yellow blossoms, and
stands only five feet tall and three feet wide. Just eight foot tall
is the rare weeping Kilmarnock willow (*Salix caprea* "Pendula
Weeping Sally"). Slightly bigger than that is the white weeping cherry (*Prunus x* "White Fountain"), which attains fifteen
feet eventually; it is a cascade of white flowers in spring. If you
have the width, go for a tree form of hydrangea (*Hydrangea
paniculata* "Grandiflora"). It will give you a ten-foot-wide
canopy of big white flower clusters that turn coppery pink in
fall. Wisteria is another rampant beauty that can be trained
into a garden tree.

Then comes color. Japanese maple is one of the handsomest
trees on the market. Small bush varieties are charming but
take a lot of ground space; small tree types have space for
flowers underneath. Two that suit a garden are the coral bark
(*Acer palmatum* "Sango kaku"), whose twigs stay red in winter; and golden full moon maple (*Acer japonicum* "Aureum").

In autumn, the golden full moon's chartreuse leaves turn orange, red, and purple.

Fall color fireworks like this make us think the garden is still in bloom. This holds true with the sourwood tree (*Oxydendrum arboreum*). First, it shows off with fragrant white flowers in panicles. Then, in September, the oblong leaves turn scarlet and the cream-colored seed pods imitate flowers. A warning: This tree is so brilliant that you must be careful of what is used near it.

Bark and trunks can turn out to be a tree's greatest attraction, especially if highlighted by a background of evergreens or snow. The hawthorn, *Crataegus succulenta x oxyacantha* "Paulii" ("Toba"), has a gnarled, twisted trunk right out of Grimm's fairy tales. The slightly larger American river birch (*Betula nigra* "Heritage") is popular for its distinctive peeling bark, and the Amur cherry (*Prunus maackii*) for its shiny, exfoliating cinnamon brown skin.

Special attributes like horizontal limbs make trees favorites. Dogwood and the beautiful Mt. Fuji cherry (*Prunus serrulata* "Shirotae") are wonderful examples. Long-term flowering is another bonus, but few trees stay in bloom longer than one to two weeks—except the small, vase-shaped crape-myrtle (*Lagerstroemia indica*). Choose it for a summer of bloom, in either white, pink, or magenta.

Pinchpenny gardeners should search around the yard when they need a small tree but don't want to buy one. They can turn to an overgrown bush out of place, carefully prune the bottom branches away, and emerge with a small tree perfect to pop into the perennial border. The winged euonymus (*Euonymus alata*) is an ideal candidate for this, with its radish-red fall color and graceful long branches. You will get spectacular results trimming a purple-leafed smoke bush (*Cotinus coggygria* "Royal Purple") into a tree. Even after the leaves fall, the big, fluffy seed pods will add charm to your garden all winter long.

There is a smaller tree, woodsy in nature, that thrives almost everywhere in the continental United States—the serviceberry (*Amelanchiar alnifolia*). Its beauty spans four seasons, from the delicate white flowers in spring, roseate leaves on loose branches in summer, radiant peach and red fall color, and dove gray branches in winter—an ideal garden companion.

25

The hot-tub experience on Mary Mougey's patio was just what Louise needed. She propped both arms on the edge, then let her body slide into the blazing hot water and dozed while Mary Mougey and Louise's sixteen-year-old daughter chatted like magpies about everything under the sun: art, literature, music. Despite her semiconscious state, she was amused to hear Janie sounding as erudite as any adult she'd talked to lately.

By the time they got home, Louise had lost the temptation to take pills and sleep and instead turned out to be good for the whole evening. Mary had persuaded her that she should talk to the neighbors and share the fact that police were questioning her on Madeleine Doering's death. After all, it would be better to prepare them in case Detective Johnson or one of his men dropped in on them asking questions about her.

On her part, Mary said she would pick up everything she could from her personal grapevine about Marty, the station manager, and Bruce Behrens. Just out of curiosity, Louise also suggested she try to get a list of cement plants Behrens operated.

First Louise phoned Sam Rosen, who lived next door. He dropped over with his small dog Missy tucked under his arm and told her that just on general principles he would tie Missy out in the patio at night so she could bark freely at the moon and at strangers.

"But, Sam, I'm not in danger," she protested. Missy wiggled obsequiously over to Louise to see if she could join this lady up on that nice, soft couch. Louise scratched the dog firmly on the head until it got over the impulse to jump. Sam's chubby face had darkened.

"Look, Louise, I heard about how Janie was chased home from school that day—Bill told me. The neighbors will be outraged that police would consider you a suspect in any crime. But whenever you're mixed up in murder and you don't know who the murderer is, you need as many alarms and watchdogs as you can find."

Through his teeth he gave a high whistle to his mutt, and she trotted over and leaped up into his arms. "Now, Missy here is a fine, barking dog." He leaned forward, and she could see a handsome man under his twenty extra pounds. "Louise, I've been working on the Hill for a dozen years now—I know a helluva lotta people in this town. Do you need information? Any time you do, I can get it for you." She thanked him.

When she phoned Sarah Swanson, the potter reported that she had finished sculpting the pottery jardinière for which Louise had posed. "We start production in the studio to-morrow on 'The Gardener'—that's what I call it—so it will reach the stores soon, maybe by Mother's Day. I have lots of orders. And, my dear, had you ever considered promoting through your program? It would be a natural as part of that little graphics lead-in at the beginning."

"I could check on that," Louise said, noncommittally. It was a little hard to talk to Sarah. The fact that Sarah's husband Mort was one of Peter Hoffman's attorneys would make a wider and wider gulf between the two women, especially as the trial approached in July. That was only two months away.

After a silence, Sarah said, "Let's get right to it, Louise. You're my friend, no matter whom my husband represents. His business is quite apart from me, and its moral under-pinnings sometimes are quite beyond my understanding. If you need me for anything, character witness, anything, I'll be right there for you, my dear. Don't forget that."

Louise could picture the big, blond woman, generous and jolly. "Thanks, Sarah," she'd said.

She did not call Nora. She missed their friendship, in spite of the woman's advances toward Bill. When she saw Chris or his sister, Melanie, she invariably inquired about their mother. Once, Chris answered, "Oh, she's head over heels, as usual, in poetry," and studiously avoided looking in Louise's face.

If this murder ever got solved, she might have time to put that matter straight.

26

"You're right," said Bill, his binoculars steady on his face, "there is a disturbance in the domestic situation." He handed the glasses to Louise. "Look at them. The quarrel continues all over the house."

She and Bill, wearing dark jogging suits, were slumped down in the front seat of her old station wagon, which had been parked for half an hour now across the street from Marty Corbin's house in Chevy Chase. It had seen better days. Set among colonials, it looked like an architectural refugee of the 1950s with its large floor-to-ceiling windows and unwieldy angled roof designed to resemble bird wings. The garage door was open, revealing the need for a good cleanup.

The drapes were not closed. Louise was appalled at the way they were observing Corbin family life. She said, "It's almost as if we were peering into a glass-sided ant house. Gosh, Bill, do you realize our house is just as much of a fishbowl as this one? If anyone tramped through the woods near our house, they could stand there and stare at all our family doings."

Bill reached over and took her hand. "There have always been windows in houses, and always been people willing to stare into them. The only solution for people is to pull curtains."

"Seal up your house like a mortuary," said Louise, "but who wants to do that?"

"Exactly."

"So what we're saying is that people are fair game if they don't draw their curtains."

"Precisely."

"One more of those, Bill, and I'll accuse you of being a prig."

"And rightly."

She wished she was as lighthearted as her husband, but she felt more serious: The Corbin house was the first of three stops tonight during which Louise hoped to learn something that would turn the floodlight of guilt away from her, and onto the actual murderer. That thought wracked her with a guilt that made her stomach feel hollow. But what else could she do? It wouldn't be her fault if one of her coworkers was the murderer.

Later on, they would swing by John Batchelder's place. Then, they were to meet their old friend, Detective Geraghty. Unwilling at first, the detective finally agreed to meet away from the police station to give them what information he could on the investigation.

When she and Bill first drew up to the Corbin house tonight, there was no movement visible. Later, they spied Marty and his wife in the back of the house, darting back and forth. "Doing dishes, I think," said Bill. "I'll just continue to hold your hand to alleviate my boredom," he said, fondling her fingers in a pleasant way.

Now, at last, there was action. Marty came and sat down in the room with the television, but his wife followed him and stirred around him like an angry hornet. "Her name is Steffi," said Louise. "A little heavy, isn't she, but a sweet face. She's a credit counselor for a consumer credit league. I've been told she's a nice, low-key kind of woman. But she doesn't look like that now." The woman's dark hair was disheveled, and her green pants suit, which appeared to be made out of velour, was loose and sloppy.

"I hate to say it," said Bill, "but she looks like a large marauding animal, coming in for the kill. Wonder why she's so upset."

"I think I know," said Louise. "Monday, I was called away to go to the Fairfax County Jail to talk to the detectives. Now, today, Marty disappears in the afternoon; he didn't tell anybody where he was going. At least he wasn't publicly embarrassed like me. But don't you suppose he got questioned again? That would explain all that activity in there."

Steffi was not letting Marty Corbin relax. She stood with arms akimbo, arguing with him, then led him into the living room where together they searched for something in a desk.

"Wonder if she got questioned?" Bill suggested. "You know what Janie said. This woman might have had more grounds to kill Madeleine Doering than Marty did."

She returned the binoculars to Bill. "Your turn, dear." She could still see the couple near the desk. They acted as if they had found something.

The furtive watchers could almost hear the angry shouts of the couple, as they obviously exchanged harsh words. Then the woman dropped her head on her chest as if breaking down in tears and rushed up the stairs.

"Look!" said Bill. "She's going upstairs now. He's following her. Something's bound to happen!"

There was a light on in one of the bedrooms. Here, too, the curtains were open. The woman in green came in the room, and her husband, still in office garb of white shirt and dark pants, followed. He grabbed her and shook her. Louise gasped. "My God, Bill, what will we do if this turns violent?"

Then they watched as Marty took his wife in his arms. "Look for yourself," said Bill, handing her back the glasses. She put them to her eyes and witnessed close up a big smooch between the Corbins.

All her nerves came alive as Bill slid a hand on her thigh.

Then, as if finally remembering the fishbowl features of their home, Marty broke off the embrace and went to the window and pulled draperies across, blocking out further view for Louise and Bill.

Her husband grinned and moved his hand higher up Louise's thigh.

"What's that big grin for, and what's the hand action?"

"I don't know Marty, but from what I can see he's a really cool guy. Knows how to problem-solve, certainly. Suppose that argument was all about how he might have killed Madeleine. Or suppose it was all about how she might have done her in. Doesn't matter. He handled it in the age-old way that men solve domestic disputes."

"Hmh," said Louise, "but it doesn't prove anything one way or another." Just then her husband reached over and pulled her close. "And what's this all about?"

"Just a little insurance, a little romantic memory for you to refer back to when you get mad at me. Besides, voyeurism is a turn-on."

"Hmm, you *are* over your broken leg, aren't you? Okay, Bill, a couple of kisses, but no fooling around. First of all, this is Chevy Chase; we're liable to get arrested." She peered at her wristwatch. "Anyway, we have just enough time to swing by John's apartment, and then we have a date with Geraghty at ten o'clock, one hour from now, in Ernie's Crab House."

"I can do all that," said Bill, sliding his hand underneath his wife's sweatshirt and loosening her bra.

Louise giggled as she and Bill swung up the sidewalk toward the door of Ernie's Crab House. "I told you the police would snoop around."

"We were just making out," said Bill, giving her a wink. "It probably won't have impregnated you, dear. But you better be prepared for the fact that Marty might have peered out the bedroom window when the cops flashed those blue lights; he might figure out someone was spying and he could have recognized your car. At least the cops didn't give us a ticket."

She smiled and shook her head. "You did a good job of talking yourself out of one, I've got to give you that. When that officer was standing there, I could just see the headline in the *Washington Post:* 'State Department official and gardening show hostess wife arrested for indecent exposure in Chevy Chase.' "

"Honey, we were still in *some* of our clothes. Hurry up now, let's see Geraghty; we've got unfinished business when we get home."

She looked at him in wonder. "Bill, you are so wild tonight. What's happened to my careful, conservative husband?"

Bill's eyes were merry as he stumped along on his walking cast. "Getting off those damned crutches is like getting out of the damned Agency. It's the end of being crippled!"

They walked in the door and passed a young man standing behind enormous pots of boiling water with a long ice pick. He plunged the steel instrument into each crab's stomach, to initiate a reflexive action that prevented the animal from jettisoning its claws. Then, he threw them into the boiling cauldron.

"Agh!" said Louise, "all that killing going on in here. But it makes you hungry, doesn't it?" She rubbed her stomach. "Yummy crabs."

Bill's eyes sought out the detective. "He said he'd sit in the back section." They saw him sitting in the farthest booth. The man's large hands encircled a draft beer; his brilliant, marble-blue eyes looked at them across the two rooms. Then, a smile broke in the reddish face beneath the shock of short white curly hair and he lifted his glass to Louise and Bill, as if in tribute to something they had done or were about to do.

27

Mike Geraghty wiped his mouth with a big napkin, taking a breather after eating his first few crabs. Louise and Bill were still in progress on their second. "So it looks like you two are still in love," said the big detective. His gaze rested on Louise with that same intensity that had made her convinced last fall that he would find the mulch murderer. And Geraghty had tried hard and in fact had been there at the end, when the murderer finally showed up at the Eldridge house.

"You betcha we're in love," said Bill, looking boyish as he dipped a big piece of crab flesh into the vinegar and popped it in his mouth.

"You're gonna need each other," said Geraghty, looking at the pile of uneaten crabs, and selecting one and sliding it into place in front of him on the tan butcher paper. He held his metal claw cracker in one hand, but didn't use it; instead, he leaned forward and said, "Any investigation involves the process of elimination. So far, Detective Thompson has very little on anyone: Marty Corbin, John Batchelder, Madeleine Doering's ex-husband . . ."

"You haven't even mentioned the janitor," Louise complained. "I saw him, or someone who looked like him, at the scene . . ."

She stopped, hopelessly. "Go ahead; I'm sorry to interrupt you."

"Nebulous figures you've seen are not helpful. It would have been more useful if you'd had a positive I.D. on that person you saw near the site of the killing. Now, back to motive. You could say several others in addition to you had motives. But as far as evidence goes, the only one Detective Thompson has anything solid on is you, Mrs. Eldridge."

Suddenly she felt her cheeks burning, probably the combination of beer and crabs and sharp vinegar. Her shoulders began to weigh heavily on her frame. "Isn't it permitted to call me Louise, especially since you're being such a good friend to us?"

He smiled and said, "I'd like to call you Louise, but believe me, it's better if I don't."

"Okay. Now let's talk about evidence. That's the most important thing that ties me to this crime."

"Ever see the stats on murders?" asked Geraghty. "Many convictions are based on circumstantial evidence only." He frowned. "But beside that, evidence isn't all that ties you to the crime: Your motive looks stronger and stronger—to some of the staff. Madeleine Doering unfortunately hit the nail right on the head in that memo she wrote. Went right to motive."

Louise and Bill just looked at him.

The big detective looked embarrassed. "I know you aren't fancy livers, and I don't know why you have a two-hundred-and-twenty-five-thousand-dollar mortgage; your house isn't that big."

"Not very strange in the Washington area," said Bill. "It's called being cash-short. We were overseas for so many years we never bought a house until last year when we moved to Washington." He looked down at the mess of shells in front of him on the paper, and with short, jerky motions shoved them into a bowl. "It's a wonder you didn't examine my losses from the neighborhood poker game."

Geraghty raised his eyebrows. "You got big losses there?"

Bill tried hard to curb his disgust. "Sure," he said with a sneer. "Sometimes fifteen dollars a night. And we play twice a month."

Geraghty looked at him in silence.

"The fact is," said Louise, "while other Americans were

trading up houses and making their little fortunes, we were overseas working for the government. We didn't get involved in all that, and it was a mistake—because when we finally decided to buy, it was a struggle to handle the financing." She shrugged her shoulders. "So what if our payments are two thousand four hundred dollars a month? We are house-poor, I'll admit it. But we get by, especially since I'm making money now."

"And then the girl at Northwestern: That must cost a bundle," said Geraghty.

Louise looked at him resentfully. "It's a well-balanced financial package. Granted, a lot is borrowed, but part of it is a scholarship grant, some was paid up front, and Martha earns a little at a part-time job. Again, what's wrong with that? We're just Americans, you know, Detective Geraghty. Debt is an invitation that like a couple of ninnies we used to refuse, but we can't any more, since we want what everyone else wants: a house, and a good education for our children. Besides which, Bill loaned a lot to his brother for medical school, and it probably will be repaid soon."

She stared at the detective she used to think of as a friend. If she hadn't been so angry, she might have cried. Quietly, she said, "Detective Geraghty, how would you like to be on the receiving end of this? How would you like me to judge your guilt on some matter on the basis of your honest debts? You do have some, don't you?"

Geraghty put up both hands. "Wait a minute. Remember, we're talking about you. The police do these financial checks for a reason, not just to harass you. They see X amount of debt. They look at you and see you contending with this Madeleine Doering for a cushy contract in TV."

"Yes," said Louise. "Well, that's quite another matter."

"Twenty or thirty thousand dollars of easy money . . ."

"It isn't *that* easy," protested Louise, sitting forward, her bottom lip jutting out. "And where did you hear the contract was worth thirty thousand dollars? I heard it was worth twenty thousand."

Geraghty gave a massive shrug. "Twenty thousand, thirty thousand—what's the dif? Either way, it's a lot of money. And Madeleine Doering stood there in your way."

"Oh no," insisted Louise in a strident voice, "I don't think so. Gosh, you sound just like Detective Thompson. I told him and I'll tell you. Just go talk to the people waiting around that day, talk to that mower company executive."

She looked at her husband. "That's it! Bill, why don't I talk to the president of that mower company? He could tell the police better than anyone else."

Geraghty lowered his head. He half-heartedly twisted a claw off his crab and laid it aside. Then he looked up at Louise over his heavy brows. "Sorry, Mrs. Eldridge, Detective Thompson didn't tell you. He's not just speculating. I thought he discussed all this with you. He's already talked to all those people. Everyone witnessed what they called a fight between you and Madeleine. And the mower company guy, he put it right out there. He liked you a lot, but he liked Madeleine better. Apparently you left the auditions before Madeleine and a number of others had theirs."

Louise sat back in the padded booth, pinned there by the force of truths that changed her whole world. "My God," she said.

Bill sat forward and looked at her. "Honey, are you all right?"

Louise firmed her jaw; she wasn't going to let this get her down. She looked the policeman straight in the eye. "Detective Geraghty, is there anything else I should know?"

The big man looked carefully beyond her, out into the empty restaurant. "Oh, a couple of little things: A young woman, I forget her name at the moment, but hair like this"—he held his curved hands up about a foot beyond either ear—"was in the auditions. She talked to you for a long time. She allegedly confirmed that you didn't like Madeleine, that you seemed to have a grudge against her."

"Oh, no!" she moaned. The girl with the leonine hair. "God, Bill, who will turn against me next?"

Her husband reached over and took her hand, but said nothing.

"Wait. What other little things?" she asked Geraghty, with a wary look.

"Oh, a police profile, done after you were in for that long interview the other day. The psychologist, well, psychologists just give indicators: motivations, that sort of thing."

"What did the psychologist say?" She remembered a little audience with the man, who had an unattractive trimmed beard that reminded her of a short-mowed lawn.

Geraghty waved a dismissive hand. "Oh, just some stuff about how, since you'd been involved in one violent episode . . ."

Bill sat forward, angry. "Where she tanked a guy with a poker stand because he was going to kill her?"

Geraghty put up his hands, defensively. "Hey, Bill, I don't think your wife has killed anyone. I'm only telling you what . . ."

". . . what some two-bit shrink had to say about my courageous wife—who brought in a murderer for you guys not six months ago!" Although his voice was low, his blue eyes blazed, and his fist was tightly clenched on the brown paper tablecloth. Louise felt like reaching over and covering it to restrain it from landing in Geraghty's face.

The detective sat forward and spoke quietly. "Bill, now, cool down. No one appreciates the irony of this whole situation more than you and me and Louise. Do you want to hear what else the guy said?"

Louise put a hand on Bill's fist. "Yes, we do."

"He said once you've committed violent acts like that—Hoffman's eye put out, his face burned, his head fractured—the next time is easier for you."

Louise gasped.

Mike Geraghty put up his hand again, like a behavior cop trying to stem a flood of emotions. "Now, Louise, I know this sounds crazy and that you actually caught Hoffman, and that you were acting in self-defense . . ."

"Yeah," said Bill in a dangerous voice. "Go on with what this guy thinks."

Geraghty looked at Bill carefully, then returned his gaze to Louise. "Well, he maintains once you'd been the victim of an enemy who was a stranger, you might have construed this Madeleine character in the same category—enemy, stranger—and struck out at her because the woman was constantly harassing you and threatening things you wanted, like that TV ad job."

In a quiet voice, Bill said, "Total and absolute bull."

Her gaze traveled down to the messy crab feast in front of them, which somewhere along the line they had all abandoned. Then she said to her friend Detective Geraghty, "Do you ever help keep track of Peter Hoffman?"

The detective nodded. "I take my turn driving by, once in a while, seeing if he's home . . ."

"How ironic that we're both in the same boat now," she said bitterly. "Both of us murder suspects. The only difference between us is that I haven't been charged yet."

28

With two swift jabs of her shovel, Louise chopped out a small clod of liriope, a small fountain of grass-like foliage with a perky purple flower in the center. She picked it up in her hand and admired it, not minding the dirt particles that ran down her arm. She looked at the vibrant little clump and realized that, once she plugged it and others like it into a new garden area, she would soon have a new carpet of the attractive groundcover. After doing that, she would assault the delicate sweet woodruff that frolicked under the azaleas, and spread the fragrant, white-flowered divisions to less privileged parts of the yard.

This rather mindless transplanting was a good way to take her mind off her problems.

Slash into the earth with her sharp shovel. Tamp down hard to shove the earth back into shape. Get down in the garden with her bare hands and force the plants into place in the rich, tilthy earth. Violent, earthy, sensuous: a little akin to sex.

At least it meant she didn't spend her day off brooding like the little man who walked around with a dark rain cloud over his head.

She straightened; her back told her it was time for a break. She put her shovel on the wheelbarrow, alongside the clumps of sweet woodruff and liriope, and decided to take a little garden walk around the house. Gone were the days when she would garden ferociously all day and end up on a heating pad in the evening.

The azaleas and rhododendrons and narcissus had faded,

and tulips were now king. In one corner of the woods caught by the sun, she had planted a tall white French variety, looking like bright swans moored incongruously on the forest floor. She wandered on, through the woods along the side of the house, to another open patch of woodland. Next to some cedars was a group of Queen of the Bartignons, her favorite, pink with blue markings on their insides.

She strolled past the wild sassafras and baby cedars to her front garden near the street, which also had half a day's sun. Set against a backdrop of mahonia bushes was a display of May Wonder tulips, big and magical. They were pink today, but some day soon, probably tomorrow, they would turn bright yellow because of a special chemical in their system.

She touched one of the flowers and considered picking a few for the house, then decided to leave them because they looked so beautiful there. Her gaze wandered to Nora's house across the cul-de-sac, and she was startled to see a dark figure standing in the front window. It was Nora. She waved gracefully to Louise. Louise returned the wave unenthusiastically. "Well," she muttered to herself, "that sure was a half-hearted wave." She felt guilty, but it was all she had to give to a treacherous friend.

As she turned to go back to her gardening work, a car pulled into the driveway. A large woman got out and slammed the door. It took a moment for her identity to register with Louise: Steffi Corbin, Marty's wife.

"Hi. You have to be Louise," said the woman in an abrupt voice. "I'm Steffi Corbin." A dark eyebrow curved upward. "You just may recognize me. This is business, so let's not waste time on pleasantries." The woman looked elegant in a mauve-colored suit specially designed for the bigger woman, with a square jacket and accented with a flowing chiffon scarf in pale pink that was worthy of Isadora Duncan. She had large brown eyes and dark, curly hair, just like her husband. Louise reflected they could have been twins. Steffi's eyes were anguished. Louise could see this woman was fighting for control.

"Um, Steffi. I'm pleased to meet you. Why don't we go right in. I'll find us a glass of iced tea or something, and we can talk."

"Fine," said the woman, and without another word she followed Louise up the path to the front door.

How past actions can come back to haunt a person, thought Louise, her heart sinking. She led the woman into the house, feeling as self-conscious as a teenager, in her dirty striped T-shirt and navy shorts and working boots. She swept a hand across her messy hair in a futile attempt to make it look better.

Finally settled with tea in the living room, Steffi confirmed what Louise was afraid of. Their detective efforts at the Corbin house had been discovered. "It wasn't very hard to find out, you know," the woman said, staring over at Louise. "We have a substation in the neighborhood. And you know Marty. He's friends with all the cops after twenty years of living there." Her mouth turned up in an unwilling smile. "The boys said you two were making out." She snickered. "I can't believe it."

Louise shook her head in total embarrassment. "Yes, it was foolish, to be there in the first place, to be kissing, just kissing, you know." She looked pleadingly over at Steffi Corbin. "I wish you could understand. We were just kind of driving around, seeing where people lived, trying to figure out things."

Steffi sat forward aggressively. "Like whether Marty or I killed that Madeleine?" Suddenly, the woman's eyes filled with tears. "It isn't as if I didn't feel like it, the way she got her talons into Marty and wouldn't let go."

"Oh, gosh. I could see something like that . . ." She added hastily, "I mean, the not letting go . . ."

"And he was trying to get loose of her lately, trying and trying again." Despite the tears that were flowing down her face, the woman seemed unashamed, and totally open in her anguish. "The only thing I'm afraid of is whether Marty did it, out of sheer frustration. And then you two come by, as if to corroborate it."

Her chest heaved, and Louise went over and sat next to her on the couch and put a tentative hand on her shoulder. "Steffi, I am so sorry."

Then she went out on a limb. "I don't really know you, but I know Marty. I'm sure you or Marty could never do such a thing."

"Well, that makes it mutual," said the producer's wife, "because he's sure you couldn't have murdered anyone, even her, although I hear you and she did not get along over the past few months."

Didn't get along. Over the past few months. Louise pulled in her breath. "Steffi, it was Madeleine who didn't like me. I didn't have anything to do with our not getting along."

The woman looked at her curiously. "No, outside of taking her job. I can see why you are sensitive, especially since Marty says there's some evidence, or something, involving you."

Louise folded her hands carefully in her lap. She needed to calm down, quit worrying about her own hide, and learn things from this woman. "Have the police been troubling you, like they have me?"

Steffi nodded her head of brown curls. "Oh, yes. Marty's been questioned twice. And they want him to come in again tomorrow." Her eyes grew moist again. When she spoke, her voice broke in a sob: "And I guess that's what I'm afraid of, that there's something hidden there, something I don't know."

"About Marty's involvement with Madeleine?"

"Yes," said Steffi, her shoulders rocking a little with quiet sobs. "You see, I've found a lot of things around the house. Marty is sloppy. I've found papers that show he's been tangled up with that woman for years. He spent money on her. He even took her on a vacation while I thought he was out of the country on business! And all this, after what happened to . . ." Steffi looked suspiciously at Louise and shoved a hand out, as if shoving a thought away. "That's long gone and forgotten."

Every curious bone in her body was alerted. But she realized Steffi would tell her no more. She said, "Do the police know about this long association with Madeleine?"

"No," said Steffi, looking at Louise anxiously, "and please, I hope you won't tell them! No one else who happens to know at the studio would tell, because people are loyal to Marty—to a fault. And I know I shouldn't make you promise such a thing. But the police . . . they can do their own investigation and find out what they can." The woman's eyes did not leave hers. "Let them find out if he did it."

She didn't promise Steffi she wouldn't tell about Marty's tangled romantic past. But she did just as well: She remained utterly silent. Loyalty could command a high price.

The woman looked at Louise with gratitude.

Then, Louise said, "Was Madeleine the only one?"

"Oh, no," said Steffi in a low voice. "You and I know she wasn't. I'm sure he made the obligatory pass at you; you're too cute for him not to have. It's just something in Marty. But we were getting back together, closer"—she gave Louise a knowing glance—"and Marty's getting . . . older—he's even got gray hair in that curly mop of his. Except the Doering woman wouldn't quit, just kept hounding him, making his life miserable." She turned to Louise. "So don't be embarrassed to be caught necking with your husband in a public place." Tears swept down her face. "I thought it was wonderful."

Louise drew the woman close and hugged her and let her cry out the grief of those years of husbandly betrayal.

Relieving Stress:
Color in the Garden

Color in the garden strikes our emotions and lifts us up above the trials of our day-to-day lives. It is a garden's most appealing feature. We begin with a framework that includes the opacity of evergreens and deciduous trees and the solidity of other garden features such as stone walls, rocks, and pools. Into this framework we place our plants and shrubs, like an artist placing colors on a canvas.

But color is more than just an element in the light spectrum. Plant textures transform these colors and remind us of natural and man-made objects, sometimes animals, often fabrics, occasionally even glass. The rose tempts us to touch it, and when we do, we find it feels just like velvet. With the greatest of care, we handle the silky poppy, so much more frail than silk. We know just by looking that the tulip, with its glaucous, luminescent petals, must have inspired Tiffany during his creation of Art Glass. Silver sage *(Salvia argentea)* sprawls about on the ground like a gray velour Victorian parlor pillow, while gray pussytoes *(Antennaria parvifolia)* and lamb's ears *(Stachys lanata)* poke up out of the garden, amusing us with their similarity to their animal namesakes.

Combined colors are powerful, sometimes too powerful—as when we assemble a prairie garden rich with the reds, oranges and purples of gaillardia, rudbeckia, salvia, purple coneflower, liatris, and native penstemon. Our senses cry out, "Help!" The answer is soothing white, which we can provide with white coneflower and wild phlox.

Much more restful than mixtures is the studied monochromatic effect. Garden catalogues now feature and sell sophisticated mixtures of plants, but any gardener can put together such a group. Assemble your own white-gray mixture to echo Vita Sackville-West's famous moon garden at Sissinghurst. Start with a gray-toned weeping pear *(Pyrus salicifolia)*, and let a white rose clamber up it. Plant moonflowers *(Ipomoea alba)* to scramble over a nearby pine. Mix in the solid white of the *Phlox carolina* "Miss Lingard," add vertical foliage with a stand of translucent white-bearded iris, and soften the scene with baby's breath *(Gypsophilia)* or *Achillea ptarmica* "The Pearl."

Finish it off with the large white translucent faces of the prickly poppy *(Argemone polyanthemus)*.

Monochromatic may be modish, but most of us mix colors wildly. If, as you stand in your garden, you don't want to feel as if you're surrounded by a clutch of women in bright party dresses, then don't forget this old adage: Repeating colors creates unity. Place a cluster of pink flowers in one spot, then echo this pink—using enough plants to make a real color impact—in two or more other places in the garden. Any large patch of color helps anchor the garden. Oriental poppy *(Papaver orientale)* or mallow *(Malva)* serve this purpose well because of their big, bright blooms.

For depth, go to the neutral-toned plants: the graceful, waving ivory-flowered goat's beard *(Aruncus dioicus)*; plume poppy *(Macleaya microcarpa* "Kelway's Coral Plume")*, its pale coral flowers set against grayish foliage; snakeroot *(Cimicifuga purpurea)*, with pure white snaky tasseled flowers on purple stems; Russian sage *(Perovskia atriplicifolia)*; and frothy-flowered meadow rues *(Thalictrum)*.

Every garden needs exclamation points. Try two products of the onion family, *Allium aftlatunense*, with its big round purple seedheads; and the shorter *Allium christophi*, with picturesque, elongated yellow seedheads. Others are red hot poker *(Kniphofia uvaria)*; *Polygonum bistorta* "Superbum," with pink, popsicle-like flowers rising above a fountain of low foliage; and polygonum "Firetail," aflame with red blooms. The attraction of *Ligularia dentata* "Otello" is not its flowers but its round, shiny green leaves and reddish stems and underleaves. When gardeners think of chartreuse, lady's mantle *(Alchemilla mollis)* comes to mind. Even more eye-catching is wavy-leaf mullein *(Verbascum undulatum)*. It has been described as "pale yellow felt as if dusted by sulfur."

If you like pastels, there are many choices, including the bluish-pink Japanese anemone *(Anemone japonica* "September Charm")*, pale-pink–bloomed *Clematis montana rubens* "Odorata," and sky-blue *Amsonia tabernaemontana*. Amsonia is a little-known garden treasure, with beautiful starlike flowers in handsome clusters called umbels. It further rewards the gardener with a three-foot-high fountain of green willow-like leaves that turn to a golden waterfall in autumn.

Let's forget their short-lived blooms and rejoice only in the virtues of daylilies *(Hemerocallis)*. Unlike some flowers, they always look comfortable in the garden. They also belong on the list of color anchors.

And finally, there are the hybrid lilies, long-lived and graceful as swans. A stand of trumpet lilies, *Lilium* "Anaconda" will give you bronze beauty at the end of six-foot stems for a month. What can top that? Well, possibly the tall, rugged, snow-white beauty of the Oriental lily "Casablanca." Yet you can't please everyone: One garden pundit complains that Casablanca's sweet, heavy fragrance is too much, and smells like a "French lady of the night."

29

Louise had been surprised—and she had to admit, relieved—when Nora wandered across the cul-de-sac as she returned home from the grocery store. She hated being on the outs with friends.

Louise's groceries now perched, disregarded, on the ground nearby while they sat together near the front garden bench on the edge of the woods. Bill had made the bench for her out of heavy flagstones, in what she called "Stonehenge" style. They sat there and talked, and it was like a small reunion of friends who had not seen each other for, oh, such a long time.

Nora gestured toward the May Wonder tulips, their pink hue now reflecting the setting afternoon sun. "I love those. I can see them from across the way. They seem to grow bigger, somehow, every day." She turned to Louise, her gray eyes smiling and friendly.

"I planted them partially for you and the other neighbors. I know you all love flowers." It felt strange to be talking to Nora at last, after all the discomfort caused by her hovering around her house while her husband was an invalid on the couch.

Nora leaned forward, her hands clasped in her lap, her dark hair falling and hiding her face again. As usual, she wore casual clothes, black slacks and a sweater. It was as if the woman had chosen the site of her own little confessional, and was now confessing. "Louise, I think I'm more stable now; that medicine has helped me settle down, helped me not feel so crazy."

"You don't have to say anything. I understand."

Her neighbor straightened up on the bench and looked at her. "You do?" she asked curiously. "But why? How? I really didn't think you could. You're much too good a person to understand anyone like me." The gray eyes narrowed, and the mouth looked sad. "I have some very dark patches in my personality."

It was now or never. Louise put a hand around Nora's wide shoulders. "We're friends, and that's that, Nora." Then she considered dropping her hand, not knowing if it were welcome. At that instant, Nora reached up and squeezed it. "That's what I mean, you are so good. I treasure yours and Bill's friendship."

Then Nora broke away, and stood up, facing Louise. This figure in the woods was totally unself-conscious, her hands fallen simply to her sides. "And that's why, despite my embarrassment, I had to come over. I've heard from Mary Mougey about you and the police and this murder. I am very worried, Louise. I think you may be in grave personal danger."

"Why?"

Nora took a few paces in the woods, the leaves crunching gently under her feet. Then she came back to where Louise sat. "When I was over visiting Bill one day, I studied a picture of you. Your hair was long, and it exactly resembled Madeleine Doering's hair in the photograph that was in the paper."

"But I cut my hair almost as soon as I joined Channel Five."

"What if it were a case of mistaken identity? Is there someone around there who would have liked to get rid of you?"

A tingle went through her body. There could be more than one person who filled this category.

Slowly, she said, "I can think of a few people."

Nora came and sat down next to her again. "Louise, all I

know is I sense danger. And I would hate to see you have to live through an ordeal like the last one with Peter Hoffman."

"Oh, so would Bill and I. But I don't know what I can do about it."

"Call the police. Call those people who seem bound to accuse you of the crime."

"You don't understand. The police have a high degree of incredulity as far as I'm concerned. They don't exactly believe me on anything, Nora." For a moment she felt like crying. "I swear, it's like I'm walking through quicksand, and I can't get out of it."

Nora took her hand in hers. "Look at how proud you should be of yourself. Look what you've done for yourself lately. You've charged right into a new career, and you're doing beautifully. You have a wonderful family that loves and admires you. Believe me, I know. At the very least, you need to call these people who are heading the investigation, and tell them. I don't mean to be a worrywart, my friend, but I can't have anything happen to you."

With that, they twined their arms around each other and sat there in a quiet embrace on the stone bench.

Detective Thompson was not available when she phoned. Yes, she said, she would leave a message on his voice mail. She did, and thought dispiritedly, that would be the end of that.

"Detective Thompson, I just had a visit from my neighbor," she started, and then went into the theory of mistaken identity. She kept the message short, because she was convinced Thompson would take a scratchy note on this message and set it aside. Then she got back to business. Tomorrow was her show on transplanting and propagating, and she needed to study the script. There had to be some quality to her life, and to her work life, even though she was losing hope that she would avoid a final collision with the police. She estimated she now had about two days left to find out the real murderer of Madeleine Doering.

She went to the coffee table and buried herself in the thick pages of *Perennials for American Gardens*. She knew a lot of the plants that could be multiplied, but this reference might tell her of some that she had overlooked. Becoming a television garden show host didn't mean she suddenly knew everything there was to know about plants.

It was almost midnight, and she and Bill had been asleep for an hour. Then, Missy started barking next door, making the first intrusion into her deep, blank, dreamless sleep. Next, the phone rang, and that cinched it. She grabbed the receiver before the ringing woke Bill. It was Martha. "Wait a minute, dear," whispered Louise, untwisting her silk nightie on her body, and slipping her feet into pink mules.

She took the phone to the living room and unfolded the Scotch wool throw and snuggled beneath it in a corner of the couch. "Is everything all right, Martha, my dear?"

"Ma, it's about Bed-Stuy."

"Yes."

"I've decided instead to go to Detroit and help Father Harrington with the City Project."

"Well, there doesn't seem too much difference." She weighed her words carefully. She didn't want to say that it made little difference which urban ghetto she chose, Bedford-Stuyvesant or the heart of Detroit, that they were all going to be dangerous to her daughter's bodily envelope. "I know you admire Father Harrington."

"He's made a real difference in the city. Detroit is such a *crummy* city, but it's improving because of people like him. And Ma, did Mary Mougey tell you?"

Louise's skin began to feel scratchy under the wool throw. "Tell me what? I just saw her. She didn't tell me anything concerning you."

"Well, she's going to try to get me a summer internship next year in Africa."

Louise felt dizzy. "I know you like and admire Mary Mougey, but, my God, that's dangerous. Do you realize . . ."

Then she lay her head back on the couch and gave it up. "Martha, it sounds wonderful. I always dreamed of doing something like that. I am so happy to have a daughter who's not just dreaming about things, but is actually doing them."

"Meantime, Ma, don't mention it to Mrs. Mougey—Mary, I call her now—until she brings it up with you. You can tell Dad. But better not tell Janie yet. Don't mention Detroit either. I think my little sister's already a little resentful. She wrote me a letter; it was pretty funny. You know what she wants to do this summer?"

"No," said Louise, warily. "Do you?"

The dizziness had developed into a dull headache. She had never felt so out of touch with her family.

"Hold onto your hat: She's looking into a program through the high school, where kids work all summer in Mexico City with the poor. Mary Mougey was the one who told her about it."

Mexico City. Poverty. Crime. And worst of all, the child's lungs probably would be ruined by the smog! Besides, she doubted the family budget could handle the expense.

Louise was now hyper-alert, but she kept her voice calm. "A little copycat in that."

"Maybe. Now, don't tell her anything I told you, promise?"

"No, of course not."

"Or mention this Africa stuff to Mary, 'til . . ."

"I know—until she brings it up."

Of course she wouldn't say anything to anyone about anything until they mentioned it first. Why, someone might mistake her for a person who helped her children make decisions!

30

Louise thought she could get used to power lunches. She hadn't been having much fun lately, but this was fun.

Demmi's was the Capital's favorite new lunch spot and it had a varied menu that ignored northern Europe. "You can choose Tex-Mex, high-Mex, Afrique du Nord, or health food," Mary Mougey had said in offhand power-lunch shorthand. Mary was one of the room's main attractions, and Louise could tell why: a combination of beauty and power. While Louise probably came across as girlish in a flowery rayon dress, Mary looked smashing in a dull-blue silk suit that illuminated her empathetic eyes and golden hair. And anyone could observe the power, from the way a parade of important people stopped at their table to say hello.

Louise was tying into grilled salmon on a bed of tangy greens. It had delightful accoutrements: a salad with jicama, kiwi, and fresh mandarin orange slices; and deep-green arame flecked with shaved carrots and sesame seeds in which she could taste the flavor of rice wine vinegar and sesame oil.

Mary was eating a haute Mexican version of venison served in a puddle of tangy black bean sauce. Both had ordered a squid appetizer in a tongue-burning red pepper sauce that Louise could have sworn was Spanish. Mary shrugged her silky shoulders. "Spanish, North African. Same difference."

Conversation was wedged in between chats with Mary's passing friends. Louise brought up the matter of the girls first. "I understand you've talked to both of them recently about summer activities."

Mary's eyes widened as she leaned toward Louise. "Do you mind? I was going to bring those things up today."

Louise patted Mary's hand and laughed. "I thought you might. And I consider you the best of influences. I even approve of Martha going to Africa, in case she's awarded an internship there. But don't tell Martha I mentioned this to you." Two could play this "don't-mention-it" game, she figured. "I just wanted you to know how I feel."

Then she updated Mary on the murder investigation. "Have you talked to Nora?"

Mary's expression was solemn. "A few days before Nora talked to you." She pointed a graceful finger at Louise. "After she told me her theory about mistaken identity, I redoubled my efforts."

Mary checked her peripheral vision to see that no visitors were approaching. She spoke quietly. "The general manager is definitely out of the picture—I hear—not even on the scene. And I couldn't find anyone who knew much about Marty, except he had a wife before this one who died in an accident."

"Oh?"

"But about Behrens: I called his former wife—she's still in the Washington area. My guise was the big donation he's giving the Children's Fund, as if I had to check, you know, to assure it was free money." She smiled engagingly. "Besides, I used to know the woman before she got divorced and plunged into the real world where she had to get a job."

Louise held a forkful of salmon in midair. "So, what did she say?"

In an even lower tone that forced Louise to lean forward to hear, Mary said, "The man has had problems"—and then pointed a delicate finger at her head.

She must mean mental problems, speculated Louise.

"I'm sure you've known a person with mood swings?

Well, Bruce has them; I should have guessed. Lately it's some question of not getting his lithium just right."

"But mood swings don't make you a murderer."

Mary sighed. "Oh, dear, I hope not. Half the people in the Capital have mood swings, from President Jack Fairchild on down"—she giggled—"or *up*, depending on your feelings toward the President. But there was something else—spousal abuse! He laid his hands on this woman."

Mary's eyes grew cold. "I can't think of anything more demeaning to a woman than to be manhandled by a man— even though violence is thought to be right there in their genes." She threw one hand out in a tragic gesture. "A lamentable programming in the brain." Her face reflected her feelings for all men thus afflicted. Then, a delicate, self-conscious smile broke over her elegant face. "I am so blessed. Even in lovemaking, my Richard is so gentle. I am forever grateful I found a man with not the tiniest streak of cruelty or roughness."

Louise had always thought of this woman's mate, Richard Mougey, as slightly effeminate, but perhaps it was just his artful Modigliani face and languid poet's body. She was reminded of Mencken's book on the dispersion of male and female traits among the two sexes, and thought Richard Mougey might have been allocated a few extra female genes, with the outcome just fine for his genteel wife.

"So Bruce was . . . a wife beater?"

"Well . . . wife *slapper*, shall we say? They went at each other, apparently. Then, one night, when she dropped him with a bookend or something, he tried to choke her, as if she were a chicken." Mary smiled and looked furtively around. "She kicked him in the balls. To say the least, this wife is vindictive: She hopes she did him permanent damage. Wonders if the breakup of the second marriage didn't have something to do with that." She giggled again. "You know, young wife to please, and the old peter not doing its job the way it should."

Then Mary shook her gentle head of curls, as if to reprimand herself for this descent into crudity. "At any rate, that was the end of that sorry marriage."

Louise was silent. Mary was seeing this cruelty through a distorted lens. "Mary," she said, smiling gently, "think about what you just described. It sounds like both parties were at fault, or even that she was tougher than he was."

Her neighbor was shocked into contemplative silence.

After a minute, she cocked her head at Louise and said, "You know, my dear, I think you're quite right—and I was jumping to unfair conclusions. And I'm glad, since poor Bruce is always being bad-mouthed except when he's giving money."

Louise sat back and put down her fork, a little discouraged. "I hate to say it but this idea about mistaken identity is going nowhere. It's so farfetched the police haven't even bothered to call me back to talk about it. Yet there are still these other people hanging out there, none of them with iron-clad alibis. The creepy janitor. Marty Corbin, who had a five-year affair with the dead woman. John Batchelder, my cohost, an occasional cocaine user at the very least, and goaded on all the time by his aggressive TV news anchor girlfriend."

Mary scoped the room. "News anchor—which one? I can see two, right now, in this room."

"Cheryl Wilding. Six o'clock news on Channel Eight."

"How serendipitous!" exclaimed Mary. "Cheryl's sitting right in my line of sight. Turn around discreetly and you can see her."

Louise dropped her napkin, making it an excuse to turn and survey the crowd. Cheryl was seated facing them, two tables away. "Want to talk to her?"

"I surely would. While we were brainstorming, Bill suggested this news anchor had a motive for doing away with Madeleine. The office receptionist told me about her, and then my family saw her in action scolding John in public."

"John Batchelder is a darling-looking man, to be sure, from what I've seen of him on your program. Quite pre-Raphaelite, like a friend of Dante Gabriel Rosetti's. But one wouldn't kill another human just to open up a job for one's boyfriend . . ." The expression in her eyes hardened. ". . . or would one?" Louise looked sheepish. "Sounds dumb, but I'd at least like to meet her. The funny thing is that I've gotten fonder of John lately in spite of everything. I hate to think he murdered Madeleine. He's become like my naughty kid brother who might have a chance of shaping up."

"Well, I know Cheryl," Mary assured her. "We've made such an impact with this African refugee relief that everyone wants a story again. I'll get her over here," she said, confidently. She sat a little higher in her chair and focused her attention on the table. When the woman looked her way, Mary waved, her hand high, like the pope giving a blessing.

"They're nearly finished," said Mary. "She'll probably stop on her way out. In the meantime, Louise, none of this sounds good." She ticked off the facts on her slim fingers with their pale-polished nails. "No direct witnesses to the crime. Circumstantial evidence pointing to you. Other people with much better motives but no handy way to prove it."

Louise said, "There's one more straw to grasp at. I've been wondering whether the police are doing all their homework. Such as checking out the hypodermic needle. Such as checking out people who may have been inquiring about poisons." She frowned. "Although Geraghty won't even give me details about what poison was used. But I'm sure it was something like Diazinon."

Mary reached over and grasped Louise's wrist. "My dear, you're so smart about those things. Do it. There's not much time left. Maybe Geraghty will help fill you in. Surely the police would check as to where someone got the murder weapon. Big hypodermics. Nurses? Yes, nurses. And horse stables. Who has horses?" She thought for a moment. "Why, Bruce, of course! That young wife of his had a few. I bet he still has them, or at least has the gear. After all," she said, ruefully, "it's probably easier to get rid of a second wife than a passel of Arabians." She raised a knowing eyebrow. "They're no longer a tax write-off, you know."

They looked up. Cheryl Wilding was approaching. She was about thirty, with a flat blond pageboy and china blue eyes, the perfect looks and clothes for a TV personality.

After being introduced, or perhaps before, the woman quickly made the connection. "Louise Eldridge, well, hello. I happen to know all—to know people who know you." She focused on Louise like a laser beam on a target.

Louise nodded. "Yes."

"Like John Batchelder." The woman smiled secretively. "He's m'honey," she said, in a Southern accent, making the words sound cozy and manipulative. Suddenly Louise realized this TV wordsmith had to be the source of John Batchelder's editorializing back when they taped the first shows and John kept adding things to his own script lines. There was an inherent innocence to John, a sort of klutziness to him despite his exotic good looks, that had made his little tricks puzzling. But it was easy to see this woman giving him guidance to perform small acts of skulduggery.

What other bad things might Miss Blue Eyes put him up to? Could Louise believe the absurd scenario of this woman coming over to Channel Five—in disguise, of course, mingling with the volunteers—and injecting Madeleine with that lethal dose of pesticide? Cheryl was probably paid a hundred thousand or more as an evening anchor in one of the most important news towns. She would be anxious to have her gorgeous live-in boyfriend earn more—at least enough to pay half the rent on their upscale condo. What would one death mean to this woman? And were those incredible eyes just a biological chance, or a genuine reflection of an empty soul?

Then the young woman came right out with it. "Pretty bitchy over there at WTBA, isn't it, Louise, with an unsolved murder? Well, John's out of it; he was out having a beer."

"Oh?" said Louise serenely. Both she and Blue Eyes knew the bartender couldn't pinpoint the time exactly.

"I hear you were there, though, when it happened." Cheryl continued to look at Louise with blatant curiosity, knowing no doubt she was a suspect. It was all there in that contemptuous look: "Here's Louise Eldridge, next to go, locked away for murder."

"Let me guess," Louise said puckishly. "You're thinking this whole thing could open up a couple of job opportunities for John."

Cheryl gave out with a phony little gasp that caused Louise and Mary to exchange involuntary glances. "Oh, my gosh!" said the news anchor, "I don't know exactly what you mean. My John is not just standing around, waiting to clamp onto opportunities provided by someone else's murder. Of course . . ."

"Of course someone has to do it," said Louise, blandly.

Cheryl smiled and shook her head as if in regret. "That's what I told my Johnny. Someone has to do it."

Now there was no doubt in Louise's mind—this woman was capable of at least contemplating murder, if not executing it. She acted like the worst of Generation X: materialistic, power-hungry, probably stashed by her mother in front of a TV set during those important childhood years when someone should have been teaching her values.

Those pretty, blank eyes told it all.

But what would the police do if Louise hurried over with this new angle? She knew exactly what would happen. They would laugh her right out of the station.

Once back in the office, she had only about fifteen minutes before a story conference with Rachel—fifteen minutes to tie up some important loose ends.

She picked up her office phone and dialed Mary Mougey. At lunch, she had forgotten a crucial question. Fortunately, Mary had returned to her office. "I forgot to ask you," said Louise. "Did you find out what cement plants Behrens Enterprises operate?"

Mary said, "Oh, I know just what you're looking for: Yes, Bruce owns several, among them the Maryland plant where that production manager fell into that large open hopper.

Ghastly. But he's not hands-on at his cement plants like he is at his chemical plants. Louise, please. By the end of our luncheon you'd convinced me I was wrong about Bruce's being a ruthless wife beater. I have stopped suspecting him of anything. According to his former wife, who should know, this kind of accident wasn't the only one at their cement plants. I got the impression they're kind of like steel plants, rough places where big chunks of rock get carried around on steep conveyor belts—that type of thing. They struggle with safety regulations to keep people alive, but occasionally they lose one. As they did in this case."

"The man who had the bad luck to be dropped into that hole and crushed into little pieces—he wasn't just anybody. He was a whistle-blower, willing to tell the truth about the way they dumped into their furnaces pesticides that didn't measure up to industry standards. Part of it went right out the chimneys in smoke!"

"I see what you mean," said Mary. "I missed the story. I'll see if I can pick up anything else."

Louise thanked her and promised to keep in touch.

Now for the next hanging question. She went down the hall to the personnel office, where she had a clerk friend whom she would dun for a favor. She was a motherly older woman who had been amused at Louise's "gee whiz" attitude when she came in to fill out forms relating to her new job, her new office, her new paycheck.

Louise collected the clerk in a corner of the office, and kept her voice at a near-whisper. "I . . . wanted a little favor. Is there any chance of finding out—just the basics—about Marty Corbin's first wife?"

A look of complete understanding passed over the woman's plain face.

"Just a minute." The woman hesitated and looked around at her supervisor's office. "This is not really a secret, but on the other hand . . . why don't you go to your office and I'll phone you."

"Thanks. I guess you realize I'm a little desperate."

The woman smiled sympathetically. "That's what I hear."

She strode down the hall and went into her office and closed the door. It seemed bare and cold in its undecorated state. But wasn't it a waste of time to decorate unless she knew what was going to happen to her life?

The phone rang and it was the clerk. "There's not much here, Louise. Marty Corbin's first wife was named Sally. There's a note that she died in 1985—June. Then, there's another notation that he married Steffi in 1987."

"I can't tell you how I appreciate this."

She knew the story conference with Rachel would take the rest of the afternoon so she phoned Bill for help.

He told her that yes, he did have time to go to the Library of Congress. There they had microfiche of the *Washington Post* going back for years. She gave him the month and year of Sally Corbin's death. He promised to get the job done.

Rachel flipped through the colorful brochure, and her thin, droll face creased with a smile. "Some people get their jollies reading dirty literature; others get theirs reading rose catalogues."

Louise, sleepy after her big lunch, slumped lazily in her flowery print rayon dress and perused a catalogue just as flowery. "Look at this one," she exclaimed, pointing out an old-fashioned white climbing rose. "I have to have one for my garden."

"That's just what I mean," said Rachel, tracing little circles in the air with her number two editing pencil. "Passion: That has to be the central theme of our rose program. Americans are passionate about roses."

"But they're so much trouble. We have to tell them how to raise them without poisoning the earth. I never can forget the rosebushes in the yard next door when I was little. They had big, gorgeous flowers, but the neighbors completely covered them with gross green rose dust, so you could barely tell what color they were."

The writer looked over her big glasses at Louise. "Oh, so

that's how you got this way, traumatized by rose dust at an early age."

Louise smiled at Rachel. They both felt fatalistic. If Louise were arrested for murder, any show they taped on roses with her as hostess might never be shown.

Just then Bruce Behrens opened the conference room door halfway. Smoothly, she said to him, "Oh, I would have thought you would have knocked on a closed door." She laughed frostily. "It's an old custom."

"Sorry, Louise. Sorry—Rachel, is it? Two beautiful ladies, indeed." Now he was all the way in the room, standing there as if they were about to entertain him. "What're you working on now?"

Louise felt her face turn red. She almost bit her tongue, to keep from saying something she would regret. This man had seemingly climbed in bed with Marty, but she'd be damned if he was going to climb in bed with her.

Rachel, crisp in her pale beige linen dress, answered neutrally, her eyes cast down. "Today is roses day: how to grow them with natural fertilizers including, you won't believe it, epsom salts! Plus all sorts of other organic sleight-of-hand that eliminate the need for any chemicals at all." Then she looked up and smiled sweetly at Bruce Behrens.

"I can hardly believe it," said Behrens. "Then I suppose there's no room for mention of that valuable product, rose dust?"

Louise chimed in. "I don't think so, Bruce. You know, since I've been researching this whole subject of pesticides, have I told you just how many people I meet and talk to who have built up sensitivities to chemicals?"

She got up and walked over to Behrens, her wide flowery skirt swaying ominously. She stood, hands loosely hung on her hips, and looked up at him. "The latest person I heard about, just last week, is a man who worked on a yard chemical spraying truck for years. He's more than just chemical-sensitive: He's dying of lung disease. Contrary to what your industry says, the stuff seeps right through heavy shoes into people's systems."

Bruce put up his hands, as if to ward her off. "That man in Kensington? Don't rush into something you don't know about. They haven't *proved* any connection."

"Not yet," said Rachel, "but they're getting close."

His mouth turned down. He said, "You women are on a tear. I think I'll leave you on your own." Then he backed out of the door and closed it.

Louise looked at the writer with admiring eyes. The scriptwriter was about five-foot-two, maybe one hundred pounds or less. "Rachel, you're a tiger."

"So are you, Louise. But maybe we should have kept our claws in. As I see it, you have two problems: staying out of jail, and getting funding to keep your show going. Staying out of jail is pretty much your own problem. But between the two of us, we kissed good-bye to Behrens underwriting."

Louise slumped in her chair and looked at the writer. "Maybe I shouldn't have been so tough. After all, funding is funding. So why do I feel as if I'm out from under an enormous burden?"

Rachel looked at her evenly. "You're like the poor, starving man who tells the rich, corrupt man to shove it—he doesn't want his handout." She smiled faintly. "That still leaves him starving, of course."

Roses, and Other
Passions of the Heart

What would we do without the rose? So much trouble, but so worthwhile. Every garden should have a few. Here is a flower that arouses passion, exciting our senses like no other. It is part of history. Sixty-million-year-old fossil remnants of roses are displayed in museums. Early Christians shunned the flower, linking it with the excesses of pagan Rome.

By the Middle Ages they had climbed onto the rose bandwagon, along with kings and dukes, and adopted it as a symbol of the purity of the Virgin. Poets gush over roses. One, Gertrude Stein, was struck practically dumb by the flower, and could only write, "Rose is a rose is a rose is a rose."

All we have to do is look at the flower to see that here is something special. It is horticulturally complete, even to the beguiling, paper-thin protective leaves that curl over the lush buds. Maybe this is why some people put roses by themselves in rose gardens. This seems a mistake, since they make every other nearby flower look good. They bring out the luminosity of the iris, the intricacy of the delphinium, the frilliness of the baby's breath, and the sentinel-like calm of the foxglove.

The practical gardener who looks for the most mileage from plants can choose repeat bloomers, although the ones that bloom only once should not be excluded from the garden any more than a lilac. Another asset of the rose is its handsome foliage, which we will enjoy all summer long and will cause us to congratulate ourself on our wise choice.

Fortunately for rose lovers who hate chemicals, there are more and more disease-resistant varieties. If we happen to choose wrongly and bring home a specimen that attracts bugs and disease, we know what to do: If a rose offendeth you with its propensity to disease, rip it out.

Tough, thorny roses bloom earliest, around May. One that will stop traffic if you plant it at the front of your house is the Austrian Copper Rose. Then in June, roses become the stars of the border, bursting forth along with dozens of our favorite perennials.

Those who want carefree roses turn to the fragrant old-fashioned varieties, which do wonderful things like climb trees and walls. Among the best are the white damask "Madame Hardy" and the white rugosa "Blanc Double de Coubert"; the purple "Reine des Violettes," which will happily clamber up a tree for you, to eight or ten feet; the very round pink "Reine Victoria," a Bourbon rose; and "Jacques Cartier," with three-inch fluffy pink flowers.

Also known for its robust health is "Koenigin von Danemarck," a deep pink, first introduced in 1826. You can brew up its rosehips into tea. "Souvenir de la Malmaison" is a Bourbon rose steeped with history that appears in a famous old French painting; it has four-inch flesh pink blossoms.

Unlike the days when tea roses had to be pampered like a rich man's mistress, today there are disease-resistant varieties. Among them are "Double Delight," a red and white bicolor; coral-red "Fragrant Cloud," medium-pink "Queen Elizabeth," white "Pascali," red "Precious Platinum," pale orange "Folklore," and pale apricot "Maid of Honor."

One could talk on at length about David Austin roses, a recent breakthrough. They combine the qualities of old shrub roses, and floribunda roses. We'll mention just one, the enticing "Heritage." It is a perfect example of the cupped Bourbon rose, richly pink in the center and shading to shell pink. Like many new varieties, it has something that was lost in the roses of recent years. It smells like a rose.

Rosarians clutch to their hearts their own little secrets about growing the flower. One basic principle is to distribute a cup of superphosphate in the rich, compost-laden soil in the planting hole, since phosphate aids bloom and doesn't travel well downward through the soil. Treat roses well during the season, with abundant water and fertilizer. Then, don't forget how much you want them to survive, and tuck them carefully in for the winter. Make them little overcoats by building up a foot of soil or heavy mulch around them after the first frost.

31

He had on opaque sunglasses so that his eyes could not be seen. His hair was slicked down straight to remove the curl, and he wore a good sports jacket with a dress shirt open at the throat. She wore sunglasses and a slouch hat with her hair tucked inside, and a nondescript cotton dress that she had filched from the Goodwill bag.

The Eldridges were in disguise.

"This time we'll do it my way."

"Okay. What's your way? Wait—don't tell me. It will have some cloak-and-dagger in it."

"Maybe cloak, no dagger. I'm not anxious to break the law in the name of this investigation, which probably will be fruitless, anyway. You wait here and watch. Keep your hat and sunglasses on in case John leaves the building. I'll try to get inside."

She giggled. "You sound like a Watergate burglar." She waved a hand in the direction of the Potomac River. "And look, there it is." Within a block of John Batchelder and Cheryl Wilding's shared apartment was the famous Watergate, with its double eyebrow construction.

Bill braced his hands against the open window of the car. He looked the way he wanted to look: quasi-official.

"This is a high-rent district your friends live in," he noted.

"I bet she pays most of the rent," said Louise. "She has to, considering the way Channel Five pays its staff."

Bill waggled an index finger. "And that all goes to motive."

He gave her an exaggerated wink and walked toward the large apartment building.

In less than twenty minutes he had returned.

"So?"

"Well, it paid to dress up, and my State Department Security Committee card didn't hurt any, either." He got in the passenger side of the car, looked over at her and smiled.

"You pulled rank."

"Darn right. So, what Sam Rosen said was true."

Before they had started out on this Saturday morning surveillance, their next-door neighbor had come over for coffee. Louise had idly asked him if he knew Cheryl Wilding.

"Do I know her—hell, I went to high school with her!"

Suddenly, the blond news anchor aged in Louise's mind into a—what? Forty-year-old? Not a Generation Xer after all, but a late-end baby boomer.

Sam could see her mind working on this, and saved her the trouble. "We're both thirty-nine. Graduated in 1974 from BCC—Bethesda–Chevy Chase High School."

And then he had proceeded to tell about Cheryl Wilding, who grew up in one of the poorer houses that stuck out like a sore thumb in affluent Bethesda, and scrabbled her way to success in the television industry. "She worked harder than anyone. The family had no money; the father was gone, somehow. I always thought he just deserted them. Wouldn't date much—too busy studying or jogging when she wasn't building up a tough, beautiful body. Or taking the lead in a school play. She wasn't brilliant, but she got herself a scholarship to Indiana University Journalism School. Then those looks"—he rolled his eyes as if no one could fault them— "plus some genuine writing skill, got her started off in a small market. She graduated to a midsized market, Buffalo, freezing her ass off every winter, as she complained to everybody. About seven years ago she got her toehold in Washington."

He'd described her reputation since coming to Washington: "It's 'Don't tread on me.' She's still competitive as hell, and from what I hear she doesn't have a lot of friends in the industry—especially among the guys and gals at Channel Eight." He smiled sympathetically and spread his hands out. "She didn't have time to learn how to be nice."

"But is she ruthless?" Louise had asked. "Could she be involved in Madeleine Doering's murder?"

Sam Rosen's gaze wandered out into the woods. Louise suddenly realized that he might never have recovered from the crush he'd had on Cheryl Wilding when they were in high school. "I can see her fighting for anything she wants, let's put it that way. They say she's always promoting that kissy-faced boyfriend of hers, but you know him—John Batchelder's your cohost. Killing? Cheryl? Or even helping someone else do something like that? Hell, that's carrying it pretty far." His brows knit below his balding head. "Please don't ask me to make a judgment. It's somehow . . . too close to me."

And now, in addition to Sam's poignant memories of Cheryl, Bill had breached the ramparts of John's and Cheryl's building.

Bill gave her his report. "By a fluke, the regular doorman was there. Regular doormen are of course much more knowledgeable than weekend doormen. Putting it simply, Cheryl and John lead the high life—go out a lot to clubs, exercise a lot, have one other couple over regularly as company, but no other friends to speak of." He gave her a significant look. "And no family visits here. Get the import of that?"

"I guess so. They don't care a hoot about their families." She looked at Bill, whose slicked-down hair was beginning to assert its natural waviness. "They're *ashamed* of their families?"

As if he were Holmes and she were Watson, he gave her an arch, faintly disapproving look. Then he broke into a grin and said, "Maybe." Then he continued: "Loud and contentious noises often come out of their apartment—mostly from the lady. She also quibbles with management a lot over small things that go wrong in their twelfth-floor living quarters."

"Wants the most for her money," said Louise. "Well, I can relate to that. Sometimes I wish we had a building manager to complain to about things around the house."

She guided the car from downtown Washington to Chevy Chase. Bill paid no attention, lost in thought.

"So, what are you thinking?" she said, finally.

"I wonder how she—or they—could have done it. Those are two exotic TV creatures there—like a couple of tropical birds. People note their comings and goings. Pretty hard to think of either one of them slipping into that women's room without someone noticing. Our killer had to have had a high degree of anonymity to leave the police high and dry like this."

"Yes, but think disguise, Bill: The very fact that she had lots of theater experience tells me that they could have worked up a good disguise."

He looked at her soberly. "Well, keep her on your list. But after what I found out yesterday, I think I'd reconsider your producer.

"Where do you think we're going?"

Suddenly he realized they were heading north to Marty Corbin's residence. He nodded in approval. "Good idea."

He had spent Friday afternoon in the Library of Congress, quickly finding in *Washington Post* microfiches several stories about Marty's first wife, Sally. He printed them out for Louise.

The woman had fallen down the stairs in their home in Chevy Chase, the same shopworn home Marty lived in now with Steffi.

The clippings revealed that there had been a brief period when Marty was under suspicion, since he and Sally had been separated and were in the midst of a nasty divorce. He no longer lived the house, but was visiting so he and Sally could talk terms. He was watching television in the living room while she went upstairs. When she started to come down, she allegedly tripped on some loosely tacked carpeting, fell and broke her neck.

A later story said the death was ruled accidental.

The picture of Marty published by the *Post* showed a strikingly handsome man.

How interesting, she reflected: A shove down the stairs was just as good as a shove into a stone crusher—both methods of murder left absolutely no clues.

Detective Geraghty didn't call her back until Monday evening, and when he did, he sounded a little desperate.

In a quiet, reasonable voice, she catalogued for him the information she and Bill had picked up on the weekend.

"Yes, of course they checked on that," he said, when she mentioned the origination of the syringe that held the pesticide. "It's standard. It's used with large animals, vets and such, hospitals, research laboratories. It could have come from anywhere."

"Um, Bruce Behrens, I discovered, happens to have horses," said Louise, in a halting voice. "I . . . I suppose you know that." Even though Mary Mougey discounted it, she also mentioned the death at the cement plant.

There was silence on the end of the line. Louise could picture Geraghty in his too-small office in the Fairfax police substation on Route One, sorry and disgusted with her for grasping at straws.

But when she mentioned Cheryl Wilding, Geraghty said, "Well, that's new. Tell me what you know about her, and her relationship with Batchelder."

So she did. She was sure he would cross-reference this with the list of volunteers who were at the studio the night Madeleine died.

She also told him how she had called every library in the Greater Washington area in a fruitless pursuit of anyone who might have inquired about poisons.

She nearly told him about Marty Corbin. Her increasing store of withheld information gnawed at her more each day.

She blurted, "And, there's another little tidbit of information . . ."

"Yes?"

She found she couldn't utter the words, that Marty had been conducting a long affair with Madeleine, that Marty's first wife met her demise in a violent fall.

And that he had a cache of old poisons carefully tucked in his messy garage, which was what she and Bill had found out in their weekend snooping.

She was silent for so long that Geraghty jumped into the breach. "Are you trying to tell me something about your producer—that he had an affair with the deceased? That his first wife died in a fall down the stairs while he was sitting around in an armchair having a drink?"

"Yes," she said quietly, "but I didn't want to be disloyal. And you already found out about those things. . . ."

"We did, and we take them seriously. Now, what else is on your mind?"

Then she went into her theory about mistaken identity. That appeared to be too much for the detective, for she could hear him breathing heavily in exasperation.

"Detective Johnson and I have listened to you. He cannot believe any of your theories so far, especially that this Doering murder was mistaken identity. There's about three inches difference in your height, and maybe five inches difference in your hair length. Mind you, I'll check immediately on this Cheryl Wilding person; anything is possible in this case. But I'd put that mistaken-identity speculation aside, if I were you.

"Now, Louise"—his voice was softer now—"you know I like you. I'm trying to be kind, and not to get upset with you. I can't believe you did this, and I don't know who did inject a banned pesticide into Ms. Madeleine Doering. Nevertheless . . ."

"Banned pesticide?"

"Well, if you must know, it was malathion mixed with methyl parathion. Parathion's been banned in the United

States for about twenty years, but people still stash some in their garages."

A flush of understanding came over her: "Parathion" was clearly marked with skull-and-crossbones on one of the ancient bottles she unwrapped when she and Bill were in Marty's garage.

Geraghty had gone on to his next indicting statement: "*You* had a bottle of it among those old remedies you dragged to the studio the day of the murder, which doesn't help your case much. So right now you're in trouble, Louise. I wish you wouldn't quote me, but as a kind of friend, I'm telling you. Have in mind a good attorney, in case you're charged."

Quickly, she sorted out the Marty situation. Why would he have kept the poisons once he used them on Madeleine? But then, why would the police think she would do the same nutty thing?

Her shoulders drooped, too tired to stay erect. She didn't answer the detective.

"What I'm saying is, there are few viable suspects. And you know what's up against you, having been seen right there with the victim. . . ."

She sank into a silence again. Geraghty waited a second for her to say something, and when she didn't, he told her he would call her if he heard anything.

She put the phone on its stand. "Bill?" she cried out. "Where are you?"

There was no answer in the empty house.

She finally found him, out in the woods, splitting wood with his ax. She felt immediately more composed being in the out-of-doors. "Hi." She went to him and he enclosed her in his free arm.

"More bad news?"

"Geraghty. He thinks it's time to hunt up a lawyer."

"Then we'd better do it, hadn't we?"

She pulled away from her husband's embrace and stood, hands folded over her chest. "No. Think of what it will do to our budget."

Her woodsman-like husband was posed artlessly with the ax drawn down alongside him, like a blond Abe Lincoln. "A wife who's headed for jail and is too cheap to hire a lawyer: What do you want to do, Louise—defend yourself?"

She thought about it for a moment. "Maybe."

Bill looked at her in exasperation. "Look, in a few minutes I'm headed to my physical therapy class at the gym. Want to come? Either come with me, or I'll stay home. I don't want you or Janie home alone any more."

The rank, smelly gym on a warm May night in northern Virginia didn't sound appealing.

"I have an anarchistic idea," she said, some of her good humor returning. "Why don't you kick over the leg therapy, and we just go to a movie? Janie can go across the street and do homework with Chris and Melanie."

Bill slung his ax over his shoulder, grabbed her arm and led her to the house. "It's a deal; we'll get our minds off everything."

"Especially hiring lawyers. We can think about that tomorrow."

32

With travel time to the Connecticut Avenue theater in the District of Columbia, they were gone more than three hours. Louise felt guilty; she had made Janie promise not to return to the house until they came back from the movie.

Bill walked across the cul-de-sac to get Janie at the Radebaughs' house, while Louise walked up the front path, aware once more that they needed to get more lighting out here. The front porch light beckoned, but provided barely enough illumination for the dogwood-bedecked woods path.

She was groping in her purse for her key when she heard the noise. A dull thud. She froze for a moment, then instinctively turned and ran back along the woods path toward the street. There, she saw Janie and Bill crossing the cul-de-sac and practically fell into her husband's arms.

"Bill," she whispered. "Someone's in the house!"

Then Missy, the dog next door, was let out and began to bark. Missy's owner, Sam, also threw on his second team of floodlights, suddenly making the nearby woods into a DeMille production set. Bill looked at her. "I think whoever it is has probably gone, with all that light. Maybe I'd better call police."

"Dad," moaned Janie, "I'm so tired. I have a French test tomorrow. Can't we just go in and confront the crooks, and make them drop the bags of money they're taking?"

"Oh, very funny, Janie," said Louise. "Let's go out to the patio; I think I heard someone there. They're undoubtedly gone, so it must be safe."

As they carefully made their way around the back of the house Bill pulled his cellular phone out of his sports jacket, dialed 911, and gave their address to the police dispatcher. They walked up onto the flagstone patio. The tall glass sliding door was wide open.

She pulled on his arm. "Wait, Bill. Maybe we had better not go in until the police come. They could still be in there." Then she looked down. Her husband was holding a pistol. "My *God*, you're armed."

He gave her a painful look. "Did you think I was just talking when I said I thought you were in danger?" He carefully edged himself into the house, as she and Janie stood aside at Bill's direction. He looked like a policeman himself, as he dodged into the house, then flipped every light switch he passed. After a couple of minutes, he returned to the patio and said quietly, "All clear. But don't touch anything."

The two officers who arrived acted as if they had special instructions. They looked at Louise intently. No anonymity here. Blushing, she realized the entire Fairfax police substation knew of her and her possible involvement in Madeleine's murder.

How could they fit a break-in at her house into that equation?

"Well, folks," said one of the officers after a quick look around, "nothing taken? Nothing disturbed? Electronic stuff is most popular. Check your TV, your stereo, CD-ROM, stuff like that."

Bill smiled. "No one would steal ours," he said, looking at the ancient TV and sound equipment he could see standing untouched in the recreation room. "It's bottom-of-the-line."

Louise had checked on the most important things first: her reference books and computer in the hut, which she used as her office. At Bill's suggestion, she went to the bedroom and found her jewelry undisturbed in her bureau. Then each of them went to their respective desks.

"Papers," said Louise grimly, pointing out the Windsor

desk in the living room. "Whoever it was riffled through the those papers on my desk."

An officer stalked slowly on big-booted legs over to the white-knobbed old pine desk. Two piles sat on its writing surface, with the top papers out of line. He looked at Louise doubtfully. "You mean, you keep them neater than this?"

"Yes. I keep them in perfect piles." Janie had to get it from somewhere.

The officer grinned, or was it a grimace? He took note of it on his little pad. "What else?"

Louise hurried around, as hyper as if she had consumed half a dozen coffees. She realized she had a heavy day of work tomorrow at the TV studio and little promise of sleeping well tonight.

Then she noticed the bouquet of tulips sitting on a side table. "The person rearranged the bouquet," she said in a tight voice. As soon as she uttered the words, she knew they wouldn't believe her.

Sure enough, the officer looked skeptical. "How would you know that?"

"Because I just arranged it today, and all the pinks were on the right, and all the whites were on the left, and the branch of dogwood to the right middle back. A special effect I was trying."

The officer sighed and wrote it down on his pad. He looked at the three of them. "Why don't you check every little thing out and call us tomorrow?"

"You're not taking prints, then," said Bill.

"Well, sir, we don't take prints on break-ins unless something is taken." The officer smiled. "Sometimes we don't even record them as break-ins."

Bill's voice was testy. "The police well know our opinion that Mrs. Eldridge here, being involved in a murder, and not having murdered anyone, might in fact be in jeopardy herself. I was scheduled to be gone tonight; it was just luck that my wife wasn't here alone."

The policeman looked at Bill with a wary expression. "Sir,

if it was someone intent on hurting Mrs. Eldridge, I'm pretty sure they would have worn gloves."

Louise looked at Bill, her eyes wide with fear. Was Madeleine's murder coming right home to them?

33

It was a lazy spring morning, the kind that invited children to skip school and adults to kick over work and go to a ball game instead. Only a whisper of Washington's unlivable heat and humidity was in the air, waiting for a few weeks to envelop humanity in the Metro Washington area and bring it to its knees.

Sylvan Valley seemed quiet and pastoral, a charming backwater handy to the Capital City, safe enough so many people didn't even double-lock their doors.

But Louise and Bill had learned differently.

So this morning they ignored the beauty of the day and the gardens and woods surrounding them. They were all business as they sat straight-backed in garden chairs on the patio and drank their coffee and made notes on a pad of paper.

They were discussing ways to make their house safe.

"How about floodlights all over the front yard," Bill suggested.

"Sure," said Louise dryly. "And then let's put them out back, too, all through the woods. It will make our yard look just like a used car lot."

Bill's expression rebuked her. "I'm only concerned for your safety, Louise. So what do you suggest?"

She leaned over toward him, eyes shining. "Let's be adventuresome! Let's have fun while we're getting safer. How about a dog?" She sensed this was a once-in-a-lifetime opportunity. "Or better still, how about two dogs?" She leaned back in the chair and gazed up at the overhead canopy of trees. "You know my life's ambitions: It's never to move again. It's to quit worrying about the state of the house as we foreign service wives are wont to do. It's to have several dogs and one or two cats. They would frolic around the house, dirtying the floors with their muddy paws." She smiled dreamily. "No one would mind. I'd mop up once in a while . . ."

Bill rolled his eyes. He didn't really like pets, especially dogs. "You know me, Louise. Owning a dog is like getting a life sentence of poop removal. But okay, I'll go along. *One* dog. And who's going to stay home and toilet-train the little fellow?"

She sat back and mused. "Maybe we had better get a used one that's already trained."

After awhile, Bill picked up the list with safety ideas and got up to go to the office. She said the careful good-bye that was her practice each time he left for work ever since that day in London when he narrowly escaped being blown up by an IRA bomb. It was like a good-luck charm to keep him safe. First, she took him in her arms and tenderly hugged him, then she gave him a lingering kiss.

His arms around hers were tight today. "I hope your lucky good-bye hugs work both ways," he said, looking fondly down at her. "Be careful today at work. I'll see you about six."

She tidied up the coffee things, then got in the car and backed out of the driveway, pausing at the end to look at the garden glittering with May Wonder tulips.

Last night, the tulips were pink. This morning, they had turned yellow and were almost flat out, like four-inch-wide golden saucers. She put her hand on her chin and admired the garden for a moment, trying not to indulge in the sin of pride. Then she quickly maneuvered the car into the cul-de-sac, and drove out of the quiet neighborhood.

Everyone was on edge when she arrived at the station. John Batchelder, not his usual self, hovered around her with a nervous expression on his face, absently chewing on his fingernails. It was as if he were reverting to some childhood behavior, for here was a man proud of his comely hands.

He cornered Louise in Marty's office before the story conference. "Look, we have to talk. Something's seriously wrong. When can we get together?" His pupils were wide with excitement.

She agreed to meet him later for a bite of lunch at a restaurant down the street. The handsome but rather vulnerable John seemed anxious to spill his guts to her about something.

Could her cohost, by any wild chance, suspect Cheryl in Madeleine's murder? She felt fairly sure John couldn't have done the deed himself. But after all, he lived with Cheryl, and could hardly avoid knowing if she were implicated.

Or did he know or suspect something about Marty?

The producer was crabby and distracted. While the rest of them worked on the script, he was taking phone calls and reading résumés, trying to find a cohost to replace Madeleine Doering.

She didn't want to be paranoid, but Marty seemed to be looking at her with reserve if not dislike. An alarming thought came to her. Maybe he saw her and Bill cruising his neighborhood again on Sunday night. She and her husband had the treat of skulking down a leafy side street from Marty's house and parking, then doing their search of his dirty garage.

And finding those pesticides. She hadn't told police of that discovery, since it involved trespassing. She narrowed her eyes and looked at the producer, seeing if she could sense, through sheer intuition, the truth about this man. A man who was at the same time so talented and so flawed.

Today she sensed a sharp gulf between them, a sort of "it's you or me, babe." And maybe that's the way it would turn out in the end.

Later, Bruce Behrens showed up, but by that time she and

Rachel and John had done their work on the latest script, and she was getting ready to leave for lunch with John.

She was having misgivings about her last unpleasant encounter with Behrens. Though she had only been fighting to maintain the character of her program, she may have gone too far and lost the station a sponsor. And she feared she was straining Marty's patience beyond endurance so that he looked at her as a knee-jerk environmentalist, not much different than the lady from the Green Club.

"Louise." Bruce came upon her unexpectedly, while she was down the hall getting a drink from the fountain. Nearby was Henry Aikens, surly, watching.

"Hi, Bruce."

"Louise, glad to see you. I wanted you to know a couple of facts about that lawn-care truck driver with the suit. The guy may have fatal lung disease, but you may not know that he's a heavy smoker and had high radon readings in his basement for years until he mitigated it. And he still smokes, even after his diagnosis."

Louise put up a pacifying hand. "Let's drop it for today, all right? So . . . what brings you here today? More business?"

"Yeah," he said vaguely. For some unknown reason, he was avoiding eye contact with her. "Just about through with my business here at the station."

Her heart sank. Had she blown it with this monied businessman?

"By the way, Louise, I was in your neighborhood. Those are the most spectacular pink tulips I've ever seen!"

"Oh. When were you there? Because, well—when were you there?"

"This morning, dropping something off in Mary Mougey's mailbox. I have a lot of business with her, too." He said this meaningfully. The man might as well be wearing a neon sign that flashed on and off and read, "I am a significant donor to worthy causes."

The import of it struck her. "This morning, hmm? And the tulips: You like them . . ."

"Yeah, great big blobby pink tulips. My kind of flower. I always wished my mother would grow a garden like that." She pictured him, a deprived little boy with barren dirt patches where a garden might have grown. But Behrens seemed more certain now of his ground now, looking her straight in the eye.

Her heart raced. This man could *not* have seen pink tulips this morning, since these clever flowers had completely changed color during the night to bright gold. The man was lying! Could he be their intruder, someone who skulked around last night, and saw clearly by streetlight the bold pink tulips? She had to get away and tell police. One thing she knew was that flowers, unlike people, didn't lie, and this tulip's strange botanical habits had tripped up a liar.

She straightened, and tried to cover her amazement with a smooth face. "Excuse me, Bruce. I'm needed in a story conference."

Instead of going into Marty's conference room area, she ducked into her own office and shut the door. With trembling fingers she punched in the number of Detective Johnson at the Fairfax Jail. For a change found him in his office. "Quiet day, Detective Johnson?" she asked.

"Are you teasing me, Mrs. Eldridge?"

"Maybe," she said in a low voice. "I'm just guessing you're waiting for lab results, and that you expect to clean up your case soon."

There was a silence. Then he said, "That may or may not eventuate, Mrs. Eldridge."

"And when you do, I might well be charged, according to what Detective Geraghty told me the other night."

"Maybe Detective Geraghty told you too much. Perhaps you shouldn't anticipate."

"He said find a lawyer."

"That's an option for anyone being questioned by police. So what can I do for you today?"

"Well, this may sound funny if I told you over the phone. But it's important. Maybe I'd better dash over to see you. Do you have a minute?"

"Yes, ma'am. When can you get here?"

34

"Did you come to tell me about the break-in at your house last night?" Detective Johnson's face was amiable as ever, with no sign of his personal feelings.

"You've heard about it," said Louise. "So soon: I'm impressed."

The detective looked down at the worn tan desk. "We're quite alert on this case, Mrs. Eldridge. Everything about it. I got a complete fill-in on the alleged illegal entry of your house."

"Alleged. You mean, you have doubts that anyone broke in?"

His brown eyes looked across at her with perfect neutrality. "The officers who came to your house were suspicious you or your husband or your daughter may have left that patio door open."

"But there were definite signs someone was there."

"The papers out of line on the desk?"

"So?"

"The wind, maybe."

"And the flowers, rearranged in the vase?"

"Gravity. They're tulips with awfully long stems; maybe they just fell that way."

She laughed bitterly. "Well, then I can see you'll never credit what I'm going to tell you next."

"Go ahead, Mrs. Eldridge," said Detective Thompson, in a respectful voice.

She told him about the May Wonder tulips in the front garden that changed from pink to gold overnight. She told him about Bruce Behrens insisting he had seen pink tulips this morning, when they already had turned to gold.

"So Bruce *had* to have been at our house *last night.* That meant he may have been trying to finish the job he bungled if and when he accidentally killed Madeleine!"

There was a long pause, as the detective took a couple of brief notes, then tapped his pencil against his note pad and stared beyond her out a barred office window. Every window in the Fairfax County Jail complex seemed to be barred. Magistrates went to and fro in the outer office. She saw the psychologist dodge by, giving her a wall-eyed look.

Finally, Johnson answered her. It was like a judge giving a verdict. "You've built a little house of cards, Mrs. Eldridge. But one of the cards underneath is missing, so it will never stand. Your latest premise is that Mr. Behrens killed Madeleine Doering, thinking it was you. Now, none of us here, not even your friend, Detective Geraghty, believe that theory holds any water, since he has a solid alibi, backed up by several who work at his place. So how can I take seriously this stuff about tulips changing color? It—it doesn't relate to anything, I'm afraid."

She looked down at her hands, folded neatly in her lap. She felt very alone in the world. "I was afraid of this," she said. "I can see that the more implicated one becomes in a crime, the less credibility one has on any and all issues."

"I'm sorry you feel that way, Mrs. Eldridge. We have tried, and we continue, to carefully consider every piece of evidence and every incident and theory, including the break-in and you and your husband's theory about mistaken identity."

"And they don't hold water. And how about that man I saw near the lady's room who looked like Henry Aiken, that janitor?"

"That's been followed up. It was not Mr. Aiken. We have finally established his whereabouts at the time of the murder: He was seen by his supervisor cleaning in the studio, the one that Jack Lederle and his crew use for their news program. Now, that figure near the women's rest room—that could have been anyone. And we're checking on Cheryl Wilding, but nothing at all there as yet."

She got up from her chair. "Thanks for talking to me, anyway. I'm going to call my husband from here. Maybe he'll help me."

"Wait," said Detective Johnson. "One more thing: Would you want me to call the Fairfax substation and ask them to drive by your house once in a while?"

"Thanks. I'll call Detective Geraghty myself, if you don't mind." She looked at him, sorrow in her eyes.

When she got home, she rang up the substation, but Geraghty wasn't there. Detective Morton was on duty, and she was connected to him. Morton again.

"Mrs. Eldridge. What can I do for you now?"

She told him about the tulips and Bruce Behrens, and the fact that the man had to have lied to her. The policeman was silent so long that she thought the line had been disconnected. "And so," she said limply, "Detective Thompson, with whom I just talked over at the Fairfax County Jail, said you should send people out once in a while to patrol the house."

"Wait a minute. I'm still back at the tulips that change colors. Mrs. Eldridge, you've had a lot of dealings with us lately."

"Yes. And you may have more. You may in fact be over here, to arrest me for murder tomorrow. But until that time, Detective Morton, hadn't you better take the chance that I'm right, and you people are wrong? And can I ask, while we're at it, why you are so skeptical of me all the time? Is there something personal that you never believe me?"

He thought that over for a moment. "Well, it's that gardening business. It's always been hard for me to take that stuff seriously—mulching and leaf collecting, bouquets that got tampered with. And now you've got tulips that change color and prove people did the murder. And let me assure you, Mrs. Eldridge, I'm not the only one that finds it hard to believe all your stories."

She slammed down the phone, held her head in her hands and wept.

Could she be wrong? What time did those tulips change color? Could the metamorphosis have taken place within a few hours? Bruce could have swung by the cul-de-sac very early, six, for instance, and still seen *pink* tulips. She didn't pull out of the driveway until after nine. Plenty of time for this horticultural miracle to have taken place!

Why hadn't she thought this out before?

She felt defeated. Another of her theories shot down, and now she looked even more foolish and desperate in the eyes of the police.

35

Bill took the cellular phone in the recreation room and discreetly closed the door until it was almost shut. He hunched down on the couch and tapped in a number. Since it was only 8 A.M., Tom Paschen could either be at home or already at work in the White House. From the man's past work habits, Bill guessed he was at work. He got through, and the old friends exchanged greetings.

Bill got right to the point. "It's Louise, Tom. You may not know about this."

"I may know more than you think. The President was so embarrassed by the Hoffman affair that he's quite sensitive to the woman who caught him, without aid of police. He follows her career."

"So you know about her show?"

"Yeah, and the pickets. Pretty funny, actually: a knee-jerk environmentalist being called a Nazi. Never stuck, I notice. Show's doing well, I hear."

The President's chief of staff would be impatient for Bill to finish the story. "Tom, there was a murder at Channel Five, the public television station. Madeleine Doering was killed. Louise is suspected. Now, what do you think of that?"

Tom Paschen gave out a big belly laugh, uncharacteristic of the slim, muscular man. Bill could picture him, looking out of some fancy window in a fancy office down the hall from the Oval Office, rocking back and forth on his heels and chortling, not taking it seriously. "Sorry. I'm having a hard time believing that. Why would they think she'd do a thing like that?"

"Physical evidence. Louise's flesh under the woman's fingernails, her hair twined on Louise's jacket, through a totally accidental encounter just before someone offed her. A memo the victim wrote. The dead woman and Louise were competing for a juicy TV job: a national commercial."

"Hmm," said Paschen, interested. "Your wife is moving in fast circles these days. How're ya hangin'? She isn't emasculating you, is she?"

"Tom," said Bill, smiling despite himself, "do you think I'm too delicate to have a wife with a career?"

"Hell, a lot of men are. *I* was. She divorced me and moved to New York and joined Hill and Struthers and makes five hundred G's a year."

"Oh. Sorry. I didn't know that was the reason."

"It took a lot of therapy for me to figure that out. So Louise is a suspect, huh?"

"She's *the* suspect. Can you believe that? Jesus! Not much you can do about that. But here's the sticky part. Someone broke into our house the other night when I was supposed to be gone and Louise was supposed to be home. One theory is that they could have killed the wrong woman—that they were aiming at Louise."

"Who do you mean by 'they'?"

"Maybe Bruce Behrens. Heard of him? Chemicals manufacturer. His lawn-care company is suffering, and Louise has really gone after chemical pesticides in an artful but determined manner. He's said to be unstable. At the very least, the bastard may have been hanging around our house and then lying about it."

"Okay, that's one. Who are the others?"

"Louise's producer and her cohost and sweetie. In their cases, no mistaken identity would be involved. They had their motives to kill Doering, especially the producer. None of them except Behrens have good alibis. But it's only Louise who is connected with physical evidence at the scene."

"Sounds like the police don't have a handle on it, if they're zeroing in on Louise."

"That's why I'm calling you. Do you have any inside information about why Louise would be in danger? You know me, Tom. I can *smell* it. Something's up, and it doesn't make any sense. I even considered whether Peter Hoffman might not have done it . . ."

"Hold on, there!" said Paschen angrily. "Hell, they've got his nuts in a sling. Constant surveillance. He either follows the straight or narrow or loses bail. It can't be Hoffman." The chief of staff was silent for a moment. "What about the Company?"

"You probably don't know. I'm about to part with them, although they're sore as hell that I don't want to go to Vienna next year and head the station. I can't think that has anything to do with this."

"Bill, this sounds sticky. Why don't you get the local police to help you—you know, have them swing by a couple times a night and flash their lights in your yard."

Bill held his head in his hands. "I can't tell you how skeptical they are about our break-in story and our feeling that Louise is a target."

Paschen apparently was thinking again; Bill gave him some silent time. "I'll tell you what," said the chief of staff. "Your wife did us a service in corralling that old sonofabitch, Hoffman, and keeping him from being confirmed. I can justify a little federal money spent. Supposing I just send a couple of men in an unmarked car, and they hang around for a few nights. I can't continue it for too long, but it sounds like things are happening, anyway."

"You mean Louise going to jail."

"Yeah, she'll be safe there, won't she," said Tom sarcastically. "Louise a criminal: That's outrageous. Look, old friend, I'll send them out tonight. And keep me posted. I'll help more if I can, if things get worse."

"Thanks, Tom."

*　*　*

Janie slipped away from the crack in the door just as her father finished the call. Like quicksilver, she ran down the hall into her bedroom. Her mother, who was just coming out of her bedroom, caught a flash of her and said, "In a big hurry this morning, aren't you?"

She stuck her head around the corner. "You better believe it, Ma. Tests, and more tests. Gotta go. Gotta get dressed. See you this afternoon."

She closed her bedroom door and took a deep breath. This family was on the verge of ruin! Her parents hadn't exactly told her that her mother was on the brink of being arrested. Somehow she never thought it could happen.

The shame of it! She put her head in her hands. Even if her mother were found innocent by a jury, no one would ever forget it; it would ruin Janie's life forever.

She hopped into the rest of her school outfit, a short vest that went over her long white blouse, that went over her short blue skirt. Then she neatened up her room.

She had to take a couple of tests today, for which she was totally prepared. Then, somehow, she had to save this family from destruction. And how she was going to do that, she had no idea yet.

Maybe Chris would help.

36

It was a dull, overcast day, the kind that was particularly good for gardening and especially transplanting. Since Louise had the day off, normally she would have been out in the garden like a shot, dividing and moving things, in the tradition of her old grandmother. But she had more important things to do.

She tried frantically to call John Batchelder at the station. He wasn't there and he wasn't at home, and reportedly wouldn't be back until filming on Friday.

Now she had even more unanswered questions that bugged her: deepening suspicion of Marty; Behrens's lies; John's undiscovered secret.

With the excitement over the May Wonder tulips, she had forgotten yesterday to get back to her cohost and find out what was disturbing him to the point where he demolished his fingernails.

She hunkered down, drinking coffee and thinking.

Few people called her besides her neighbors, Mary Mougey and Nora. They asked her how she was, and when she responded noncommittally, they understood and rang off.

Finally, by afternoon, hunkering down grew boring. She decided she would cook something good for her family's dinner. Curry, the recipe courtesy of Mary Mougey. Cooking, which she cared little about since she had gotten into this job, would give her a chance to sort out what she would do next to find the person who actually killed Madeleine Doering.

As she started her chicken and chopped scallions, she looked out into the deep woods, dark with the threat of rain. The three of them, Bill, Janie, and she, would eat this nice final meal together. And then the police were liable to come and collect her tomorrow.

Was she going to put up with that? No, she thought, and the French chopping knife increased its speed: She would be damned if she would go quietly; she still had a few cards up her sleeve. She wouldn't take the word of the police regarding the alibis of other suspects. And she would continue to believe in her own sensibilities. It came down to the question of whether she had faith in herself.

She put down the chopping knife, washed and dried her hands, and considered whether to go out to her writing hut to make a few exploratory phone calls.

Before she could leave, the phone rang in the kitchen. It was Bill, with a conflict. "Louise, I got the call I've been waiting for! My contact has arrived in Washington."

"Does it involve tonight?"

"Is that all right? The guy's stopping in Washington on his way from London to L.A."

She was disappointed; she needed Bill tonight. But she didn't tell him, at an important time like this. "Where would this job be, Bill? Tell me not L.A."

"No, not L.A.," said her excited husband. "That's the beauty of it. It's an international start-up company, and you and I could stay right here in Washington. Keep the house, and everything. Keep Janie in school where she is now. I'd travel part of the time, but, well, is that a good tradeoff?"

"It sounds pretty good to me." What a lukewarm answer that was! "What I mean is—it sounds wonderful. So, when will you be home?"

"Now that's what I want to talk to you about." Bill's voice had become fussy. "Lock the doors, and stay home. Call Sam next door and get those back floodlights turned on. Damn, I'm going to string some up in the yard this weekend. And we'll stop by the pound and get us a used dog. You and

Janie'll be okay tonight because I made a call today. There definitely will be some police types checking around, so you can feel safe. And I'll be home by eleven at the latest."

"Thanks, hon. And I hope things turn out the way you want them to."

She turned back to preparing her vegetables. This was the first decent dinner she had created for months and her husband was missing. She could invite someone to share. Her neighbor Sam deserved a dinner for all his concern and help. And then maybe Sam could come with her in Bill's place as she did a little detecting.

She called Sam at his office in the Rayburn Building.

"Sorry, Louise; I'd love to, but I'm stuck here at some fancy reception for congressmen—where we'll all fight over the shrimp until only the lettuce is left. I'll be home later; I'll turn the lights on then and put Missy out so you can feel safe."

Louise thanked him and hung up the phone. Everyone wanted her to feel safe, but she didn't. She went to the hut to make her phone calls.

Later, she went out to Bill's workroom. There, she selected a group of his sharpest, most lethal tools. To them she added several pair of scissors she found around the house and three knives, two from the kitchen, plus Bill's fillet knife from the fishing gear in his closet.

She distributed these items through the house and in the hut. She now felt better prepared to spend an evening alone without her husband. After dinner, she would encourage Janie to go across the street and study with Chris; at all costs, she wanted to keep her daughter out of this. She was pretty sure now who the murderer was, but tonight she would find out for sure by eliminating the other possibilities. Then, all she would need was some proof. . . .

She and Janie ate dinner in the recreation room while listening to the local television news. Her daughter was unnaturally quiet.

"Were your tests okay today?"

The girl nodded, her mouth full of curry. "Cinchy."

"Do you like the dinner?"

"Fab."

"Hmm," said Louise. "Whatever happened to the good English you used to speak? Oh well, never mind. Be prepared to eat curry forever; I think I made too much."

Janie darted her a glance that told her she didn't care a hoot about food and had her mind on something a million miles away.

It was the Channel Eight news, and there was Miss Blue Eyes, back in town. It meant John was back, and she ought to be able to reach him tonight and get some questions answered.

It was as if Cheryl Wilding hypnotized her audience. Even Louise found herself mesmerized. The woman displayed none of the malice Louise had felt when she met the woman in Demmi's Restaurant.

"Fairfax County police tonight said they have received results of forensic evidence, and are considering making an arrest in the case of Madeleine Doering's brutal murder."

Louise stared at the woman and stopped eating.

Then she flipped the channel, wanting to get away from those blank blue eyes.

"No, Ma, turn it back!" demanded Janie. "You can't hide this stuff from me. They mean you, don't they?"

Louise turned back to Channel Eight, then turned and stared at her daughter. Janie's eyelashes, like little dark curtains, were drawn over her eyes, and tears were coming down the girl's cheeks.

"Janie, let me turn this off."

"No, no, no! I need to find out what's going on. You can't treat me like a baby."

But the crime news item was concluded, and Cheryl Wilding passed on to a news story on a dramatic new possible treatment for Alzheimer's disease. Louise sat, mouth open, trying to make a connection.

Janie grabbed the remote control and switched to Channel Thirteen, which was just beginning to talk about an imminent arrest in the Doering murder.

It was the flashy male news anchor she had seen the day when she auditioned for the mulch mower job. A low, resounding voice came out of the handsome face. "Police said they had found this one of their most perplexing cases, with no eyewitnesses to rely on but several strands of what they called 'significant' circumstantial evidence."

Louise felt ill. She got up from the couch and was disconcerted to realize her legs were trembling. Her strength was dissolving, just when she needed it most. "I'm sorry," she told her daughter quietly, "but I need to lie down, just for a few minutes. Would you just pop the curry in the fridge? I'll do the dishes; I know you still have exams to study for."

"No problem, Ma, I can do them up in ten minutes," Janie said, her moist eyes still glued to the television set.

Janie was at her home away from home, Chris's house. She flipped her French book shut. Melanie had drifted off to her bedroom, leaving her and Chris alone in the Radebaughs' study. "Chris," she whispered, and looked furtively toward the adjoining living room where his parents, Nora and Ron, sat silently over a backgammon board while classical music played in the background. "Do you want to help me tonight?"

"Help you what, Janie? Not investigate, not the night before my advanced physics exam."

Janie sighed. "My mom's about to be arrested. What would you do if Nora were about to be arrested?"

He sat tall in his chair and looked at her through a shock of blond hair that had fallen on his forehead. "I—I understand. Look, you and I have done this before. And got nowhere, I might add, when that Peter Hoffman was loose."

"He's still loose," Janie added.

Chris groaned in frustration. "No, Janie, not him again. Look, this thing doesn't have answers, like the last time, when it did." He looked at his watch. "It's ten o'clock; I still need to review some stuff. I'm buckin' for a 4.0 this semester; there's some college scholarship money riding on it."

She looked at him with wide eyes. "And that comes first?"

He slammed down his physics book. "Darn right! Be practical, girl!"

She scooped up her perfectly aligned books and stood up. She stared down at him. Her voice was low and shaky. "And I thought you were the boy I loved." Tears welled up in her eyes and she ran out of the house.

The End Is Near . . .
How to Handle the Entrance and Exit
to the Garden

The best part of a garden is that it's all yours, to do with what you please. Put the stamp of your personality on it—whether it's camp or class: flamingos, teakwood benches, or junipers trimmed to look like poodles. Do it at the entrance, then reinforce the theme at the garden's end.

The entrance to a garden needs mystery—a dry stone wall, a loose hedge, a tree—to interrupt the view, so that all is not revealed at once. Like a veil on a woman, this only entices the visitor forward. The exit to a garden must be related. It should be like the conclusion of a good mystery—exciting, bold, and finally revealing all its secrets.

Memorable entrances and exits can be fashioned with plants alone. Try a cluster of tall beauties, golden *Ligularia* "The Rocket," flanked by white-tasseled *Cimicifuga* or *Lysimachia*, for instance. Underplant these with the big white coin-faced *Anemone sylvestris* and blue *Lobelia syphilitica*. Then add a punctuation mark: the burnt orange tea rose "Brandy." Any such grouping looks even better against an evergreen background.

But why not try something different from flowers? Flamingos reflect some people's souls, staid benches others'. Or try ruins. Why shouldn't we meet an ancient concrete pilaster walking around the bend of those evergreens? Old architectural fragments—pieces of ancient fence, sculptures, posts, pots—are available in junkyards and antique stores. Victorian gardeners called them "conceits," but they make a garden fun.

It's not hard to construct your own garden decorations. Find yourself some heavy Virginia creeper vine *(Parthenocissus quinquefolia)* and twist it into a trellis form, the kind you would pay dearly for through expensive garden catalogues. Mix up a little concrete, lay it in an oval, and sculpt yourself a Cycladic face to prop in the midst of your perennial border. Make a Stonehenge-type bench out of three thick pieces of flagstone. This is as easy as going to the local stoneworks and selecting the appropriate pieces, the bench being two to four feet in approximate width. Be sure the two support pieces have a flat side, which remains up when you bury the ends, and takes the weight of the top. This primitive homemade seat could be placed near the end of the garden, a tall clump of some interesting flower like plume poppies *(Maclayea microcarpa)* as a backdrop.

Since we have to look at our gardens winter and summer, it is good to choose plants for the entrance and exit of the garden that have sculptural features that last through the seasons. *Hydrangea* "Snow Queen" is a plant that lives up to this. Its skeletal form in winter attracts the eye, with its angled elbows and tenaciously held fat brown seed heads. It makes a fitting plant to herald the end of the garden, especially if combined with an evergreen or two. To make more of an impact, plant three or five. That's following the "rule of three" that says groups of plants are better than one.

Tall ornamental grasses such as *Miscanthus sinensis* "Gracillimus" are also good; they continue to wave their tanned fronds through the winds of winter. Or let the garden trail off with a slim, irregular path—you won't need more—of the foot-tall Japanese blood grass *(Imperata cylindrica* "Red Baron"). It will catch the western sun and dramatically proclaim the end of the garden trail. These grasses could be set against a few large stones, and descend into a lower area swarming with a ground cover such as wild ginger *(Asarum canadense)* or *Epimedium.*

Trees are another fitting way to finish a garden view. A wide-spreading tree such as a hawthorn or tree-form mountain laurel could be underplanted with *Calamintha nepetoides* or *Liriope muscari* for a Bernhardt-like exit. Calamintha, gray-toned and airy, and liriope, with its smooth green grassy look, are two of nature's great background plants. Or, you could choose a clump of jaunty, woods-loving trees, and it would proclaim to one and all the informal soul of the gardener.

Just like pools, hills make gardens exciting. A pool is usually an interior focal point, but a small hill, made of imported soil for just this purpose, is a great exit line. Planted, of course, with small trees, grasses, or flowers, and—let's never waste space that can be given over to imagination!—perhaps a little Oriental touch: an orderly little row of bamboo sticks. These perform a secondary service as a barrier to keep dogs from making a route through the garden. Cut the tops in an upside-down V, as a last little fillip. It will make its impact as the last order of business before the visitor leaves.

37

Something woke her, probably the chiming of the French mantel clock in the living room. In her half-conscious state, she was disoriented and barely knew where she was, much less who she was. A horrible, bottomless feeling of amorphous terror made her want to slip back into sleep, but the chime of the clock—ten strikes—reminded her that she mustn't.

She raised her head from the pillow a little. It was pitch-dark. She was sprawled on her bed, still in the clothes she had worn to work. She rolled over and stared up at the skylight directly above her bed. The sky outside was bereft of stars and moon, blanketed with clouds, so she could not even see the tall tree that usually filled the corner of that little skylight picture.

Ten o'clock: Janie was probably in bed and Bill would be home soon. She had slept for more than three hours! Dismay swept over her: There went her detecting junket, her last chance to ferret out something about Madeleine's killer.

Now it was too late: Bill would be home any minute and he wouldn't let her go charging out into the world like Don Quixote. She turned on the bedside lamp and got up and went down the hall.

The dishes were done neatly, not a trace of the golden curry sauce tainting the polished stove or countertops. But something was wrong. There was one light on over Janie's desk and another in the recreation room. Understandable. But where was Janie?

The girl was gone.

Louise dialed Nora and got her husband, Ron.

"I saw Chris and Janie and Melanie together not too long ago, studying. But then I thought I heard her go home, maybe in a little bit of a huff, from the sound of it. Chris is in the shower; Melanie's asleep. Want me to get Chris?"

"No, thanks anyway. Just tell Nora hello. Janie can't be far away." And she hung up.

She went around to each door of the house and discovered she had been carefully locked in.

But without her daughter. The daughter who was so disturbed over the evening news that tears were coming down her cheeks. The daughter Louise wanted so desperately to protect, and who apparently felt the same way about her.

Without turning on any lights, she looked out into the dark night. Sam had not yet come home to flip on floodlights and post his ineffective watchdog.

She sank down on the couch and thought about Janie. Janie, who was resentful of her older sister's courage. Who was anxious over her changing relationship with Chris. And who was crushed by the thought that her own mother might be arrested for murder.

Then Louise remembered the girl's "suspect" list. She went to Janie's bedroom, and there it was, open to the last page on which the name "Peter Hoffman" was written in neat capital letters. Beneath that, it said, "Under constant surveillance. Police say not a suspect." The last entry was a cryptic sentence with today's date: "Don't rule him out, even if police do."

Panicked, Louise went to her room and changed hurriedly into her jogging outfit and cross trainers. She flipped off the front porch light before she slipped out the front door, nearly tripping over a neatly stacked pile of Janie's school books. A sob caught in her throat. The girl had completed one assignment, her homework, and now had plunged fearlessly into the next. As for Louise, she ran down the road at top speed toward the quickest route to Peter Hoffman's house—the Sylvan Valley Swim and Tennis Club.

38

She sprinted down the street, passing several houses including the familiar hilltop home of her friend, Sarah the potter. Then she plunged into a wooded path that was the back entry to the Swim and Tennis Club, running with hands held palms out to protect her eyes against the honeysuckle tendrils that reached out to grab her. Her only goal was to find Janie before the girl invaded the dangerous world of Peter Hoffman.

Roughly, she shoved open the entry gate and sprinted past the garden area where new trees were going in. Approaching the center of the club grounds, she noted with a shiver that under the lonesome floodlights the steep-roofed clubhouse looked like a witch's abode. Then she heard the sounds. Strange, scrabbling noises.

She looked up. Silhouetted dimly against the dark sky was a figure—her daughter. She had somehow gotten up on the wood shake roof of the clubhouse; now she stood there, perilously balanced. "Janie!" cried Louise. "My God, that roof . . ."

"Ma, look out! The guy who chased me here—he has some kind of poison!"

As if on cue, a large hooded figure, looking like a creature from outer space, stepped out from behind a group of evergreens. He had been circling below his trapped prey, but now, seeing Louise, he loped toward her with the speed of a grizzly. She froze with fright, until the smell came toward her, accompanied by a small spurting noise. Like a living presence the chemical odor surrounded her head. She fled toward the pool, straight into a cluster of scratchy old evergreens nestled against the fence. Over her shoulder she saw the plastic-hooded pursuer bearing down on her, and she lunged for a small entry she had discovered when mapping the grounds of the club. She shoved aside a juniper with needles like a thousand pins, and slid through the eight-inch space between bush and fence. Crossing the concrete apron of the pool, she dove in.

The chilly water hit her like a rock and threw her body into momentary shock. She braced herself, reached out with her strong Australian crawl, and swam facedown across its width. Finally to the other side, she grasped the ladder. She pulled in a shuddering breath, coughed, then quickly shoved her breath out, trying to get rid of the last of the poisoned air she had breathed. Peering around to see where her pursuer was, she saw the person struggling to get inside the chain-link barrier. She vaulted up the metal ladder, and, dripping water, ran to the fence and slipped back the way she came. In a few quick steps she was at the other side of the clubhouse and saw her daughter still crouching on the roof above. "Janie, are you okay?" she called in a hoarse whisper. "Can't you get down? That roof is rotten."

"Ma, never mind me," the girl whispered back. "I'll get off here later, somehow. You get out of here and get help!" And the girl slunk down onto the dark roof so that Louise could see her no more.

But she couldn't just leave Janie there: She must lure this predator away. Suddenly, she knew the answer: The holes! A garden full of generous, big, *treacherous* holes—a perfect booby trap!

She gave her pursuer time to realize she had escaped the pool and to clamber back over the fence. While she waited, all the bugs in the Virginia night seemed to settle on exposed parts of her soggy person.

She estimated a twenty-foot start was all she would need. When he came within this range, she shouted, "Come and get me if you can!" Then she streaked away toward the hilly ground where she and her volunteer crew had prepared deep depressions and pits for new plantings. She darted quickly up the incline and hurried down the other side, taking refuge in a grove of viburnum. Bending far over to relieve her strained body and lungs, she panted like a spent long-distance runner. A paroxysm of coughing overcame her, which she muffled with both hands.

Then she heard it—a cry of pain from the other side of the hill. "Oooh, Christ!" The agonized scream had an air of finality to it, as if the victim were actually dying.

She straightened up, her coughs mixed with sobs of pleasure. She could picture her pursuer lying there: His leg must be badly injured. She started back toward the clubhouse, happy in the knowledge they had found Madeleine's murderer. Now she only had to figure out how to get Janie down safely off that roof.

She had only taken a few steps when she heard the scratchy noise of bushes being pushed aside. Her pursuer had escaped the trap and was right in front of her!

"Oh, God!" she cried, and turned and sprinted away down the wooded trail, cursing her water-soaked clothes. Her athletic foe was closing the distance on the path, and there was no way to break through the wall of tangled honeysuckle on either side. Her only possible chance now was to reach Sarah's house.

As soon as she was beyond the swim club property, she ran through the scrub growth up the Swanson's hill, ignoring the fashionable steps framed of stone and railroad ties. As the thrashing noises of the killer followed close behind; she prayed that Sarah was working late in her potter's studio. She ran down the side toward the lighted studio. Sarah was there! Louise pushed at the door and it opened. "Sarah!" she screamed. No one answered. Empty.

There was a small oasis of light near Sarah's potting wheel. Beyond it was the door that led to the main house. Sarah and

Mort were somewhere on the other side of the soundproofed wall of this custom-designed house. "Help!" she cried hopelessly. "Please help me!"

Through the broad glass windows she could see her pursuer arriving at the top of the hill, coming toward the studio door. She ran across the room and pulled at the connecting door to the main house. It was locked.

She gasped for precious breath. Now she was trapped in a dimly lit pottery studio without a weapon to her name, to face a person wielding a sprayer full of deadly poison.

Despairingly, she looked around the room for something to defend herself with. Ghostly objects of uniform size stood on the many tables. Not much there to help. She examined Sarah's trappings near her potting wheel. Lying next to the wheel were several implements that the potter used to smooth the sides of clay she was throwing. Louise picked one up, uncertainly, then threw it down; it was too flimsy.

Then she saw what she wanted: Resting next to the wheel was a lump of clay as big as a man's head, still damp, and loosely wrapped in burlap. Next to this was a large bucket of water, that Sarah used to dip her hands and moisten clay as she turned it on the wheel.

She heard a loud click and looked up with anguished eyes. Her pursuer had flung open the studio door, and could see her clearly across the dark room in the only lighted patch in the whole place. She unwrapped the clay with trembling hands and sloshed it vigorously into the big bucket of water. She held the clay securely in her hands. Then she stepped out into the shadows so she would not be such a good target.

But she could see him now, through the plastic-faced hood he wore above dark overalls. She could tell who it was from the way he moved—awkwardly, like a schoolboy.

It was Bruce Behrens, his eyes wide in concentration as he attempted to kill her, the woman he had missed the first time.

She pulled herself to attention. She would have few chances of getting out of here alive and she needed all her wits and physical strength. Her only advantage was that Behrens could take but one route to reach her through the sea of tables. Moving rapidly, he pulled his sprayer into position. When he was fifteen feet away, she threw the clod of clay at him with both hands, as if it were a medicine ball.

"Shit!" She heard the muffled word through his plastic-faced hood. He obviously had not recognized what was coming at him. To her dismay, the big clay ball fell short and skidded the rest of the way. He stepped aside, missing it, then rushed toward her like an animal anxious to end the hunt and kill his prey.

He was so close that she could see the moment when his big feet slid grotesquely out from underneath him on the slippery wet clay surface. "*Owwww!*" he yelled as he fell down hard, knocking the hood from his head.

She realized this was her chance to make her way around him through the sea of closely placed drying tables. She ran to the corner of the room and discovered there was no exit lane: She was trapped. The chemicals manufacturer, sweating and as out of breath as she was, struggled to his feet and stood like an enormous barrier to the only exit. She stood in the corner and yelled as loudly as she could, "Help, help!"

Silence. She faced this killer alone.

"Don't waste your time screaming, Louise," he told her matter-of-factly. "I've got you now—after making a mistake the first time."

"So it was a mistake. You killed Madeleine, thinking it was me. But Bruce, why?" she pleaded. "We know each other—why, we even have some things in common. Why do you have to do this?"

The chemicals manufacturer laughed, a breathless laugh, and that was when Louise realized he was in intense pain. "You sound so innocent, Louise—dear Louise, whom everyone admires. . . ." She could hear him panting in between his sentences. "But you're going to pay for everything—ruining my business, making me a laughingstock. . . ."

"How could I ruin that enormous business of yours?"

"Oh, yes. Your silly program with all its good publicity . . ." Suddenly he winced, stopped and grabbed his leg.

She thought she heard a click, and her hopes soared, but then there was silence. What was left to her? Only talking.

"Not only did you murder Madeleine. You're the one who threw that poor plant manager into the rock crusher at your cement plant, didn't you? He was like me, wasn't he, Bruce? He was harming you, too, by telling the truth about those nasty pesticides you were illegally burning."

Through the dim light she could see the man's face was frozen with rage. "The two of you," he said in a shaking voice, "shooting off your mouths, trying to destroy me. That plant manager was once my friend, believe it or not!"

"But the plant manager was right—"

"He was wrong!" roared Behrens, so loud that she flinched. She realized Bruce Behrens was a man who in his own mind was never wrong.

Then Behrens coldly told her, "I needn't have had to kill you, you know: I tried to destroy you with those pickets and those letters. But then you got everything going for you— that story in *TV Guide* . . ."

Her mouth had fallen open. "You mean you sent those pickets out. You unscrupulous—bastard! And you wrote those crazy letters—do you care about nothing?"

Still standing, spray gun held in one hand, he smiled cynically at her. "You mean, the environment, or something? You with your knee-jerk reactions to everything that's green-colored—you're a laugh! I broke in your house trying to find you home—even rearranged a bouquet you'd done badly. And your daughter: Who do you think chased your little daughter from Route One—a stranger? That was me, too. I thought maybe threatening her would shut you up. Now I have to get rid of her, too, before the night is over, because she's smart—somehow she's figured out who I am."

"Bruce, look," she said, trying to keep the tremble out of her voice, "I know you've had hard times—your wife, your business—but why make it worse?" The thumping in her chest had decreased into a slower, painful beat. As she talked, she carefully maneuvered herself between two tables so it would be harder to reach her. "Think about it, Bruce. Can the police really tie you to either of those murders? I don't think so or they would have by now. But if you kill me here, you'll never go free."

"Don't try to hand me that bull," he rasped. "I gave you plenty of chances to be nice to me and you didn't take them." His voice exuded self-pity. "You just treated me shitty, like all the others eventually do, no matter how good I am to them—no matter how much money I dole out to them."

With large, competent hands in which Louise detected the slightest tremble, he picked up his sprayer, adjusting its nozzle so the pesticide would reach across the thirty feet that now divided them. He had lost his protective headgear and now had to be careful. He could not afford the broad spray he tried at the Swim Club—the fog of chemicals would poison him, too. He wanted to turn it into a thin, accurate stream for a quick kill.

What could she do to protect herself? She looked around wildly and saw the answer. The tables. That was it—she would burrow her way out of here!

Suddenly, behind Behrens she saw her daughter at the door: Janie ran in and headed straight for the chemicals manufacturer.

"Oh no, please don't!" Louise begged.

Behrens, thinking she meant him, merely laughed and aimed the sprayer at her.

At that moment, the girl leaped on his back like a small attack animal and knocked the sprayer aside and Behrens to the floor.

Louise ran forward, but by the time she had reached them, Bruce Behrens had grabbed her prone daughter and was choking her. She looked frantically around and grabbed an object on the nearby table, stood over the man, and bashed it over his head. He fell to the ground and lay there, still.

She threw down the fragment of pottery still in her hand

and ran to her daughter, who was sitting up, supported by her elbows. "Ma," she said shakily, "he's not down for long. Watch out!"

Behrens was quickly recovering from the blow on the head. Louise tried to pull Janie out of his way, but with an enormous hand the man dragged her down again and pulled her against his body as if this slim girl could defend him against Louise. His hand scrabbled on the floor like a crab's until his desperate fingers retrieved the spray gun.

Just then, the lights went on in the room, and Mort and Sarah Swanson stood in the door connecting to the main house, their eyes wide with fear. Swanson, in a satin dressing gown, held a large pistol unsteadily in his hand, pointed at the three of them.

"Good God!" cried the attorney. "What is going on here?"

"We heard enough to know what's going on," snapped his wife. "This man's trying to kill Louise! Keep that gun on him."

Behrens had struggled to his feet, still grasping Janie, with the sprayer aimed straight at Louise. "Don't come near me, anyone," he warned.

"Okay, fella," said Mort nervously, "just take it easy."

Surrounding the beleaguered attacker were several dozen drying tables, on which were lined up jardinières with a figure of Louise as "The Gardener." Only one was missing, and it lay on the floor in broken shards; it was the one with which she had struck him. He rubbed the back of his head and swayed unsteadily.

First he looked at Louise, and then at the statuary again. "Jesus, are these all you?"

"Yes, Bruce," she said, grabbing up another jardinière, "and I'll damned well heave this one at you, too, if you don't get your hands off my daughter now." She raised the clay pot and would have thrown it, but was afraid she would hit Janie.

"Now, hold on, Louise," demanded Mort. "Isn't that— aren't you—Bruce Behrens? What's going on, Bruce?"

Louise could see Behrens's wheels turning. "I have been defending myself . . ."

"No, Mort!" cried Louise. "Don't be ridiculous! Look at Janie. Look how he still holds her: Let her go!"

Mort Swanson hesitated.

Then two things happened at once: Sarah Swanson wrested the pistol from the hand of her indecisive husband, and Bill kicked open the door.

Police style, he held his automatic in both hands and pointed it straight at Bruce Behrens's heart. "Let her loose, Behrens," said Bill. "Put that spray gun down and put your hands up."

"That's right," cried Sarah Swanson, a comfy but commanding figure in her voluminous pink muumuu. "There's two guns pointed at you."

Behrens released Janie, and she ran to her mother. Then he carefully bent down and placed the sprayer at his feet. Louise realized then what deadly liquid it held, so lethal that this chemicals manufacturer didn't want a drop of it to touch him.

"Got him covered, Sarah?" asked Bill. When she said she did, he went up to Behrens and gingerly picked the spray gun. The man put hands protectively in front of his face.

"What have we here, Mr. Behrens?" asked Bill. "A prospective murder weapon?" He carefully placed the spray gun on a nearby table. Then, glaring at the chemicals manufacturer, he commanded, "Janie and Louise, come here. I need to know what's gone on. Why is Janie's head bleeding?" They went quickly to his side.

He took one hand off the automatic and gently touched his daughter's head. "Ouch," she said. "I'm all right. The bleeding's almost stopped. I fell when I was getting off the roof."

"What roof?"

"It's kind of complicated, Dad. This guy had me trapped on a roof."

Mort walked carefully around Behrens toward Bill, with his hands half up, as if he also were a prisoner. He said, "I

231

called the police when we heard noises. They'll be here soon to straighten this whole thing out. Let's not shoot anyone. This guy you'll recognize as Bruce Behrens—and I've always known him as a reputable man."

"Reputable, Mort?" said Louise coolly. "Hardly. He's the man who murdered Madeleine Doering. And another person as well."

"That's right," said Sarah Swanson. "Mort and I heard him admit to two murders—just as we were coming in the door."

The police burst in seconds later. Detectives Geraghty and Morton and several uniformed officers.

Louise looked at the detectives triumphantly. "Hi," said Louise. "I think we have some information for you." She pointed to Bruce Behrens, who was supporting himself against a table full of pottery. "We've found Madeleine's murderer."

39

They intercepted the neighbors as they went down the Swansons' front steps with the police. "Looks like a block party in the making," Louise joked, pulling on her wet sweatsuit in a vain attempt to make it more comfortable. Coming up the hill were Chris, his mother, father, and sister Melanie; Mary Mougey and Sam Rosen. She felt a warm glow come over her. These people were like her family.

She and Bill told them briefly what had happened.

"We've all been looking for you," said Chris. The eighteen-year-old put a gentle arm around the bedraggled Janie. "I'm sorry. I should have come with you. After I studied a while longer, I felt bad and decided to try and find you. But your house was open, with no one there."

Mary came over and hugged Louise, who tried to warn her she was soaking wet. "You're a drowned rat, my dear, and I don't care. I'm so happy you're safe."

Then Nora embraced her, too. "Being the typical non-communicative American family, Chris didn't tell me until much later about Janie and her . . . aspirations to go out detecting. And Ron hadn't mentioned your phone call about missing Janie until we were getting ready for bed. Then Mary phoned us, because she couldn't reach you and was suspicious. So we all piled in the car and looked for you, until the police screeched into the neighborhood."

Louise looked at Nora. Between this woman, Mary Mougey, and herself, they made a good composite mother for the fearless Janie.

Then she turned to the others and gave each a wet hug. She told them how brave Sarah Swanson had been. "She and Bill saved us," she said. "And—Mort, too, of course." Tears were coming to her eyes. "You were all looking out for us. We couldn't get along without you."

Sam, still in his dress suit, was full of apologies: "Sorry I got home late or I might have been able to help by putting Missy out."

"Maybe." Bill laughed. "But do you mind if I get a true watchdog of my own?" and they all laughed.

"I want to walk you home, Janie," said Chris.

"Sorry, son," said Detective Geraghty, putting a hand on the young man's shoulder. "The Eldridges are going to the emergency room. Mrs. Eldridge may be suffering from exposure to pesticide, and you can see your friend Janie needs stitches. Then they're going with us to the station if they're well enough. They'll be there for awhile."

"I don't care," said Chris, "I'll wait, anywhere."

"Chris," said Janie, "your physics exam is tomorrow . . ."

He pointed to his head. "I've got it."

The Eldridges said good-bye to their neighbors and climbed in the car with Geraghty. Chris piled in front, with Louise, Bill, and Janie in back.

Geraghty swung a large arm over on the back of the seats and turned to them. "I've called Detective Johnson. He wants us to all come over to Fairfax City, since Madeleine Doering's murder was in that jurisdiction. Officer Morton's taking the Swansons. We can close this case once and for all. Let's stop to pick up a quick change of clothes. Then we can take the ones you have into evidence."

"That would be great," said Louise. "And then we can go back to the county jail. At least it turns out it won't be my home away from home."

40

Louise, wearing her old striped sweatshirt and shorts, was finishing her final cup of morning coffee on the patio. Janie sat opposite her, with the large bandage on her head making her a rakish young pirate. Talkative, just like in the old days. Her slim legs, protruding from her short skirt, were waggling back and forth, a clear sign her patience was strained.

"Ma, I hate to say this, but you can't meet the press in those clothes. You have to wear something more lady-like."

"I'll change in a minute." She stretched her long legs out and the movement caused her to cough a little. "Oooh," she groaned. "I'm still coughing, the muscles in my legs are in spasms, and I'm just plain exhausted."

Janie's legs were still now. She looked at her mother intently, a hint of tears in her blue eyes. "But it's nice to be alive, isn't it?" she asked in a quavering voice. "I thought we were both going to die last night."

Louise reached over and clasped her teenaged daughter's hand. "If you hadn't come into the studio when you did, I think that man would have killed me. And no little shot of atropine would have set me to rights."

The girl tightened her grip on her mother's hand and her eyes widened, as if to bid the tears to recede. "I didn't know to be scared enough of Bruce Behrens's sprayer full of poison—that one little tiny drop was enough to kill you. . . ." She shook her head and looked over at her mother. "Sorry I got off on the wrong track by thinking it was Peter Hoffman.

That Behrens guy started chasing me the minute I started through the woods." She turned her head, but not before Louise saw her lip trembling.

"Janie. I really want you to stay home today."

Janie straightened. "No, Ma, I gotta go, at least for a few hours. I have exams this afternoon. And I have to show off my wound. How often do you have a wound to show off? So don't take too long, because those TV people out front won't wait forever, and they want to talk to both of us." She ran into the house.

Louise sighed and picked up the dog-eared script for her next show that lay near her on the patio table. She wished she could just work on that instead of talking to people, re-living all the terrible moments of last night.

A moment later Bill came out and sat down next to her. He had a piece of notepaper and a pen in his hand. "So Janie warned you. You're not going to have any peace until you come out front and talk to the newspeople. They particularly like the way you capture criminals—bashing them with bromeliads and clay pots. And how the police pooh-pooh your garden instincts and then they turn out to be right on the money."

"Those May Wonder tulips. But it was more than instinct: I looked it up in a gardening book, and then phoned Wild Flower Farms to verify it with their horticulturalist. So I was pretty sure Behrens was the one."

Bill hunched forward on the patio chair and supported his elbows on his knees. "I can't believe the sonofabitch sneaked into our house. It makes me wonder about myself, Louise. Good thing I'm quitting the agency. I must be losing my touch."

She laughed and patted his shoulder. "Honey, we aren't usually the targets of break-ins. But Behrens was devious."

"We're getting new locks, lights in the yard . . ."

"Dogs . . ."

"I'd go for one dog, Louise."

"Has Geraghty called? I see you have a list there."

"He called. He'll be over later to talk to us. Behrens—he's in a cast—has decided to confess, especially after he discovered the Swansons heard him admit killing both that cement plant manager and Madeleine. It turns out he wore a disguise to the station and posed as a volunteer. He mistook her for you, bending over the sink in that rest room."

"How did he manage such a good alibi—did Geraghty find that out?"

"He had no trouble with that," said Bill. "As the boss, when he signed in after-hours at his company headquarters, he just exercised privilege and altered the sign-in sheet. Made his arrival half an hour earlier than it really was. The police bought it, no problem, but this morning, the security guard told police the real story. And the poison he used . . . Jesus! It scares me to think of it."

She sat back in her chair and grinned nervously. "I know. That means I'm living a charmed life, and think of what a responsibility that is."

"Okay," said her husband, dead earnest. "Maybe it's better that you joke about it."

"So, who else called—did Marty call?"

"Of course he did, all apologetic, for exposing you to Bruce Behrens. Wants the four of us—he and Steffi, you and I—to have dinner together."

"And how about John?"

Bill consulted the list. "Oh, lots of people from work. Jack Lederle. He said to tell you, 'Good show.' Laconic, isn't he? And friends from all over—most of the neighbors. Yes, and John Batchelder. He was as apologetic as Marty—something about the memo they found in Madeleine's machine . . ." He stuck the list in his shirt pocket.

Louise was recalling something that Cheryl Wilding reported in last night's newscast. "I can guess what happened! Cheryl wrote that memo in Madeleine's computer, getting access to her office through John. He might not have known exactly what she was up to, until he thought about it for a while. She wanted me to be charged with that murder."

"How can you draw that conclusion with no evidence?"

"Last night, Cheryl mentioned on the news the discovery of a new treatment for Alzheimer's disease. That was in Madeleine's memo, and at the time I thought it was fishy . . ."

"Why so?"

"Because Madeleine apparently never had any story ideas of her own. She was totally dependent on the producer and the writers for show ideas. So, I'll bet that's what's weighing on John's conscience. Cheryl Wilding probably did it while she was hanging around waiting for John one evening after the murder."

"Sounds like he'd better get a new girlfriend. That one's trouble." Then her husband put his hand on his chin and stared into the woods. "Something else is buggin' me, Louise. I've been thinking about this a lot since last night. We could move. You must think this neighborhood is cursed."

"Not any more. I came out of all this virtually unscathed, not like the last time. And Janie is, well . . . I hope she's okay as she thinks she is. I don't want to move, unless you do." She cocked her head and looked at him. "After all, we have some good friends here."

"I'd miss the people around here, especially the men's poker club."

"See? So we don't want to go anywhere. Anyway, you have that job offer. If you take them up on it, it would allow us to stay here indefinitely."

"I'd be free at last." He sighed. "I'd enjoy being an American businessman engaged in overseas trade, coming and going on my own schedule, taking my family with me once in a while. And then there's Janie and Martha. They're handling their own affairs quite well, for the most part. Except Janie shouldn't be so rash; she could have been killed last night." He shook his head grumpily. "I have to talk to her. She acts like a P.I. in a mystery . . ."

". . . or like an undercover CIA agent," she added, slyly,

238

then laughed, ". . . as compared with you and me, who are sedate, law-abiding snoops, right? Face it, Bill. She's following in her father's footsteps. Seriously, though, she did it to prove that she's brave. With all Martha's ambitious plans for an urban internship, she was feeling overshadowed. But the whole thing's over now—we can all loosen up and relax." She placed a hand on the script lying near. "I can return to work on the latest episode of my show. I've called it 'The Impetuous Gardener.' "

He moved closer and looked deeply into her eyes. "Forget that for a minute, Louise. I want you to promise me something. . . ."

She leaned over and placed a finger gently on his lips. "Don't say it, Bill, I know. You wish I'd stay out of trouble. I promise—I'll do my very best."

"Good." He reached into his shirt pocket and retrieved the list. "Then I'll give you that message from the guy with the twang in his voice. He wants you as his spokesperson."

Tom Paschen knocked, and without waiting, strode into the Oval Office. Jack Fairchild, with his glasses on his nose, was reading the morning newspaper. He looked up at his chief of staff. "So she did it again."

Paschen grinned. "Yeah, Louise Eldridge has snared another killer. I think you know him: Bruce Behrens. Chemicals, cement. Unfortunately, we lose a donor—he's given us beaucoup campaign funds. But it's a damned good story."

"The woman's as good as a team of detectives," said Jack Fairchild.

Paschen smiled. "Her family helps." He stationed himself in a chair opposite the President's carved antique desk, stretched his legs out, and crossed them at his Italian leather loafers. "So, what are you going to do with this woman?"

Fairchild looked crossly over at his chief of staff. "What do you want me to do with this woman?"

"Well, you have to be grateful to her. First, she polishes off Hoffman. Now, she takes another killer off the streets." The chief of staff pulled at his chin with his thumb and forefinger. "Hoffman and Behrens sort of remind me of a poem I used to know by John Crowe Ransom: *Captain Carpenter*. The guy goes out to fight and keeps losing parts"—Paschen waved a careless hand—"you know, first his nose, then his legs, then his arms, until he has 'an anatomy with little to lose.' " He grinned at the President. "Except Captain Carpenter was a good guy, as compared to those two. While dealing with Behrens, Louise Eldridge somehow gave him a concussion and caused him to severely injure the ligaments in his knee." The chief of staff chuckled. "He'd better watch out for that woman so that he doesn't meet her again."

The President rubbed his chin with a hand. "Hmm. What happened to Eldridge's gardening show during all this?"

"It's doing very well. Turns out the pickets were phony— Behrens sent them. Also sent a lot of the negative mail. It all just served to make the show more popular."

Paschen got up from his chair, put his hands in his pants pockets and strode around near the President's desk. "I suggest you appoint her to the National Environmental Needs Commission. That way, you'd slip right into the limelight with her. Not only that, you'd position yourself on the side of the angels."

"When would we do it?"

"ASAP. There's a short lead time on the show, so probably next week."

"So, I get to be on that kooky show with those environmental nuts."

"Yeah," said Paschen, smiling. "Maybe you can learn how to talk the talk when you get there—garden talk, that is. Remember, gardening is Americans' second most favorite sport—the first is either sex or television, I'm not sure. They'd love to hear the President of the United States discussing nematodes and cutworms and stuff like that. Every American wants to know how to get rid of tomato worms."

The President looked at his chief of staff suspiciously. "Tom," he said, "you're just putting me on, aren't you?"

"Not necessarily," said Tom, with a little smile flickering below his calculating eyes. "Man of the people, gardener, willing to get his hands in the dirt. Think about it. Might help your re-election chances. Right now, Jack, as you well know, they're piss-poor."

The Impetuous Gardener

Remember your grandmother's garden? It was probably a big rectangle with neat rows of flowers and vegetables, edged with prim annuals such as marigolds.

Grandma was influenced, no doubt, by the great gardens of Europe. Today, many gardeners have kicked over the straight-line tradition, loosened up, gone a little wild, and set their gardens free of geographical restraints. They are developing gardens without formal boundaries. In America now you will find gardens in many irregular shapes, following the lay of the land, as casual and wild and congenial as nature itself.

Equipped with more knowledge than ever before from books, magazines, and catalogues, they are not only learning how to design and plant a garden that is uniquely theirs, but also maintaining this planted space without the burden of chemicals.

The millions of American gardeners have discovered that nowhere does life permit us the opportunities, the risks, and the rewards that gardening does. Whether the garden is in a backyard plot or a retirement home windowsill, and whether the gardener is thirty or ninety, they can be impetuous. They need follow no orders laid down by others, but only what is told them by their own eye and heart.

Since more people in the United States join the ranks of gardeners each year, it is safe to say gardening will never be the same, never again be thought of as cutting a rectangular shape out of the Kentucky bluegrass and planting things in rows.

As they experiment with change, people don't always agree. Some argue for planting only native plants. They favor them because they attract the butterflies, birds, and animals that are part of a whole ecosystem. Yet who can deny the magnetism of a hybrid delphinium, lily, or rose? Some gardeners keep the hybrids in special areas so they can take care of their special needs; others think the combination of natural with more exotic plants is the greatest union of all.

Grass is another debate: Turf is always thirsty. Why can't you just replace Kentucky blue with drought-resistant grass? The downside is that you lose months of green, since these native grasses don't green up until June and turn tan again in September. Some devote part of their property to these less-needy varieties, and relieve the tan spring color by studding the turf with spring bulbs and hardy native plants. In the unbound garden, there still may be a strip of mowed Kentucky bluegrass, sturdier than native varieties, leading us literally down the garden path. Others will make that path out of wood chips or stones.

Let's face it. Americans are looking for excitement in the garden bed. Not only the *shape* of the garden has changed, but the plants that go into it. We can't say, "Marigolds are out; native larkspur is in," because marigolds are never *out*. But now people may use them differently, feathery petite-flowered varieties planted in masses as part of their field flowers. They've also reaffirmed what Grandma knew, and place them near vegetable beds to keep away garden pests.

Gardeners look for forms, colors, and textures in plants that arouse their senses—and often find this reward in old-fashioned or native plants—or in new cultivars that plant producers are busily sending to market. For instance, our eye loves vertical plants, striped, dappled and mottled varieties, big-leaved flora, plants with lacy, delicate foliage, trees with curvy branches and exfoliating bark, native species we've never seen or heard of before that were there in the field, and are now available in gallon pots.

People are now recognizing that gardening is an adventure, not just work. If the garden oppresses them with its size, they make it smaller, for gardeners need time to spend in the garden, dreaming. They need time to use a magnifying glass and observe nature at work, enjoying the bugs and the butterflies, as well as the peerlessly designed flowers, shrubs and trees.

People today grow more native plants, eliminate turf, pick disease-resistant varieties that don't demand pesticides, and in general work with nature. They improve the soil but don't try to change it radically. They control garden pests, but they don't try to demolish them all. They have discovered that they have a place in the natural order of things, but are not the rulers. They are willing to nurture the earth, as they remain impetuous and passionate about all living things.